Red Dress
in
Black and White

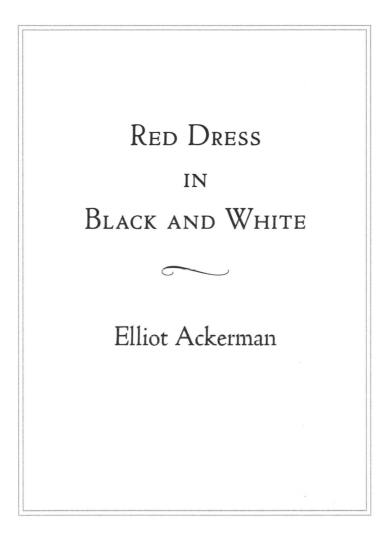

Red Dress
in
Black and White

Elliot Ackerman

Alfred A. Knopf | New York 2020

THIS IS A BORZOI BOOK
PUBLISHED BY ALFRED A. KNOPF

www.aaknopf.com

Knopf, Borzoi Books, and the colophon are registered trademarks of
Penguin Random House LLC.

Library of Congress Cataloging-in-Publication Data
Names: Ackerman, Elliot, author.
Title: Red dress in black and white : a novel / Elliot Ackerman.
Description: First edition. | New York : Alfred A. Knopf, 2020. |
Identifiers: LCCN 2019025623 (print) | LCCN 2019025624 (ebook) |
ISBN 9780525521815 (hardcover) | ISBN 9780525521822 (ebook)
Subjects: LCSH: Married people—Fiction. | Divorce—Fiction. |
Custody of children—Fiction. | GSAFD: Domestic fiction
Classification: LCC PS3601.C5456 R33 2020 (print) |
LCC PS3601.C5456 (ebook) | DDC 813/.6—dc23
LC record available at https://lccn.loc.gov/2019025623
LC ebook record available at https://lccn.loc.gov/2019025624

Front-of-jacket images: © DrPAS/iStock/Getty Images
Plus; © wera Rodsawang/Moment/Getty Images
Jacket design by Janet Hansen

Manufactured in the United States of America
First Edition

For Vail,
Coco,
Ethan
and
Alexis

Yet the most important element depicts the young woman in the red dress. Unlike the policemen, she is not protected by the usual apparel: she wears no goggles, no facemask, no helmet. Most remarkably however, her vulnerability in this tense context is further underlined by her body language: she simply just stands there . . .

—Gezi Park protests reported in
The Guardian, May 28, 2013

Contents

⁓

Part I

A Tuesday in
late November 2013

That evening, at half past nine

⌒

To William, the question of his mother is clear. The question of his father is more complicated, because there is Peter.

The night that they meet, William is about seven years old and his mother has brought him to one of Peter's exhibits. She hasn't said much to her son, just that she has an American friend, that he takes pictures and that the two of them are going to see that friend's art, which is very special. That's what she always calls it, *his art*.

His mother doesn't drive, at least not in this city, and in the taxi on the way there she keeps looking at her wristwatch. It isn't that they are late, but that she's anxious to arrive at the right time, which is not to say right on time. The apartment she's trying to find is off İstiklal Caddesi, which is a sort of Ottoman Gran Rue running through the heart of Istanbul, the place of William's birth but a home-in-exile to his mother, who, like her friend Peter, is American. As their cab crawls along Cevdet Paşa Caddesi, the seaside road which handrails the Bosphorus Strait, she stares out the window, her eyes brushed with a bluish cosmetic, blinking slowly, while she absently answers the boy's questions about where they are going and whom they'll meet there. William holds a game called Simon on his lap. It is a palm-size disk divided into four colored panels—blue, red, green, yellow—that flashes increasingly complicated patterns, which reflect off the cab's night-darkened windows. The aim is to repeat those patterns. It was a gift from his father and his father has the high score, which he has instructed William to try to beat.

An allée of birch canopies their route and they skirt the high limestone walls of Dolmabahçe Palace. Their cab jostles in and out of first gear in the suffocating traffic until they break from the seaside road and switchback into altitudes of linden-, oak- and elm-forested hills. When the sun dips behind the hills, the lights come on in the city. Below them the waters of the Bosphorus, cold and pulling, turn from green-blue to just black. The boat lights, the bridge lights, the black-white contrast of the skyline reflecting off the water would come to remind the boy of Peter and, as his mother termed it, his art.

After paying the fare, his mother takes him by the hand, dragging him along as they shoulder through the evening foot traffic trying to find their way. Despite the darkness eternal day lingers along the İstiklal, flightless pigeons hobble along the neon-lit boulevard, chestnuts smolder from the red-painted pushcarts on the street corners, the doughy smell of baked açma and simit hangs in the air. The İstiklal is cobblestone, she has worn heels for the occasion, and when she catches one in the grouting and stumbles into the crowd, she knocks a shopping bag out of another woman's hand. Standing from her knees, William's mother repeatedly apologizes and a few men reach under her arms to help her up, but her son quickly waves them away and helps his mother up himself. After that the two of them walk more slowly and she still holds his arm, but now she isn't dragging her son, and when the boy feels her lose balance once more, he grabs her tightly at the elbow and with the help of his steady grip she manages to keep on her feet.

They turn down a quiet side street, which aside from a few shuttered kiosks has little to recommend it. The apartment building they come to isn't much wider than its door. After they press the buzzer, a window opens several floors above. A man ducks his head into the bracing night and calls down to them in a high-pitched yet forceful voice, like air through a steel pinhole. He then blows them an invisible kiss, launching it off an open palm. William's mother raises her face to that kiss and then blows one back. The street smells bitterly of scents the boy doesn't yet recognize and it is filled with the halos of fluorescent lamps and suspect patches of wetness on the curbs and even the cinder-block walls. The buzzer goes off and William's mother shoulders open the door. Inside someone has hammered a plank across the elevator entry. It has been there long enough for the nail heads to rust. They climb up several floors where the brown paint scales from the brick. The empty apartment building meets them with an uproar of scattering rats and the stairwell smells as bitter as the street.

A shuttle of unclasping locks receives his mother's knock at the apartment door and then the same man who had appeared in the window presses his face to the jamb. His gaze is level with the fastened chain and his eyes are pretty and spacious, as if hidden, well-apportioned rooms existed within them. The honey-colored light from inside the apartment shines on his skin. His eyebrows are like two black smudges. William notices the plucked bridge between them, and also his rectangular smile with its brilliantly white teeth. The man is uncommonly handsome, and William feels drawn to him, as if he can't quite resolve himself to look away.

The chain unlatches and then half a dozen or so men and broad-shouldered women spill across the apartment's threshold, pressing against William's mother, kissing her on the cheek, welcoming her. When they kiss William on the cheek, the harsh, glancing trace of the men's stubble scrapes against his fresh skin. The women begin a refrain of *Wonderful to see you, Cat,* and while they escort her inside they keep saying *wonderful* over and over in their guttural voices as if that superlative is the last word of a spell that will transform them into the people they wish to be.

A blue haze of cigarette smoke hugs the ceiling. Tacked to the sitting room wall, next to a white hard hat displayed like a trophy, is a poster advertising this exhibit. It is a portrait Peter shot of one of the women. She was photographed shirtless from the shoulders up, her mascara runs down her cheeks, her lip is split, a small gash zigzags across her forehead, and her wig—a tight bob symmetrical as a rocketeer's helmet—is missing a few tufts of hair. That summer, protests had shaken the city, shutting it down for weeks. Hundreds of thousands had squared off with the authorities. William's dominant memories of those events aren't the television images of riot police clubbing the environmental activists who opposed a new shopping mall at Taksim Square's Gezi Park—seventy-four acres of neglected lawns with a cross-hatch of dusty concrete walkways shaded by dying trees—or even the way so many everyday people surprised themselves by joining the pro-testers' ranks, but instead William remembers his father pacing their apartment on his cellphone, unable to drive into the office because of the many blocked streets as he negotiated a construction deal on a different shopping mall across town.

By the time the protests had finished, the city's long-persecuted queer community had assumed its vanguard. This caused one colum-nist, a friend of Peter's, to observe, "Among those who struggled for their rights at the police barricades at Gezi Park, the toughest 'men' were the transgender women." And so, Peter had a name for his exhibit. In the poster, battered though she is, his subject's eyes hold a certain, scalding defiance, as if she can read the words beneath her: *The Men of Gezi, An Exhibit.* As William's mother wanders into the apartment she becomes indistinguishable from the others, blending perfectly into this crowd.

❊

Catherine and William have arrived at Peter's exhibit right on time, which is to say that they have arrived early. The apartment belongs to Deniz, the one who had appeared in the window to let them in. His date, who takes their coats, is a university-age girl with a pageboy haircut. She is as beautiful as Deniz is handsome. Her mouth is lip-sticked savagely, and with it she offers Catherine and William a thin smile before retreating to the sofa, where she stares absorbedly into her phone. Soon others arrive and Deniz comes and goes from a small galley kitchen off the sitting room, where his guests pick at the food he's elegantly laid out on the thinnest of budgets. Not much wine, but carefully selected bottles from his favorite bodegas, a few plates of fresh sliced vegetables on ice bought end-of-day for a bargain at last Sunday's market, small boxes of expensive chocolates to ornament each table. William can't keep track of who is who, as there are several Hayals, as well as many Öyküs and Nurs. Their self-assigned names affirm their identity, but in this political climate also serve the double purpose of noms de guerre. Who knows if one Öykü was born an Arslan and one Hayal was born an Egemen. Why so many of them had chosen the same names, he couldn't say. What seemed most important was that they had chosen.

His mother makes him a small plate and sits him in a chair by the window. While William picks at his dinner, the scented and beautiful crowd swarms around her, saying *Cat that* and *Cat this*. To take her son here, without his father's permission, so that she can be called Cat instead of Catherine, which is what everyone else calls her, endears her to the Men of Gezi. She has made a choice, just as they have. Having lost sight of his mother, William removes the game Simon from his pocket. He sits by the window and he plays.

Soon everyone has arrived and the apartment becomes too warm. Deniz walks to where William sits and heaves open the window. William glances up from his game. His eyes are drawn to Deniz's muscled arms, his rounded shoulders, how strong he is. A hint of breeze passes through. Deniz cracks a door catty-corner to the window and whispers inside, "Our guests are here." Nobody replies and he says it again. Then a man's voice answers, "Yeah, okay," and Deniz shuts the door and returns to mingle in the crowd, where William has lost his mother.

Whatever this night is about exists just beyond that door, so William stands from his chair by the window. Carefully, he turns the knob. The hinges open smoothly, without a trace of noise. Inside there is light: white walls, white floor and ceiling. The room is transformed into a gleaming cube. The scent of fresh paint hangs heavily around Peter, who stands in the room's center, his back to the door, surrounded by his portraits. William steps behind him and watches.

Peter has almost hung the exhibit. A pair of photos lean one against each of his legs. They are printed in the same dimensions as the other portraits, twelve by eighteen, and the finishes are a monochromatic black-and-white matte. In front of him a single empty nail protrudes from the wall. He combs his fingers through his longish brown curls, which he often teases into a globe of frizz while concentrating. He cranes his neck forward, as if trying to stoop to a normal person's height, which bends him into the shape of a question mark. He has pulled his glasses onto the bridge of his nose and his alternating gaze dips into their lenses and then shifts above them. None of this seems to help Peter resolve the decision with which he's wrestling. William watches him for a while, until Peter feels the boy's eyes on his back despite the many sets of photographed eyes that encircle him.

Peter turns around. His scrutiny is slow and accurate. "Who are you?" he asks. As an afterthought, he adds, "And shut the door."

William does as requested but remains silent.

"Wait, are you Cat's boy?" Peter combs his fingers back through his hair and he puckers his nose toward his eyes as if the remark had left a spoiled, indigestible taste on his lips. "She brought you," he says, like an accusation, or statement, or even a compliment. William can't figure out which, so, finally, he says, "Yes."

"Come here," says Peter. "I need your help with something." He has transformed the cramped bedroom into a pristine gallery, and William steps carefully through the space Peter has created. "I can't decide on the last photo." Then Peter crouches and tilts out the two frames balanced against his legs. William crouches alongside him. One of the two photographs is similar to all of the others: a man with long, stringy hair wearing makeup looks back, a bruise darkens his cheek, a cut dimples his chin, he wears a hard hat like the one hanging on the other room's wall by the poster. Though he stares directly at the camera, his eyes are not set on parallel axes—one wanders menacingly out of the frame.

The subject of the other photograph is beautiful.

Peter has shot this young woman in the same dimensions and lighting as the rest of his portraits. A sheet of dark hair falls straight to her shoulders. There is a bruise around her eye. Up from her chin and along her jaw she also has a cut. She wears a bright dress, whose shade in black and white is exactly the same shade as the cut. A tote bag hangs from her shoulder. Her eyes fix on William clearly, in a way that feels familiar to him, the reflection in her pupil serving as a kind of a mirror.

"This one's a bit different," Peter says. "She was born a woman."

Being a boy, William doesn't understand the exhibit, the nature of Peter's subjects or why he would mix in a single photograph of this one particular woman. But William knows the effect the second photograph has on him. He tells Peter that he likes it best. "You sure?" asks Peter.

He says that he is.

Peter hoists the last photograph onto the wall. As he takes a step back, he crosses his arms and examines it a final time. Then he crouches next to William. Peter has pushed his glasses all the way up his nose and his hands are planted firmly on his knees. "We'd better go find your mother," he says.

※

Twenty photographs hang inside of the gallery. About the same number of people mingle in the kitchen and sitting room. William recognizes many of the faces he has seen in the portraits. Peter's eyes shift among them, as if counting the tops of their heads. When it appears that he has found all of the portrait's subjects, he takes off his glasses and tucks them into the breast pocket of his corduroy sports coat.

A knife clinks against a wineglass. The noise comes from a woman who stands alone in a corner of the apartment. The party faces her. Around her neck on a lanyard dangles a blue badge with an embossed seal—a bald eagle clutching arrows and an olive branch between two furious talons. This places her in the U.S. diplomatic corps. In her photo on the badge she wears the same navy blue suit jacket with a boxy cut and powder blue shirt as on this night, giving the impression that she has only the one outfit, or maybe multiple sets of the same outfit. Her face is lean. Like that of Deniz's date, her black hair is cut into an easy-to-maintain, yet severe, pageboy. Her complexion is such that she could readily be mistaken for a native of this city. A slim and no-nonsense digital triathlete's watch cuffs her wrist. The crowd turns its attention to her. She glances down at her chest, as if she can feel the many sets of eyes settling on her badge.

Awkwardly, she lifts the badge from around her neck, having forgotten to remove it when she left her desk at the consulate. She then raises her glass. "Thank you all for being here," she says. Her eyes land with sincerity on Deniz, who's telling his date to put away her phone. When he looks up he seems startled, as if confused at receiving thanks for being present in his own home. "And thank you to my old friend Deniz, for lending us his apartment. He was one of the first people I met when I came here nine years ago—"

"The first and last reception you ever threw at the Çırağan Palace," interrupts Deniz with a good-natured smile.

Kristin gives him a look and he shrugs, settling back into his seat. Her gaze then turns to Peter and she speaks to him directly. "I want to congratulate you on this remarkable exhibit and say how proud the Cultural Affairs Section is to have helped, in our small way, to host tonight's event."

Everyone toasts.

"That's very kind of you, Kristin," says Peter, but his words stall in the forest of raised glasses, and before he can say anything more, Kristin continues her remarks, speaking over him, saying that she hopes Peter's photos will bring awareness not only to the events in Gezi Park but also to "this community's long struggle for equal rights and dignity." The room listens, politely, but by the time she finishes most of the crowd, including William and his mother, has migrated into the gallery.

Each person falls silent as they find their image on the blistering white walls. On one side are the portraits of the battered "men" of Gezi and on the other side are the women with their meticulously layered makeup and hair arranged as best as they can manage or covered with a wig for an evening out. Viewed from the doorway, a duplicate of Peter's exhibit begins to form among the guests. Then the finished product appears: a set piece, the exhibit itself as subject, portraits in and out of the frame. William can't put words to it, but he feels the effect Peter has created.

"What did you help him with?" his mother asks.

Of the twenty portraits, the only one that nobody stands in front of is the girl in the dress chosen by William. He points toward it and his mother says nothing but leaves him and wanders to its spot on the wall. Now every portrait is mirrored by its subject, or, in the case of his mother, a nearly identical subject. William turns back toward the door, where Peter leans with his camera hung around his neck. He snatches it up and takes a picture of his exhibit. Then he departs into the sitting room.

Deniz and his guests circulate among the portraits, theorizing about themselves in Peter's work, honing in on different details within the photos. William can hear them teasing one another, saying that they look like hell, or some variation on the same. The quiet that had descended so quickly lifts. The party that began in the sitting room and kitchen now resumes in the gallery. William's mother has drifted away from the photograph of the girl in the dress, even avoiding it, instead finding protection with Deniz and the others, who keep her at the center of their conversation with their *Cat that* and *Cat this*. William has no one to stand beside, so he follows Peter.

Kristin has forgone the gallery and stands by the window. With her thumbs she punches out a text message. Peter sidles over to her and she glances up from her phone. "I have to go," she says.

"You liked the exhibit that much?" Peter says self-deprecatingly. "What's the matter? Problem at home?"

"No, nothing like that. I've got to get back to work."

"It's almost midnight."

"Not in Washington it isn't, but the exhibit's beautiful. Congratulations." Kristin tucks her phone back into her overstuffed handbag, from which she removes a small bottle of Purell. She squeezes a dab into her palms, which she vigorously kneads together. Heading to the door, she nearly bumps into William, who is slowly angling across the room toward Peter. "It's almost midnight," Kristin says to the boy in a tender almost motherly tone, as if the fact that he is up at this hour is more remarkable than the fact that he is at Deniz's apartment in the first place.

"That's Catherine's boy," says Peter.

Kristin glances behind her, offering Peter a slight rebuke. Of course she knows that this is Catherine's boy. "Don't let your mother stay out too late," she says to him, then touches his cheek.

"He won't," says Peter, answering before William can. Kristin leaves and Peter and William install themselves at the window, staring toward the streetlamps with their halos.

"Take a look here," says Peter, lifting the camera from his chest.

William tentatively leans closer.

"The portrait you picked was perfect." Peter guides the boy next to him by the shoulder. With his head angled toward Peter's chest, William stares into the viewfinder. The picture Peter took inside of the gallery is a symmetrical panorama, five portraits hung on each of four separate walls, with every person a reflection of their own battered image.

"Your mom filled the last spot."

William vacantly nods.

"One of the first rules of being a photographer," says Peter, "is that you have to take hundreds of bad photos to get a single good one." He points back into the viewfinder. "This is the one shot that I wanted, understand?" He is inviting William to be in on something with him, even though William doesn't completely understand what it is.

The boy offers a timid smile.

"Photography is about contrasts, black and white, light and dark, different colors. For instance, if you put blue next to black, the blue looks darker. If you put that same blue next to white, it looks lighter." Peter flips through a few more images on the viewfinder, pointing out pictures that demonstrate this effect. Each time that William nods, it seems to please Peter, so William continues to nod. "But the blue never makes the white look lighter and it never makes the black look darker. Certain absolutes exist. They can't be altered."

Catherine wanders over. She takes Peter's hand in hers, quickly laces together their fingers, and then lets go. "The exhibit is fantastic," she says.

William reaches for his mother's hand and grips it tightly.

Peter shrugs.

"You don't think so?" she asks.

He dips his gaze into the viewfinder, scrolling back through the images.

"I'm sorry more people didn't show up," she continues. "I'd hoped a couple of critics might come to write reviews. I know Kristin tried to get the word out through the consulate, but you know most of the papers are afraid to print anything on this subject."

"Meaning photography?" says Peter.

"Meaning them. Don't be cute."

He tilts the viewfinder toward Catherine. She tugs the camera closer so that its strap cinches against his neck as she takes a deeper look. On reflex, her two fingers come to her mouth. "This whole thing was a setup for that photo?"

He takes his camera back and nods.

She glances into the exhibit, to where Deniz's guests revel at being the center of attention, for once. "Don't show them," she says.

"Catherine, I need to talk to you about something." Peter rests a hand on William's shoulder. "Give us a minute, buddy."

Catherine and Peter cross the room. They speak quietly by the front door while the party continues in the gallery. William reaches into his pocket and removes the Simon game. He plays for a few minutes, trying to match the elaborate patterns set before him, but he comes nowhere close to his father's high score. While he presses at the flashing panels, he begins to think about what Peter had told him, about contrast, about how one color might change another. He glances up from his game. As he watches Peter standing next to his mother, the two of them speaking close together, she is like the blue. William can see the effect Peter has on her. While Peter looks the same, unchanged by her, like the black or the white.

That night, two hours later

⌒

Murat Yaşar usually doesn't smoke in the house, but he is waiting. It is almost midnight. And he knows that she is out with him.

He has seen Peter's photographs and he finds them tasteless. Because he is an architect, Murat's taste is a matter of business, for it has been proven in the marketplace. His family name, Yaşar, affixes itself to enough of Istanbul's acreage that he hears it spoken as a destination more than he hears it spoken in reference to his person. So he feels more than qualified to render judgment with regard to Peter's taste. A book of his work—cheaply bound by a publisher Murat has never heard of—had been inscribed to her by Peter. When Murat read the slashing, unconstrained cursive on the inside page, he viewed it as Peter's solicitation of his wife:

> *For Catherine, I hope you find the same pleasure in these photographs as I found in our meeting. Yours, Peter*

Nearly two years before, on the night of that meeting, she had also stayed out past midnight. When she stepped through the front door and handed her husband the book, she offered it to him as if he were a child, as if by occupying his hands she might occupy his mind and keep him from probing about her evening. Thumbing through the pages, Murat asked if she'd had a nice time. He didn't ask the obvious questions, the ones he suspected she possessed no answers for: why she had arrived four hours late, or why she smelled of cigarettes, or why she had insisted on taking a taxi when Murat had texted offering to send a car for her. Provoking her lies would only put her on guard. Murat merely shook his head, mumbling "Very interesting" as he leafed through Peter's photographs. Unable to restrain herself, Catherine leaned over his shoulder and pointed to a few of the prints that she admired most.

After Catherine came home with the book, Murat chose to say nothing of her other encounters with Peter, which he never learned of directly from her, but rather heard about in one instance from the maître d' at one of his favorite restaurants, who casually mentioned that his wife had been there with "a young gentleman," and in another instance when Murat happened upon his wife's pocket calendar spread across the kitchen counter. In her rounded, girlish cursive, which had never matured into the handwriting of a grown woman, she had scribbled *P, Kafe 6, Cihangir,* with an hour blocked off in the afternoon beginning at four o'clock.

In each instance, Murat decided that a confrontation would weaken his position. A shared antagonist would only drive her closer to Peter, and it was their closeness that had first alarmed him. She had taken lovers before—or so he assumed, given his limitations as a husband—but she had never spoken openly of another man in their home, gone to lunch with him in public, in short, shown such carelessness. The nearest Murat ever came to challenging Catherine about this affair was when he threatened to throw out Peter's book after finding their son, William, sitting on the living room sofa with it spread across his lap. "He's an impressionable boy," Murat said, scolding his wife with the book flopped open in one hand as if he were delivering a sermon from its pages. Though there was nothing lewd in the images, Catherine certainly knew how she had overstepped by bringing something of Peter's into their home. She also must have known how, slowly, she was provoking her husband. Whether she knew to what end this provocation might come, Murat couldn't say, not even to himself. When she snatched the book from his outstretched palm and returned it to its place on the coffee table, among a growing collection of exclusively American magazines—*Vogue, Vanity Fair, Architectural Digest*—to which she subscribed but never read, Murat felt an inexcusable urge to hurt her. He then left the room.

It hadn't always been this way between them. When they were younger, things had been different. In the morning she used to make them breakfast while he made the bed. In the afternoon they would cross the city to meet on a bench and share from a single packed lunch. And at night—at night she would carefully wake him, her hands pleading for him, and his pleading equally for her. Murat doubts she would concede any of this to Peter. The portrait Catherine paints of their marriage must make him enough of a monster to justify her infidelity. But their past is as real as their present. Even if she says it wasn't love, or claims it wasn't happiness, Murat has proof that it existed: their son. Murat knows that each time she looks at William that past will assert itself. So always they will be married.

Years ago, when they met, Murat was living in her country, attending university, a choice his father did not support. Not because his father objected to an American education, but because Murat pursued a degree in architecture. Construction was the family business, and business was what Murat's father wished him to study. Murat believed that spreadsheets, leasing forms, labor contracts—the bureaucracy of putting up a building—could be apprenticed in any office. To make a beautiful building, or to use the words that had won over his father, "a superior product," took devout study. It was often said of the elder Yaşar that he would take the dimes off a dead man's eyes and return nickels, so it surprised everyone, and Murat most of all, when he convinced his father that a slightly frivolous degree in architecture would be more advantageous to the family's business interests. Though he had presented a convincing argument, Murat hadn't been entirely forthcoming with his father about his ambitions, which transcended the family business and its financials. He wanted to have enough skill so that the buildings he would design in his life might reflect something of it. Soon after meeting Catherine, he confided this to her. Soon after that, she stopped referring to his floor plans, technical drawings and schematics as *his work*. She began referring to them as *his art*.

Although Catherine saw Murat as he wished to see himself, not even she could provide him an escape from his family. Like his father, Catherine's father presided over a dwindling business empire, though his business wasn't construction but rather construction materials export. When the two patriarchs and occasional associates realized their children lived within an hour's train ride of New York, it was they who had brokered the introduction. Like Murat, Catherine wanted to reinvent herself outside the confines of her wealthy family. She had danced as a girl and this was where her ambitions had always dwelled. After high school, Catherine's father had given her a year's allowance to make something of her dream. When she met Murat, that fruitless year was dwindling to its end. Without her having found her way into a dance company or any steady work, the expectation was that she would attend university.

It was Catherine's body—her height (slightly too tall), her frame (slightly too shapely)—which betrayed the promise she'd shown for dance as a girl. The same limitations nature had placed on her ambitions caused Murat to feel a corporeal draw to her, at least at first, in the freedom of his university days. Catherine's father had hoped that Murat's influence might help her to resume her studies, to relinquish one dream for another. To the contrary, she soon moved in with Murat and he supported her, which liberated Catherine from her father's expectations. So she continued to dance, even though her efforts amounted to little. With Murat she too felt free, as if glancing at a menu she could choose her life. After yet another year, when it came time for Murat to return home, she agreed to join him. "What do you think your father will say?" Murat had asked. "I'll be his finest export," Catherine had responded, but malice lingered behind her words, and had Murat been a more mature person, a less trusting person, in short, the person he was now, that malice would have cautioned him. Catherine had no ambition beyond escape. And once she made that escape, it terrified Murat when he slowly realized that her ambition to escape endured, captive as her life had become to his.

When Murat returned from university and took over the family company, immersing himself in what he had once considered the apprentice work of business, he learned of the burden his father had carried all of his life: the uncertainty of labor schedules, the corruption of contracting agents and the tyranny of balance sheets. And this is when his anxiety began, a tension that despite her efforts not even Catherine could calm. Murat also learned that he had never convinced his father of the importance of his study, or *his art*. His father had humored him, a few last years of self-expression, the gift of a doting parent on a frivolous child.

Murat had come to understand that the architect with his pencil and paper was not the creator. The creator was the foreman, the contract negotiator, those whose hands touched brick and mortar. "A real job means you shower at the end of the day, not at the beginning," his father had been fond of saying. Life was not reflected in buildings, as Murat had once thought. Life was earning enough to live. He learned this before his father died, and when he assumed his father's burden, he came to regret those wasted years of study, and Catherine.

❋

Pacing his living room Murat can't help but find something amusing or, perhaps, ironic about his situation, in which Catherine is the expatriate in his country. It has been almost ten years and she has never accepted Murat as her guide, even though he had once accepted her as his. When Murat's cousins used to invite her to lunch, Catherine always had an excuse, until those invitations vanished. When he and Catherine decided on William's education, Catherine insisted on an international lycée instead of the strictly Turkish one Murat had attended. And

Catherine quit her language lessons years ago, often phoning Murat in the middle of the day, interrupting his business meetings, just for him to translate directions from her to a cabdriver. Murat has long wondered if the draw to Peter is that he knows less of this place than she does.

He must seem more like me then than I am now, thinks Murat. Except in one important way, one she doesn't yet know, or even suspect. Peter is a man of limited means, but I am far worse off than he is. I am deeply in debt.

A gust of wind enters through an open window.

If Murat were not waiting for Catherine, he would still be awake, pacing their house with a head full of troubles. Before the protests at Gezi Park, his unfaithful wife had been the largest of his problems. He longs for such simple concerns. But the riots, the politics, they have corrupted a system that was once reliably corrupt. A construction license can no longer be bought. He has a half dozen stalled projects—a glass tower in Zeytinburnu, acreage of underground parking lots, a controlling share in a new stadium for Beşiktaş football club—all of them, at this moment, little more than holes in the ground. When each project finances the other, and when none of them progress, this is a far greater problem.

Tonight she has taken their son, so he does consider phoning the police. Long ago he had the appropriate legal authorities explain to her that if she ever tried to remove the boy from the country, take him back to her home, the required papers had already been prepared so that divorce and custody would be settled in this, "their home," as Murat instructed those same authorities to precisely inform her. Although Murat has faith in the legal precautions he has made, he does not rule out the police entirely. They would certainly send a car to return her, never mentioning a word of it, but in these days it is wise to be spare in the favors you ask. However, there is one other person he could contact, someone who assures discretion.

Murat stubs out his last cigarette in the full ashtray. Peter's book rests beneath it on the coffee table, surrounded by Catherine's unread magazines. He checks the time. It is late. No matter. He punches out a text message. While Murat waits for a response, he again flips through the pages of Peter's photographs.

Tasteless, tasteless, tasteless, he thinks.

How like him I once was.

I am being beaten by myself.

Twelve-thirty that morning

Peter can't believe that she brought her boy. You don't see many second graders at house parties off the İstiklal on a school night, let alone one hosted by the luminaries of the police-brawling gay and gender-fluid community. Bringing him was yet another of Catherine's little rebellions. When he saw William wandering around the wilted crudités, Peter felt protective of the boy. He also realized that Catherine's rebellion wasn't that she brought her son to this neighborhood to be with these people, but that she wanted Peter to meet him—something the two of them had not agreed upon.

She had always said that she hoped Peter would get to know William. She had always picked her words carefully when speaking about him. "It is important for William to know men with a broad worldview," she had told Peter. This was at the beginning, before they had spent entire afternoons sprawled naked across his bed in the sunlight, wordlessly communicating and validating small emotional contracts. This then evolved into "William needs a figure in his life with a worldview that isn't as narrow as his father's." The journey between those two statements had taken nearly two years. Bringing William to the exhibit was her way of announcing to Peter that they had reached a destination.

They stand by the door of Deniz's apartment, where Peter has guided Catherine so that they might speak in private. He says softly, "I thought we'd both decide when I should meet him." He can feel the boy staring at them.

Catherine's hair is the plainest sort of brown, but with a single blond streak, which she was born with and which will likely be the first to gray. It falls in front of her face. She nervously tucks the loose strand behind her ear. "I wanted him to see your work."

As he thinks of that work, Peter's eyes traverse the apartment. On the other side of the door, his photos hang in the gallery. But it isn't a gallery, just a bedroom he has painted white with Deniz's permission. Nothing about this exhibit feels legitimate to him. Kristin has subsidized the entire event with consulate funds and for purposes Peter won't question. He has chosen subjects who crave attention, which he can give. And he is there with a woman he can never possess.

A pair of Deniz's guests stumble drunkenly toward the apartment door, debating which bar along the İstiklal they should head to for after-party drinks. When they remove their coats from the rack, they are men's coats—a heavy parka, a shapeless rain jacket. What has my exhibit revealed? Peter wonders. That these gay men and transgender women are forced to lead a double life? This is as obvious as their coats by the door. If he was trying to make some point about modes of coexistence, or double lives, he could have just photographed Deniz's friends standing by the coatrack. Or photographed himself. Either would have spared everyone the trouble of an exhibit.

He dips his eyes into the viewfinder around his neck. Peter had told William that a photographer has to take hundreds of bad photos to get a single good one. A thought comes to him very clearly: Some photographers just take hundreds of bad photos.

He stares up at Catherine. "It isn't fair for William to meet me."

"I wanted him to." She gently rests her fingertips on his forearm.

Two years before, he had been in a period of self-doubt. He had been grasping for reasons to stay in Istanbul. Meeting Catherine had given him a reason when otherwise he likely would have left. His work progressed, and although this exhibit wasn't the show he'd long hoped for at the Istanbul Modern, it had nevertheless become another reason. Now that it is over, he's left with only her. And he feels increasingly certain that she isn't enough. But he doesn't know how to tell her that he is leaving.

Then he suspects she has anticipated this. Out of desperation she's brought her son so Peter might pity her—or them both—and stay.

"Will I see you tomorrow?" she asks, coaxing him.

"What is tomorrow?"

She hesitates, as though it is a trick question, one that can be interpreted and then answered with infinite variety. "Wednesday," she says.

The moment to tell her about his plans to leave has passed. It will return again and he will do better with his next chance. "Let's talk in the morning," he says.

She has been gently holding his arm. With this answer, she releases him.

The party has begun to empty. The young woman, Deniz's date, disappears deeper into the apartment, luring one of the guests toward a bedroom where Deniz has already gone. William has wandered back over to the window. He sits looking down to where the other guests—the Hayals, Nurs and Öyküs—have gathered outside beneath the pale light of the streetlamps. They are on their way to the bars on the İstiklal. Their voices echo through the maze of alleys, whose narrow, ricocheting bends allow sound to travel further, and it seems as if they might wake the whole neighborhood with their deliberations as they struggle to decide in which direction they should go.

One o'clock that morning

⌒

She lingers at the party. While William waits for his mother to cycle through her many goodbyes, he wanders off and falls asleep on a bed littered with coats. Catherine heaves him off the bed and onto her shoulder as she climbs precariously down the many flights of stairs toward the street. In the backseat of the cab, William's head is in her lap and they will soon be home. She gently nudges him awake. William jolts upright, causing the black silk blazer Catherine had draped across him as a blanket to fall to the taxi's floor. She reaches between her legs, recovers her jacket and folds it into a pillow, which William rests his head against as he leans on her shoulder. She strokes his black hair.

William fixes his attention outside his window. They have descended from the hills and now idle at an empty intersection. A single, stubborn traffic light holds them in place. When it turns, they take a left onto Cevdet Paşa Caddesi. On one side is the incomplete stadium for Beşiktaş football club, a construction site frozen by indefinite delay. Rust encroaches on the steel I beams, whose vertical spans rend a skyward grid into the partially laid foundation. A black-and-white pennant idles in a weak wind from a flagpole that marks the stadium's entrance, but that also marks a congregation point for pallets of expired sod, stacked one upon another. The rotting sod can no longer cover a football pitch and instead it stains the freshly laid concrete. William has driven by this stadium many times with his father, who owns a majority share in its reconstruction and who usually grows silent and dismayed as they pass by.

A similar silence fills the taxi as they come up on Dolmabahçe Palace, the former home of the sultans, which remains hidden behind its unscalable limestone walls. At its entrance a towering wrought-iron gate is hinged into a pair of hulking columns, each adorned with lashing Arabic script, the remnants of the country's defunct Ottoman alphabet, which is now the unreadable language of a vanished empire. Long ranks of birch trees clutch at the star-riddled sky with their trunks white as bone and their branches obscuring a half-moon. Statues flank the wide avenue below. They stand, sentries hidden in ambush among the trees, their bronze-cast expressions frozen miserably into their vigil. Sleeping vagrants encircle the statues' granite pedestals. They keep a separate vigil, obedient as dogs.

❋

A week or so before, William and his father had passed such a vagrant on the street. It was a Monday, and Murat was stuck taking the metro. Usually, he was driven to work. The international school was on the way to Murat's office so, on occasion, he would drop off his son. The two of them would sit in the backseat of the glistening black Mercedes. The driver would crank the wheel, wending through Pera, Cihangir, Taksim, those ancient neighborhoods built into the terraced hills, and Murat would play a guessing game with the boy. He would pick out a few buildings on their route and ask William to arrange their value from lowest to highest. He would then tell William that his job, as his son, was to become the best at this game. When William would ask why, Murat would explain that this was because his job, as his father, was to be the best at it now. And Murat believed that he was the best. He knew the names of every doorman, custodian and construction site foreman. He even knew their children's names. He could look at the glittering tarnish of the horizon from İstinye on the European side to Kadıköy on the Asian side and rattle off the loan rate, scheduled completion date and likely completion date of any project. Across Istanbul's two continents, he would read the skyline like a ticker of deals, those completed, those under way and his future. This was how Murat Yaşar saw the city.

But that Monday morning his Mercedes remained parked in the driveway, and he stood underground at a metro station with his son. At a kiosk on the train platform he picked out a morning paper as he clutched William's hand. They had been forced to take public transport as another round of demonstrations near Gezi Park had brought traffic to a standstill. Murat bought a copy of *Radikal,* one of the few papers the conservative government had yet to take a controlling share in. If a thought couldn't be served up alongside poached salmon at a society dinner party in Beyoğlu, it couldn't navigate its way through the elitist and leftist editorial team at *Radikal.* Murat had spent many evenings perched silently next to his wife at such tables. These were her people and he read their paper and went to their dinner parties because he thought it made good sense to keep tabs on those who might undermine both his business interests and, as he began to suspect, his personal interests.

A train hurtled into the station, its brakes whining along the track. Murat handed his son a five-lira note. The boy placed it on the kiosk counter and was given two lira in return. He glanced back at his father, was rewarded with a nod and then pocketed the pair of coins. Murat thought it was important for the boy to get used to handling money. They rushed to the platform. William liked riding the trains and waited eagerly for the doors to open. His father hated the cramped cars and the indignity of standing shoulder to shoulder with strangers. He held his son close, pressing the boy to his legs.

After the first stop, two seats opened up. Murat and William sat alongside one another. Murat handed his son the funny pages while he leafed open the business section. A column in the margin referenced his unfinished football stadium, specifically the latest delays in construction. Since the Gezi Park riots, Murat had been unable to place his other projects as collateral against the loan he needed to erect the superstructure, to say nothing of the interior—seating, concession stands, turnstiles, restrooms, electrical fittings—a crippling assortment of minutiae. The unfinished stadium sat along the main thoroughfare of Cevdet Paşa Caddesi like a ruin viewed in reverse, a monument to what had never existed.

A midlevel functionary from the Ministry of Interior had given a quote to the newspaper: "Yaşar Enterprises's share will be bought out at a fair price if funds cannot be secured to continue this project." The loans Murat needed would have to come from a government bank, yet the column made no mention of this fact and its bearing on fairness. A couple of years before, the government had petitioned Murat to partner with them on the project during a citywide revitalization initiative, yet the column also made no mention of this fact and its bearing on fairness. The phrase "loss of confidence" appeared in print several times with Murat's name appended to the allegation. Then the piece ended with a final quote from the football club's general manager. "Murat Yaşar sold us a shell, not a home."

Murat folded his paper in half and tossed it under his seat.

Look at us all, he thought, crammed onto trains, unable to drive because of the gridlock created by our own childish dysfunction. If it weren't for last spring's protests, my stadium would have been built. The government has overreached. The protesters have overreached. They are all equally guilty.

A woman searching for a seat stepped on his foot. She apologized halfheartedly to Murat and then hoisted up the toddler perched on her hip. The train carriage rocked. Murat thought to offer her his seat, but, irritated as he was, he didn't and instead watched as the woman stumbled along, burdened by the weight of her child.

You have little in common with these people, he assured himself.

They had one more stop before Şişhane.

Murat put his arm around William, and then glanced down. The light from the fixtures above them was shabby. It fell bitterly over the compartment and it shorted off and on, flickering as the darkness outside in the tunnel contested with it. Father and son fixed their shared concentration on the dimly lit funny pages. They began to laugh and the sound of their laughter rose above the unrelenting noise of the train.

※

A pair of boys, Arabs or gypsies, played a game at the station's exit. They raced up the down escalator, pulling after one another's shirttails, nearly tumbling on the treacherous steps. Murat and William rode up the escalator the correct way, silently passing the playful boys, who examined them with desperate eyes. As they came out of the station and into the combination of fresh air, low morning sun and blue sky, Murat's gaze shifted to a vagrant lying on the sidewalk. The man held a cardboard slat with a message penned in black marker, soliciting money for food. Next to him was a collection of empty lager cans, some tipped over, some still upright. The vagrant's rheumy, glacial eyes stared toward the tall buildings whose dead windows shone high above, and in the way he searched vacantly upward he appeared like a defeated mountaineer stranded at an inescapable base camp, his lager cans like so many depleted cylinders of oxygen, the evidence of his many failed attempts at the summit. His gray beard hung to his chest. His saliva-tipped mustache curled into his mouth. And the small bloodshot pustules of alcoholism congregated on his cheeks like freckles on a fair-skinned child.

Murat stopped and glancing down he took William by the shoulders and pressed him to his legs as he had done on the train. He held him in front of the vagrant. "Do you see this man?" Murat asked his son.

William nodded.

"This man has nothing. Now look at me."

William turned over his shoulder and stared up at his father.

Murat wore a tailored suit, as he always did, today it was a conservative charcoal gray, a white handkerchief meticulously folded in the pocket, a creaseless full-Windsor knot cinched at his neck; he had shaven at six a.m., his hair was cut the first Tuesday of each month.

That morning he looked the same as he did any of the other mornings that his son had known him.

"That man is half a billion lira richer than I am."

William looked again at the vagrant.

"Do you understand?" Murat asked.

William nodded, as if trying to comprehend his father's debts. Murat crouched next to him on the sidewalk, stooping to eye level with his son. He had confused William and he regretted it. The boy couldn't appreciate such debts, and shouldn't have to, at least not yet. The silk hem of Murat's suit jacket brushed against the street. He and the vagrant were close, their bodies almost touching.

Murat dragged William away by the hand. They wandered onto Istiklal Caddesi and Murat pointed out certain buildings, quizzing William about their value relative to one another and sharing insider details of many—the confidential plans for a new shopping center here, a landlord who bribed building inspectors there. They then passed Galatasaray Lisesi, the oldest school in the city. Engraved on the iron gate was the year of its founding: 1481. Murat explained to William that this was not even thirty years after Sultan Mehmet the Conqueror seized Constantinople from the defending Christians.

"Did he build the school?"

"No," said Murat. "His son Bayezid did."

"Bayezid," repeated William, slightly mispronouncing the name, the influence of his mother's American accent showing.

"Bayezid the Peaceful," added Murat, and his clear pronunciation served as a subtle rebuke to his son.

The story, or at least the version recounted by Murat, was that when Bayezid inherited his empire he took it upon himself to revitalize the city after his father's bloody conquest nearly destroyed it. To understand his new capital Bayezid would roam the streets disguised as an ordinary citizen. On one of these secret walks he found himself in a garden filled with red and yellow roses. A young man in simple dress who had a reputation for great wisdom tended the garden. After

Bayezid revealed his identity, he asked how to improve his empire and
its capital. The gardener advised the sultan to educate his people and
explained that his own wisdom had come through quiet contemplation
among his roses. He then suggested that Bayezid build a school there,
which the sultan did. The gardener became the first headmaster and
administered Galatasaray Lisesi until his death.

Murat could see the roses. They still grew just beyond the gate.

"How did the gardener die?" William asked.

"Like his father, Bayezid turned to conquest as he grew older. At the
sultan's request the loyal gardener—now the headmaster—recruited
his students to become soldiers. He then led them in a campaign for
Bayezid and died in one of the battles."

"And Bayezid, did he die in the battle?"

"No," answered Murat, "he died some years later."

"How?"

"He had a son, and that son betrayed him."

Murat stared out into the garden. His eyes shifted from the broad
Corinthian columns flanking the entrance of the lise, to the sturdy
masonry of its three wings, to the terra-cotta-shingled roof and, finally,
to the cobblestone footpaths lined with benches where students reclined
against their backpacks reading books that were flapped open across
their chests like flightless birds.

"This must be the most expensive building on the İstiklal," announced William, as if solving the riddle that his father had laid before him.

Murat smiled at his son but absently. When he was with the boy
he felt both burdened and unburdened at once. To prepare William
for an unkind world, he needed to be firm. But he also needed to equip
him with the reservoirs of approval and affection that would sustain
him against the same unkind world. His responsibilities as a father
conflicted with one another. He could love the boy too much, or he
could love the boy not enough. If a tension existed between Murat and
his son, it was a reflection of these two conflicting impulses, and Murat
believed that this tension, which dogged him, was also the proof that

he was a good father. Anything aside from tension was a failure. He took an appraising, final look at the lise.

"I'm not certain that you're right," he told his son. "The lise would never be for sale. I guess you would say that it is priceless."

"But that means *it is* the most expensive," said William.

"Perhaps," Murat answered. "When the value of a thing exceeds an amount that money can capture, that's when it becomes priceless, but, of course, this can also mean that something is merely worthless." Then Murat scooped up his son, who looped his arms around his father's neck. As he carried William the last two blocks to school, Murat noticed the time and nearly broke into a run. Waiting on a leather sofa in his office was a lawyer who had come to see him about the football stadium and who billed one thousand lira per hour. Murat did the math in his head as he hurried down the İstiklal. He would be at least thirty minutes late, so five hundred lira. Try as he might, he could not help but calculate what this morning with his son had cost him.

※

William rests his head on his mother's shoulder and watches the city unspool as they return from the party: dark side streets interrupted by channels of bright wet filth, the moon's white reflection brushed across the ambling current of the Bosphorus, the bridges with their spans studded in lights. Catherine types furiously, grasping her phone with both hands, as if she's captured a snake by its neck. Her expression is drawn, strained and afraid. William shuts his eyes. He tries to sleep.

The clanging house gate slowly rolls open. William sits up and Catherine tucks her phone back into her folded black silk blazer. The taxi pulls along the curved driveway. Murat stands waiting under the arch of a white colonnade that leads to the front door. His look is heavy, a mix of worry and anger, as vacant as the bronze sentries William had observed outside the walls of Dolmabahçe Palace. Gravel crunches beneath the taxi's wheels. Then they stop.

The driver announces the fare. But before Catherine can pay, Murat has opened the driver's door, as if he might drag him out from behind the steering wheel. Instead, he drops a hundred-lira note in the man's lap. Murat then opens the back door. He grabs his wife just above the elbow and pulls her onto the driveway. Catherine reaches after William, but Murat swats her arm away and hoists the boy from his seat.

William lunges for his mother. Murat lifts William by the waist and then plants him like a stake in the ground. Then he snatches both of their wrists and leads them inside. The last thing William hears before the front door shuts behind them is the taxi's wheels churning at the gravel as the driver speeds out to the street.

All of the lights are on in the marble foyer. A porcelain blue-and-white temple jar filled with white orchids rests on a mahogany center table. The table is aligned beneath a crystal chandelier and the house smells heavily of cigarettes and flowers. Murat stands with his wife on one side of him and his son on the other, their wrists each cuffed in his firm grip. He breathes from his chest. He sights down at Catherine and then at William. He struggles to direct his sense of betrayal and anger away from his son.

He is unable to ease his breathing.

He drags William upstairs.

Catherine tries to follow them.

"Don't," snaps Murat.

She hasn't succeeded in taking even a full step. Caught in the foyer, she clutches at her silk blazer, pulling its lapels across her body as if warding off a chill. Murat stands in the stairwell and flips the light switch.

William watches as the chandelier above his mother goes out.

Half past three that morning

His apartment has a view. It seems they all do. This is an advantage of living in a terraced city, one that reaches into the hills. The window by Peter's bed looks out on the First Bosphorus Bridge. Its spans and cables are ornamented with turquoise LED lights that reflect off the water, which glides past like black oil. The strong current swirls in the light and the surface of the deep strait swims with color.

Forty years before, the bridge's construction had been touted as a great triumph, even though an unspoken shame surrounded its completion. Why had it taken more than a millennia to connect the two sides of this city? Looking at the bridge, he thinks of his exhibit from earlier in the evening, of Deniz and the others—including Catherine—staring at two disconnected versions of themselves. These many years later the bridge has not had the desired effect. After Gezi Park, the country is riven with divisions and in this way Peter can understand the shame associated with a bridge built too late.

His head is on the pillow as he watches the current, hoping it might hypnotize him to sleep. The sunrise is still a few hours off, yet his mind roams, keeping him awake. Catherine knows he plans to leave. He feels certain of it. He feels equally certain that she can't come with him, even if he wanted her to, which he doubts. She is bound up in Murat and their son. Perhaps this is why he had succumbed to their affair in the first place, because he knew that it could go nowhere, that it had to finish in this way, and since he already understood the nature of its ending he could be absolved of responsibility, for they both knew this was the inevitable destination.

As Peter looks at the bridge, his thoughts stray to what he considers their first night. Although they had met for dinner once before, at the Istanbul Modern, this meeting occurred a few days later, when they had bumped into one another at a gallery opening for the controversial artist Taner Ceylan, whose violent, sexually charged and hyperrealist paintings resembled photographs. After the event they had searched the crowded streets for a taxi and had then wandered onto the bridge, which was more like a highway, and usually closed for people to walk across, but it was open that day, so they had chosen to cross it together and, perhaps with a bit of luck, to find a ride home on its far side. In the center of the bridge, she had approached the railing, staring two hundred feet below at the dark, churning current. She waved Peter toward her so that he might look as well.

"Come here, Peter!"

He remained a few steps from the railing and didn't move.

"Don't you want to look? We're right between Europe and Asia, we're not on any continent." She leaned deeply over the railing. "This bridge is my favorite place in the city."

"This whole city is a bridge," said Peter.

"Maybe so," said Catherine. The Bosphorus ran dense as mercury beneath them. Peter glanced to its banks, to the two continents, to Istanbul, a city so illuminated that it vanished the power of the moon. "But you can't live on a bridge."

"Why don't you come back from the railing?" Peter suggested.

"Are you afraid of heights?" she asked. The wind was quick to carry away her voice and he could barely understand her. "Everyone has one existential fear," she continued, but now she wasn't looking down, instead she stared at him and he could see the light from the water reflected from below, its projection playing off her eyes. "For instance, my husband, his fear is that he won't be a success, or at least that he won't measure up to his father." Peter offered a confused look, revealing the absurdity of this fear for a man whose business conquests riddled the skyline. "It's not as ridiculous as you may think. None of us see ourselves as others see us. If only we could. Our vision of ourselves is like our voice. The world hears us one way, but inside our head our voice sounds entirely different. There's no possibility of recording that voice, of sharing it with anyone. We go our whole lives without another person ever hearing us the way we hear ourselves. How people see themselves is the same, and there is no clearer way to understand that differing vision than to understand those insecurities, to understand that one fear." It had rained the hour before and the bridge lights shone on the wet pathway.

He asked what her fear was.

"Why should I tell you?"

He took one cautious step and then another, shuffling his feet as he transferred his weight, as though at any moment while he was drawing closer to her the ground beneath him might fall away. Then he lunged forward and gripped the railing as desperately as if it were flotsam on the open ocean. He glanced up at her, smiling the heedless smile of an idiot, his eyes searching for some reaction, as if she might reward what he perceived to be his conquest of fear or, put another way, his courage when grasping the railing even though he was paralyzed by heights. That night as they stood on the bridge, the wind kept snatching away their voices. Peter had needed to lean in close to Catherine so that he could be heard. "The idea of falling terrifies me," he confessed. "I can feel the vertigo in my stomach."

"The vertigo isn't from your fear of falling," she said. "It's from your hidden desire to jump. That's why we feel vertigo."

Peter pressed his body against the railing and took another deep look at the water below. "So are you going to tell me your fear?" he asked.

"You weren't paying attention," she said. "I just did." She told him to feel how her heart was beating. He reached for her wrist, to take her pulse, but she said, "We aren't children, are we?" and placed his hand elsewhere.

They had continued their crossing and on the far side they finally found a cab. He held open the door for her and they climbed inside. Peter gave the driver his address. When he glanced back at Catherine, so that she might give her address as well, she said nothing. Their taxi climbed the steep, wending roads and through her omission they both made their way back to his apartment. Neither of them spoke. Their eyes avoided one another's in the backseat. Past the door a rocky bluff plunged hundreds of feet below. Peter was turned toward his window, away from her. He couldn't help but look at the drop.

⁂

Is it two short knocks and then one long one? Or is it one long knock and then two short ones? Peter always forgets, and in the weeks after Catherine first spent the night, he often stood in front of his own door trying to remember before he knocked. When he'd come home, he could always hear her slight, hurried movements inside his apartment—the clinking of dishes, footfalls against creaking floorboards—the quiet patter of someone trying to remain silent. She would visit on evenings when Murat was out of town for business, or in the afternoon between the errands she invented to consume her days.

She had once asked Peter for a key, but he had demurred. Affairs by definition had an element of adverse selection when it came to trust. Could you trust someone who was untrustworthy enough to be making such liaisons with you? So Catherine didn't get the key. On days when she planned to visit, he would leave it under the mat for her and they would implement their system of secret knocks. Catherine had insisted on the knocks in case someone else came to the door while she was there alone. Peter had thought it a bit overcautious. He had told her that no one ever stopped by his apartment. But he realized her insistence wasn't really about the knocks, but rather about having a code between them—something only they shared. She then came up with one short, two long.

Or, he wonders as he lies with his head on the pillow, looking out at the First Bosphorus Bridge, trying to sleep, was it two short, one long? He could never remember the combination.

It all began with Kristin, and that was more than two years before. He had come to the city to live cheaply and to assemble a body of work that would signal his transition from photojournalist to artist. Peter's photo credit had, for some time, been a regular microprint feature in the Sunday supplements of several major newspapers. That work had felt like a continuous vibration between gravity and air. Gravity: journalistic assignments covering elections in Venezuela, earthquakes in Haiti and Tibet, the occasional war zone embed, et cetera. Air: commercial assignments shooting starlets at media junkets, insets for glossy music magazines, home décor arrangements for various catalogs, et cetera. The et cetera in his portfolio was the problem. If a photographer transforms the fleeting into the permanent, he wanted to create a lasting body of work, not just magazine snaps. "If you don't make a vessel for your life to pass into," a mentor of his once said, "it will simply pass into an urn."

When Kristin first returned his call, following up on the grant application he had submitted to the consulate's Cultural Affairs Section, he had run through most of his savings and was about to return home and to journalism. He had never wanted money from the government, as he thought it would taint the objectivity of his work, or at least how that objectivity was perceived. But he felt that he had no choice. To return to journalism meant to return to the ceaseless stream of body-bagged GI's, a fondue of suicide bombers, natural disasters, man-made disasters, all of it: senseless. Like Warhol—whom Peter despised—just the same images repeated over and over until they lost all meaning.

When he arrived at Kristin's office on the top floor of the consulate, a seven-story fortress in İstinye buttressed by concentric circles of security, he felt the same reservations as he had when he'd submitted his grant application on a lark. He still wasn't certain that he wanted to exchange his independence for a partnership with the cultural attaché's office. Then Kristin slid the terms of the grant across her desk and allowed Peter to look them over.

"The terms *are* generous," she said, loading her emphasis onto the verb so that the weight of that emphasis would cut off debate.

While Peter read, she mixed a chocolate-powder nutrition shake in a large plastic cup with a special twist-off lid. She sneezed as some of the powder got up her nose, and it was a squeaking sneeze, a noise like a sneaker stopping suddenly on a lacquered basketball court. A pair of running shoes sat at the foot of her desk with sweat socks balled inside their heels.

Peter's chin sunk toward his chest as he read. The terms were generous, uncomfortably so. It was enough to support his work for at least the next year, likely a bit more if he minimized his expenses. Kristin sipped her breakfast shake and checked a half dozen cellphones laid out in a single rank across her desk. She typed a text message on one and then set the phone down. It vibrated again, but she ignored it, and instead reclined in her office chair and finished off her shake, digging a straw from her cluttered desk drawer to suck up the dregs. Her landline rang. Chatter came from the other end. Kristin replied, "And you got that reading from her mouth or armpit?" She then listened intently with the receiver cuddled between her shoulder and ear. "If her temperature is that high, you need to take her in." She shifted in her seat. "I don't care what the doctor thinks." Peter had finished reviewing the contract and his eyes met Kristin's. "Listen, I'm in the middle of something," she said, her voice descending into the phone. "Promise me that you'll take her in." Kristin looked down at her desk, away from Peter. "Yes, I love you too." She set the receiver back in its cradle.

"If you're busy, I could come back," Peter offered.

"It's nothing, just family stuff," she said. "So what do you think of the terms?"

"You're offering quite a bit." Peter's eyes canted upward, as if he was looking at a bank of clouds hovering just above their heads.

"You say it like it's a bad thing." She rested her clasped hands on the desk between them. "We could always offer you less . . . if that'd make you more comfortable." A table fan in the corner circulated the air, which carried the delicate scent of Kristin's sweat. "You're an excellent candidate, Peter." She swiveled in her chair toward a computer on the corner of her desk. Her fingers danced across the keyboard as she opened his application. "Exeter and then Yale"—she turned the screen toward him, revealing a Google search of his photo credits—"plus your portfolio to date, which is quite impressive. You're here, you want to do good work, and your government wants to help you. Also . . ." She paused and motioned for Peter to hand her back the terms of the grant. He slid the contract across the desk. She took her pen and indexed it on the payment, ". . . I think that you need this. I don't think anyone else is supporting you here and I don't think you want to go back home. This buys you time. You need time."

Kristin wasn't pushy, but she was persuasive. Sitting behind her desk with her government-issue badge on a lanyard around her neck, she possessed an unquestionable authority. She was part of a diplomatic mission and, unlike Peter, had a profession, a real job, and one that didn't require the pittance of grant money. Nothing about her was freelance. She spoke with the tenderness of an older sister advising a younger brother. But she also spoke with the same type of subtle, yet cruel, diminishment offered up between rival siblings.

This country persisted as a riddle to him, a tangle of conflicting signs. And yet it seemed like the easiest of passages from his life in New York to his life here—a plane ticket, a month-to-month lease, a visa. The entirety of him, at least to her, was what appeared on her screen. She likely wondered what his family thought about his decisions. A decade after he had left university, did they feel as if he had squandered their investment in him? If they still supported his work, would he have found himself sitting at Kristin's desk, broke and ready to return home? His credentials which so impressed Kristin were far in the past and as useless as everything else in the past. He wondered if she could understand why he had traded that world for this one.

Her pen was still indexed on the grant payment printed across the contract.

Peter took back the sheet of paper and read aloud from the mission statement: "The recipient will collaborate with the consulate to provide artistic programming that advances relations between the United States and the host country and which furthers cross-cultural dialogues."

"You got it," said Kristin. "We call it soft power."

The same cellphone vibrated again on her desk. She ignored it, waiting for him to sign so that they could begin their work together. Then another cellphone went off right next to it. "Are you going to answer either of those?" Peter asked.

"If they're important, they call me on my landline." She picked up one of the phones, giving it a cursory glance, and then she set it back on the desk as if confirming her suspicion that it was, in fact, no one of importance. "Are you still interested in the type of project you outlined in your proposal?"

In his application, Peter had described in some detail his current project of portraiture, which was an expansive survey of the city's inhabitants. Peter recognized that it lacked focus. He had been wandering the streets like a paparazzo, but instead of hounding out celebrities he was hounding out the most obscure citizens. He couldn't say whether or not this work was any good. He hadn't figured out the thrust of his project and he suspected this was why Kristin had selected his application among a multitude. If the project remained undefined, she could help craft it to her own purposes. While determining exactly how to answer Kristin's question, he reviewed the paragraph he had submitted a few weeks before, the one headed "Scope of Work." He could already see the flaws or, as Kristin phrased it, "What you have outlined is ambitious, Peter."

"You don't think it'll succeed," he answered, not without some defensiveness.

"That's not what I said," she corrected him, "but I want you to pare it down."

"Into what?"

"Maybe a book? An exhibit? Or both? We don't have to figure that out today. What we do have to figure out is whether or not we're going to move forward together." She glanced insistently at the contract.

Peter leaned over her desk and signed.

"The right choice," said Kristin.

Her comment did nothing to assure Peter. "What do we do now?" he asked.

Kristin reached into her desk drawer and handed him a business card with the same eagle she wore on the lanyard around her neck embossed in gold. She scrawled a number across the back. "Use that if you need to be in touch." She then turned to her keyboard and began crafting an email. "I'm going to make a few introductions for you. It will help get you momentum as you start your project."

"I've already started it," Peter grumbled, reminding her of this.

"Of course," she replied. "Also, you should meet Catherine Yaşar, an American who's lived here for some time, nearly a decade. She used to dance in the ballet, though I'm not sure which company, perhaps one in New York. She married a Turk and is now a patron of the arts. Her husband is a well-known developer. I'll set it up. She'll take an interest in your work."

"What makes you so certain?"

"Because your work is interesting."

Kristin turned back to her computer and continued to craft the email to Catherine. While she typed, Peter punched the number on her business card into his cellphone. He pressed dial so that it would save to his contacts. The call connected. A cellphone in the batch that sat on Kristin's desk began to ring. Without shifting her glance from the computer screen, Kristin reached over. She silenced the phone.

❄

Peter's head is still on the pillow. He continues to watch the bridge and with the least possible gesture the gray morning light reveals its spans. The traffic comes in an unsteady drip. He counts the cars, reaching one hundred. The headlights curve out of the snaking residential streets, up the on-ramp, and then hold steady, pressing straight ahead into the rush between the two continents. The road across is a lonely no-man's-land.

Peter keeps counting the cars.

From the easternmost hills of Europe, he looks over the water and watches the westernmost hills of Asia take shape. These are the minutes before dawn. The lights on the First Bridge have served their purpose and, as if set to a timer, they extinguish. The buildings on the far bank, lightly sketched in fog, shine with the sun behind them. The strait is a mirror. His window has no curtains. This high above, who can see in? Traffic picks up. As the lanes begin to fill, Peter loses count of the cars and quits. He reaches for his phone on the bedside table to see the time. He needs to be up in an hour. His ringer has been off and he sees a half dozen missed calls. Before he can check who it is, there is a knock at his door—one long, two short.

One-thirty that morning

⁓

Three Persian rugs cover the wooden floor of the enormous room where the boy sleeps. His father rarely puts him to bed, and that night Murat stands at William's dresser rifling through the drawers for a pair of pajamas. He eventually finds a matching set. William is old enough to dress himself, but it has been some time since Murat participated in the nighttime routine, so he strips off the boy's shirt and bottoms, not allowing William to do it on his own.

He stands naked in front of his father.

Murat fumbles with the pajamas, putting the shirt on his son backward. William is fearful of further upsetting his father so he makes no correction. Murat finishes and crosses the room to the bed. He flings open the covers. William climbs beneath them. Murat does not kiss William or say good night, or say anything for that matter. Yet when Murat turns out the lights, he does remember to keep on the small lamp alongside William's nightstand. There is a great deal in William's life that Murat is oblivious to, but he never forgets that his son is afraid of the dark. He once had the same fear himself and, at times, in other situations, he still feels sweat breaking out on his forehead and the back of his neck, he still feels his mouth turn to cotton, and he still feels that tight panic in his center, as if a big, invisible hand were pressing open-palmed onto his rib cage.

The door shuts behind Murat and William listens as his father's heavy footfalls sound down the hallway and then down the stairs to the foyer. William strains to hear either of his parents in the silence of their grand house, yet he hears nothing. His eyes wander. Piles of untouched toys—train sets, stuffed animals, a thousand colors of molded plastic—jam the corners of the room like a fugitive's wealth hoarded away in a cave. He has arrived at that age where, slowly, he has lost interest in these possessions. Above the dresser his mother has arranged photos of the three of them—a reminder not of her, or of his father, but rather of the general idea of a family.

A door slams somewhere in the house. More footsteps. He hears his parents' voices intermingling in sharp whispers. Another door slams. Then another. He no longer wants to hear anything. Or see anything. He wants to be hidden. He reaches over to his nightstand and turns off the lamp.

He lies in the dark convincing himself that the dark can no longer hurt him.

It is still dark when his mother wakes him. Her face is very close to his. The trace of her perfume lingers, it is the scent she had put on before Peter's exhibit that evening. She gently shakes William by the shoulders. He rolls over and reaches for the bedside lamp, but she stops him. "We have to go," she says. Before he can sit up, she has already flung away his blanket and is cramming his shoes onto his bare feet. He walks hand in hand with her, down the hallway, still in his pajamas, toward the stairs. He knows to step quietly—heel to toe, heel to toe. They make their way. The lights are out. They descend the stairs one at a time so that they don't stumble in the dark, so that they don't interrupt the early-morning silence. Then they stand in the foyer, next to the table with the porcelain vase filled with white orchids.

The chandelier above them turns on.

William is holding her hand and he can feel a jolt course through his mother's entire body. She squeezes his palm in hers.

"Where are you taking him?" His father has appeared at the top of the stairs.

She backs up into the table. "We have to leave," she tells William.

The boy won't look at her, or his father. He stares only at the white orchids in the blue-and-white vase. Murat descends the stairs two at a time. Catherine moves briskly toward the door, taking her son with her, but she never breaks into a run. It is almost as if she wants Murat to catch her. Her husband places himself between her and the door.

"Tell me where you're going?"

"I don't know where," she says.

"You know it's no use."

"Move aside."

"Then take some of your things."

"These are all your things."

Catherine steps around him, trying to pass through the door. Murat grabs William by the elbow. In the strength of that grip, the boy can feel his father's desperation. William thinks to snatch his arm free but doesn't. He allows his father to hold on to him, though it hurts, until, slowly, he feels the grip release. Murat crouches next to his son, as he had done before, when the two of them had stopped to look at the vagrant lying in the street and he had tried to explain to William the many debts he owed.

Catherine holds her son's hand, but he is gently pulling away from her. Murat looks as if he has something to ask the boy. William waits for whatever that thing is and he won't move from where he stands, not until he hears it. He isn't yet ready to follow his mother, so he gives his father this last moment.

Murat says nothing.

Catherine takes her son and leaves. But when she tries to close the front door behind her, Murat won't allow it. He sticks his foot in the jamb and makes certain that the door will remain open.

❀

Dawn strikes all at once and the day sets in. The water trucks have already made their rounds, their sprinklers tamping down the morning dust. William and his mother stand at the bottom of the gravel driveway, on the edge of the street. The passing, indifferent traffic crowds them from the curb. Eventually, an off-duty taxi stops out of courtesy, or curiosity. When the driver rolls down his window, he gives Catherine a pitiful look, his eyes seeming to ask: Who is this stranded woman with her child wearing nothing but his pajamas? When Catherine and William climb into the backseat and the taxi pulls onto the road, the driver leaves his meter off.

Catherine gives him an address. She puts her arm around William, whom she has again covered with her blazer. As she holds him, she slips a hand into its pocket. In her rush to leave she has brought nothing other than her phone and wallet. She dials a number. It rings and rings. No answer. She taps out a text message. Then she dials the number again. Voicemail picks up. "Hi, it's me," she says, and then she swallows away the emotion that threatens to overtake her voice. "I don't know where you are . . . I need to come over . . . something's happened. And I have William. Please call."

She hangs up and clutches the phone to her chest as if it is a rope that she has ascended halfway but no longer has the strength to climb.

"Where are we going?" her son asks.

She cradles his head in her lap, and then bends over and kisses its top. Above them, big thick clouds hurry east, toward the country's interior. William gazes up, tracking their navigation across the sky.

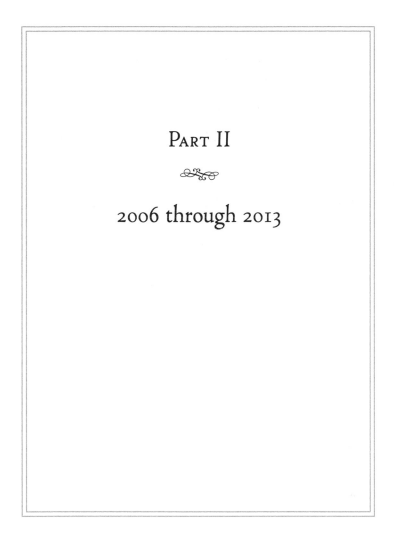

PART II

2006 through 2013

July 25, 2006

◦——◦

Murat held a paper ticket in his hand. It read 319, his number in the queue. He sat in a row of four metal chairs bolted to the linoleum floor in the consular services waiting area. A digital counter hung on the wall and a television played Hollywood comedies on mute with a ticker of subtitles. A few people watched. Nobody was laughing. Every minute or so, the digital counter advanced by one. Murat wore a khaki summer suit, which he had found at a Brooks Brothers outlet while attending university in the States. It was many seasons out of fashion and seldom left his closet. The jacket needed to be let out and also the pants, and although the suit no longer fit he thought it was the right choice for an appointment with an American embassy official.

He had come on behalf of his newly adopted son. The boy was ten weeks old, but they had had him for only two weeks. Murat looked forward to a month and a half from now, when the boy would be sixteen weeks and one day old. That's when he and his wife, Catherine, would have had him for more than half of his life and in Murat's mind they would then be majority shareholders.

Murat's secretary had made this morning's appointment for him online. The consulate's website had assigned him a single time slot—10:30 a.m.—over which he had no say. He had a conflicting appointment, a meeting with a potential investor. He had called the consulate personally to request a different, more convenient time. After he'd been placed on hold for what he felt was unreasonably long, an operator had connected Murat with an official in Immigration Services. Before requesting another appointment, Murat liberally aired his grievances about the wait. When he eventually did make his request, the official predictably refused.

The morning of his appointment Murat's driver dropped him as close as he could to the consulate's entrance, which still didn't prevent Murat from having to walk through a vast serpentine of concrete barricades until he eventually encountered a Turkish security guard who wore the navy blue uniform of a private contracting firm and who stood, with metal-detecting wand in hand, grumbling to Murat that regulations prohibited foreign nationals from carrying cellular devices on the premises. The security guard then took Murat's phone and handed him a plastic token, like those used for a coat check. Without his phone and stranded in the waiting room, which had no clock, but only the red digital counter, Murat had no way of telling the time. A Filipina woman sat next to him, her arms crossed over her chest. He asked if she had a watch.

She glanced at Murat's wrist. He wore a slim white gold Patek Philippe on an alligator-skin band with two indentations from the clasp. The first indentation was for a very substantial wrist. The second indentation, which was where Murat wore it, was on the slightest setting. While he was alive, Murat's father had never given him the watch. It had come later, as a de facto inheritance, gifted without any parting message that might have validated it as an heirloom passed from father to son. He held its face to the woman, to show her that its second hand didn't move. And although the watch was broken, Murat put it on each morning. A few jewelers had examined it for him. If it would ever again tell time, the entire internal mechanism would need to be replaced. This would leave behind only the original casing and watch face. Murat preferred the old parts, even if none of them worked.

"A man who wears a broken watch is a—" said the Filipina woman.

"Is a sentimental man," answered Murat, finishing her sentence.

"Is an idle man," she replied. She then read from her digital Casio. "It is twelve forty-two." She wore a Mickey Mouse T-shirt with the word *Orlando* etched in an excited, looping script across the bottom. Murat thanked her and the two of them sat silent alongside one another, he in his Brooks Brothers suit and she in her Disney T-shirt, both of them having had a similar idea of how to dress in order to impress an American diplomatic official.

Murat resented the idea of having to impress anyone, particularly a government functionary—no matter the nationality—whose work happened out of a waiting room with linoleum floors and among a crowd who had to take numbers on tickets in order to be seen. That Murat was part of that crowd had no bearing on this prejudice. He had suggested on several occasions that Catherine handle this appointment. "William can, after all, only become American because of you," he had told his wife. "If you came, we could skip waiting in line and just go straight to U.S. Citizen Services."

Predictably, her refusal assumed the form of inaction and silence. Within days of adopting William, Catherine had fallen into a depression. Murat could not give her a child and he would not allow her to use a donor, which he likened to her having another man's child, so they had chosen to adopt. Her son committed her to Murat and to the resulting fate of being left childless.

Murat recognized the root of this depression. How many conversations had they had about adopting? How many agencies, go-betweens and even traffickers had they spoken to? Only now, once a midwife had delivered the boy to a family in Esenler, a neighborhood they had always avoided, and from a mother whose name they would never know, only now did his wife finally reveal her true reservations. Murat understood Catherine's crippling disappointment. Were he able, he would have given her a child in the normal way. But on assuming his father's burdens, he had lost the ability to become a father himself. He of all people understood the psychic paralysis of wanting something too much, so much that you cannot even say what it is you want. Yes, he understood. But he had yet to forgive her for wanting something that he could not provide.

Murat glanced toward a cordoned-off section of the waiting area. Enclosed behind a soundproof glass wall and door were a dozen or so padded recliners and a table of refreshments—coffee, pastries, fresh juice in large glass carafes. Inside, a separate digital counter hung on the wall. The number displayed was far lower than the one in the waiting room for foreign nationals. It was set at 016. The few people inside the glass room lingered, watching a television that was not bolted to the wall, but rather stood on a console, and that played movies identical to those outside, comedies mostly, but with no subtitles. This was the waiting room for U.S. Citizen Services.

Murat glanced at the paper ticket in his hand. He tried to calculate how much longer this would all take. The soundproof door opened. A teenager with a cascade of floppy brown hair and a polo shirt tucked into his khakis departed, holding a new passport. A wake of noise trailed behind him. Murat could suddenly hear the movie in English and the voices of the few people ensconced behind the soundproof walls. All of them were laughing along.

❋

Eventually his number came up. Built along the far wall of the waiting area were a half dozen interview booths, where on one side there was a counter and on the other side there was a consular officer perched on a high chair. The interviewee didn't have a chair, but rather stood, presumably so that the interview didn't last too long. A thick glass pane with a circle of pinkie-size holes drilled into its center like a shot-out target partitioned the booth so that the two parties could speak to, but not reach, one another. Beneath the glass was a slot to pass documents. The setup reminded Murat of the visiting station in a prison.

Murat had brought his leather attaché, which was a fine calfskin case Catherine had given him the year before, after his father's death, when he had finally taken control of the company. She had thought the gift might boost his confidence as he assumed the role of chief executive, or so she had told him, and he now clutched the attaché in a double grip like a player about to toss a forward pass. As he hoisted it onto the counter, he felt uncertain about whether he had ever found that elusive confidence. From its satin interior, he removed a sheaf of documents. While he quickly sorted through them, the consular officer opposite him turned over her shoulder. Another officer stepped behind her, a young man with a side part in his blond hair wearing a Brooks Brothers suit similar in style to Murat's own, except in the fit, which was more carefully tailored. He cupped his hand to his mouth and whispered something into his colleague's ear. She then gathered her things while the young man installed himself across from Murat and asked vacantly, "Size nasıl yardım edebilirim?" He logged on to the desktop computer in front of him, hardly even glancing in Murat's direction.

Murat continued to silently leaf through his documents. He didn't want to answer the young man in Turkish as his English was impeccable, something he had worked at over many years. Reading the language had come far more easily to him than speaking it. When he and Catherine had first lived together, Murat would, with religious devotion, watch *Mister Rogers' Neighborhood* each morning. The slow cadence of the show helped him to pick apart the spoken language. When he had an early class, Catherine would diligently record episodes for him, herself becoming engrossed in the show, finding appeal in the contained world it imagined. The two of them took to watching episodes together, making whole nights of it with popcorn. And his English gradually improved. When a guest of theirs once noticed the episodes on the DVR, Murat turned ashen. Without hesitation, Catherine said she was considering a degree in child psychology. She was watching for research, with an ambition to one day create her own children's program. With no prompting at all she had come to her husband's defense, understanding implicitly the importance of preserving his fragile dignity, at least back then, before he'd so damaged her own.

Standing in front of the consular officer, without his American wife,

Murat felt the English he had struggled to master might now help his son, so he didn't respond in Turkish, but waited for the consular officer to repeat himself, which he did. "And how may I help you?"

Murat placed his open attaché on the floor so it leaned against his leg. He slid his documents beneath the glass partition. "I'm here about my son." He explained that he and his American wife had recently adopted William and that they wanted to submit the appropriate naturalization forms. "The N-400 I believe is correct," said Murat, while the consular officer reviewed the sheaf of papers Murat had submitted: his own birth certificate, William's adoption certificate from the Turkish Central Authority, a copy of Murat's university degree, his Turkish marriage license, a few bank statements. Murat hadn't collected the documents according to any criteria. He had made his own criteria: an assemblage of what he thought were the essential bits of paper that established his life.

The consular officer became lost in the confusion of documents, sorting through them with both hands as if he were tearing away tissue paper to find the prize at the bottom of a gift-wrapped box. He gave less than a second's consideration to each, returning them facedown to their folder until he had cleared them from his desk.

He glanced up at Murat. "Do you have your wife's passport?"

Murat reached into his suit jacket's internal breast pocket, where he'd tucked her passport for safekeeping. He slid it under the glass. The consular officer flipped through the book. He swiped the bar code on its front flap through a scanner. A readout of data flashed up on his screen.

A pleasant gust of breeze landed against the back of Murat's neck. He turned around. Above him a ceiling fan had begun to churn the waiting room's stale air. The fan's mechanism wobbled and it made a metronomic clicking sound. He watched the consular officer, while the rhythmic *click, click, click* of the fan kept the time.

The consular officer swiveled his computer screen toward Murat. "From what I gather, you and your wife have resided here the last three years. However, I don't see an American marriage license. Do you have one?"

Murat bent over and searched his attaché case, as if perhaps the nonexistent document could be in there. He hadn't known what the complicating factor would be for William, but he had felt certain one would present itself. His son had no greater claim to American citizenship than he did, despite the boy's given name, despite who his adoptive mother was. Murat had, from the outset, thought there was something unnatural in him petitioning for this favor of citizenship and, when presented with this obstacle, Murat felt relief that his efforts might fail and that his son, like him, might remain with but one nationality, that the boy might remain pure in this way. But as he lifted his glance from the attaché, so his eyes met those of the consular officer, that sense of relief shamed him. How could he deny his son anything? He then shook his head, conceding that he did not have an American marriage license, but only a Turkish one.

"Both you and your son would need to establish residence in the U.S. for a period of two years before either of you could submit an N-400 naturalization form. That would then take another year to process. These cases are complicated, but usually that's the protocol." The consular officer gathered up Murat's papers.

"I can't do that, my business is here," said Murat.

"I'm sorry then"—the officer glanced down at the top sheet, reminding himself of Murat's name—"Mr. Yaşar, this isn't something we can solve today, perhaps . . ." Then he did a double take down at his form. "What is your business?"

"Construction."

"Are you that Yaşar?"

"Excuse me?"

"Are you part of the Yaşar family?"

He didn't want to disabuse the young consular officer of the belief that there still was a Yaşar family and not just a collection of inherited real estate holdings that he could hardly afford to maintain, or manage to sell. He was like a vanquished noble—his suit, his calfskin attaché, his father's broken Patek Philippe—and like any vanquished noble he clung to dreams of reestablishing a bygone order.

Murat nodded.

The consular officer meticulously returned the papers in the exact manner Murat had presented them. He then clutched the folder in both hands, holding it like a tablet of commandments. "Your case is obviously complex," he said. Behind Murat the fan in the waiting room continued its wobbling rotations: *click, click, click, click.* This was the only sound between them as Murat waited for the officer to finish his thought. "Under such circumstances we could take a closer look at your case file . . . If you'd be willing, I'd like to schedule another interview with someone in my office in which we'd have more time to discuss the matter." He glanced past Murat, into the waiting room. His gaze fell somewhere near the Filipina woman. "We can do it at a place and time that's more convenient for you. That will afford a bit more discretion."

Murat thanked him and agreed. He also couldn't help himself and made mention of how inconvenient scheduling this appointment had been, to which the young officer readily apologized, happy to indulge Murat's grievance if doing so would facilitate a next meeting. He copied down all of Murat's contact information. He then handed back the file of documents as well as one of his business cards. Its seal was gold embossed. Murat read the consular officer's name, but also the name of his office, which was listed right below: Cultural Affairs.

❋

Murat went from the consulate to his office, where he put in a few hours' work, before returning to a dark house. A window had been left open and a breeze passed through the foyer, making the crystal chandelier's pendants tinkle and chime in weak celebration, like many gently toasting glasses. Murat stood very still, trying to hear where his family was. A few months before, he had taken out a sizable mortgage to finance the home. The furniture from their walk-up in Cihangir couldn't fill the new house. The living room had a love seat instead of a sofa. The dining room had a small, round kitchen table. The walls were mostly bare. He had often thought how he might fill them, but less so in recent days.

He climbed the stairs. The door to his room was shut and Catherine was likely asleep on its other side. Further up the hallway, he could hear William cooing. Murat entered the vast nursery, which they had yet to carpet. The unpolished floorboards creaked as he approached his son, who rested on his stomach in a wicker bassinet beneath a window without curtains. It was a mostly empty room and there wasn't a chair for Murat to sit in. He flipped William onto his back and then stroked the boy's primitive whorl of black hair, allowing it to slip through his fingers like fine sand as he considered his son's dark complexion. "Do you really want to be an American?" he whispered to the boy. Murat glanced up at the high ceiling. "Such a big, lonely room."

William clasped his father's pinkie and began to suck, searching, it seemed, for the breast he didn't have. Murat reached for a nearly full bottle of formula tucked into the bassinet's corner. He offered its rubber nipple to William, who refused it, preferring instead the nub of empty flesh. Murat continued to pet the boy's head, allowing him to suck. When he pulled his hand away, William began to cry. Murat again offered William the pinkie, which he took. This silenced him.

Murat couldn't leave now. He crouched over the bassinet, glancing around the room's four corners for a toy, or anything that would occupy an infant. Murat found nothing, so he unclasped his watch. He dangled it from its band just above William's nose. Outside was overcast and dim moonlight filtered through the clouds into the room and when that light caught the watch's gold case it glinted softly. William reached at the air, making little fists as he clutched after the glinting light.

The floorboards behind Murat creaked.

Catherine wore a black silk robe, its tie loosely knotted in the front. Her smooth, bare legs revealed themselves up to the thigh as she approached him, as if with each step her body was suggesting a first naked movement from behind a curtain. Her lean stomach was exposed and her small breasts cupped against the silk. She was a mother but had sacrificed no part of that body for her child. However, on closer inspection, her husband could see that this wasn't true—her depression had taken a physical toll. Her eyes were red rimmed, though she slept more than her child did. Her cheeks were gaunt and pallid, as if she had lost every nutrient in her blood. Dim as the nursery was, she was squinting—the room she had come out of was far darker.

Catherine crossed her arms and glanced into the crib. "Don't let him ruin your father's watch," she said, observing her son, who now gummed on the white-gold case of the Patek Philippe.

"The watch has always been broken," said Murat. "What else can he do to it?"

Six o'clock on that morning

Peter opens his apartment door barefooted. Catherine steps over the threshold, clutching William, who is asleep with his cheek cradled against her shoulder and his arms hung behind her neck as limp as a pair of heavy wet ropes. Peter helps her into the living room, where they lay the sleeping boy gently across the sofa. She has managed to carry William from the taxi up four flights of stairs. Catherine stretches her back and Peter watches the curving, upward articulation of her body. Neither of them says anything, not wanting to wake him. Peter then disappears down the hallway and returns with a blanket. Catherine tosses her black silk blazer across the arm of the sofa where Peter's camera bag hangs by its strap. The two of them creep into the bedroom. They sit on top of the mussed sheets where they have lain through many afternoons insensate from lovemaking with the sun pouring in from the westerly window across the bed. But now, in the morning, the room is dim.

"Just a day," she whispers, "enough time for me to get William some clothes and to book a flight to the States." Her voice accelerates as she speaks, becoming exasperated. "Murat says he's going to file divorce papers here and then it'll all be over, then I'll have to stay. Not even a day, really, just enough time to get us sorted out, to get William out of here with me. Is that okay? Not even a day—"

Peter raises a hand to quiet her. Catherine's nervous hedging, asking for something while she insists that she asks for nothing, is about to wake William.

"Get cleaned up," whispers Peter. "Then let's talk this through."

Her eyes fix beyond the bedroom door, to where William sleeps. The two of them return to the living room. She kisses William's head and tucks the blanket up around his shoulders. She then walks into the back of the apartment. The shower turns on.

Peter sits in a chair across from the sofa. William begins to stir. Beneath his eyelids strange images seem to flicker and die. He appears to be dreaming, floating or falling through some world contained entirely inside him. He kicks away Peter's blanket and now his feet poke from its bottom. They hold the large, awkward promise of how much the boy has left to grow. A familiar twist of anxiety cinches down in Peter's stomach. He had never wanted to meet William because he had never wanted to obligate himself. He could know Catherine and keep her at an arm's length, but he couldn't treat a boy that way.

William tucks his knees to his chest. His feet disappear under the blanket.

Peter sits very still in his chair. Past the window a gray mist lingers in the already gray streets. Satellite antennas jut from the baked, broken angles of the rooftops. Clotheslines sag heavily with yesterday's wash. The morning is becoming brighter. As Peter begins to draw the shade, allowing William to sleep a little more, a muezzin calls the prayer from a minaret a few blocks away. When the first thin note crackles from the speakers, a small flock of birds leaps from their perch several houses down. They fly straight and then all at once make a sudden turn, wheeling over the street and disappearing into the glare from the sun, which sweeps across the rooftops.

William wakes up.

Lying on his back he stretches his limbs. Then he opens his eyes. His gaze rebounds through the room and lands on his mother's blazer slung across the arm of the sofa. He crawls over and snatches it to his chest. This knocks Peter's camera bag to the floor. "She's just in the back," he says, nodding deeper into his apartment. William glances down the hall, but keeps his stare cautiously fixed on Peter, who slowly, as if trying not to spook a skittish animal, picks up his camera bag. "Why don't you let me hang that up?" Peter points to the silk blazer William clutches to his chest. The boy lets go and Peter crosses the living room and drapes it on a coatrack by the apartment's entry. He notices William glancing at the camera bag. "Take it out," says Peter. "It's the one I showed you last night."

William opens the bag's canvas flap. He stares inside but doesn't reach after anything. Peter sits next to him on the sofa, removes the Nikon and places it in the boy's hands. To turn the camera on, the shutter release and power button have to be held down together. The manufacturers implemented this cumbersome sequencing to keep the battery from inadvertently draining, but the result is a camera that requires practice if one is to use it for quick-action shots. William has to awkwardly stretch his fingers so that they can simultaneously reach the two buttons. "Hold it like that," says Peter, as he wraps the boy's small grip around either side of the Nikon. "Now press."

The flash goes off, surprising them like an accidental gunshot.

"I'm sorry," says William. He is sitting up, his bare feet hanging off the side of the sofa, the elastic from his pajamas cuffing his ankles.

"With a little practice, you'll get very quick with it." Peter steps to the living room window. He draws open the shade and motions for William to follow. The two of them gaze out across the cityscape. The sun has risen and its glare has subsided and no longer sweeps the rooftops. The light is clear and the birds Peter had noticed before are perched in long single rows on the windowsills and gutters of the adjacent apartment buildings. Peter points them out to William. "See whether you're quick enough to catch a photo of a bird as it either takes off or lands."

William stands at the window, the camera strap looped around his neck, his grip stretched across the Nikon so that only the very tips of his fingers brush against the edges of the power button and the shutter release. When a garbage truck passes beneath them, its heavy engine spooks a half dozen birds, which take flight and swoop in parabolas above the street. William snatches up the camera, but doesn't manage to push the two buttons in sync with one another. Nothing happens and the boy misses the shot.

"That's okay," says Peter. "Just wait and try again."

William glances up at him, and then registers a determined nod.

"Stay there," says Peter. "I'll be right back."

He leaves William by the window and walks deeper into his apartment. He knocks on the shut bathroom door. No answer. Peter can hear the static hiss of the running shower. He lets himself in and takes two steps before he can see Catherine through the steam. She is faced away from the water that jets against her back. She has leaned her arm on the tiles, resting her forehead in the crook of her elbow. Her expression is clamped, the eyes sealed, the mouth shut and the jaw clenched against the shock of the water, whose rivulets trace the contours of her toned shoulders, her full hips, her strong thighs. Watching the water course over the athletic body she crafted years ago, which ultimately failed her artistic ambitions, Peter notices a slight tremor run through her, the only indication that she is crying.

"Peter, please!" She doesn't turn toward him. Her forehead still leans against her arm. Her eyes remain shut. The mascara she'd worn the night before streaks in jagged lines from her cheeks to where Peter can see it on the edge of her chin.

"William's awake," he says, glancing down.

"Okay."

He stands motionless, his feet fixed to the tiled floor.

"Peter—" she snaps.

He lets himself out of the bathroom and stands in the hallway, still holding the shut doorknob as if trying to hold on to her nakedness, something she has never denied him until this moment. How useless his hands seem. He hides them in his pockets. The shower turns off.

Peter returns down the hall. Light fills the living room. William stands at the windowsill in his pajamas as he fumbles with the camera, straining his fingers around the grip to reach the pair of buttons. Peter leans against the arm of the sofa. The birds from before remain on their nearby perches. William has the camera angled toward them. He watches their jerky movements—the occasional flap of their wings, the spastic craning of their necks—and he waits for them to take flight.

The bathroom door slams shut.

A pair of the birds bounds off the ledge. Like a miracle, one of the birds is completely black and the other is flawlessly white. William snatches the Nikon. His synchronized fingers find the shutter release and power button. He snaps a photo. The two birds extend their wings, catch a gust of wind, and glide out over the gray street, rising in an orbit above the stuttering traffic. "Look," William says, showing the photo he has taken to Peter, who toggles the camera from color to black and white, observing no discernible change between the two settings. Through either accident or instinct William has managed to create a photograph in which every color and shade stands in equilibrium with every other. The balance is perfect.

"What are the two of you doing?" asks Catherine, who has padded barefoot into the living room. Her hair is drying in a towel that is turbaned around her head.

Peter tells William to show his mother, and the boy holds the Nikon up to Catherine. "He's getting the hang of this," says Peter as her eyes dip into the viewfinder. "The photo's pretty remarkable, every part of it is in perfect balance." He smiles toward William and looks back at Catherine, who continues to examine the image of the two birds. Watching her, Peter realizes that he has hardly, if ever, seen her without makeup on. Over the run of their two-year affair, or "friendship" as Catherine insists on calling it, she has never once been able to stay an entire night with him, and because of this he has never seen her fresh from the shower, or just awake in the morning. Until last night, he had also never seen her with her son.

When Catherine finishes looking at William's photo, he raises the camera up to his mother and takes a candid of her. "Please," she says, and her voice is tight in her throat, holding the same pitch Peter heard when she asked him to leave the bathroom. "Don't point that thing at me."

She makes William delete the photo.

He goes back to the windowsill. The pair of birds, which had left their perch together, continues to orbit over the street. Then they turn, beating a few powerful flaps of their wings as they flare backward and come to rest right in front of William. The boy raises his camera. He is ready. He would stay where he was. And he would watch them until they chose to take off.

❋

They drive to Akmerkez, a shopping mall ten minutes away. When they exit the taxi, it is nearly time for lunch. William still wears his pajamas. He asked to bring Peter's camera, which Peter has allowed, and so the Nikon hangs around the boy's neck by its strap. Peter has never shopped for children's clothing before and he hovers over a glass-enclosed map in the atrium. The mall has many of the same offerings as in the States. It also has most of the same brands. There is a Gap Kids on the ground level.

They ride the elevator down and a family steps inside with them: mother, father, little girl. The girl is about William's age, with a long dark braid running along her back and her foot planted on a red scooter. William snaps her picture. Catherine holds Peter's hand. She also keeps stealing glimpses of the other family. When the doors open on the ground level, they head in opposite directions.

From the display table inside of the store, Catherine picks out a few pairs of jeans for William. When presented with his options, he doesn't like any. She asks him to choose something else on his own, but he refuses. "I want to wear my clothes from home," he says.

"How about these?" offers Catherine, holding up a pair of khakis.

William creeps away, dipping beneath a rack of sweatshirts, where he sits cross-legged, his elbows propped on his knees and his face cradled in his palms. Catherine continues to browse. "Or these," she says, crouching low and offering her son another alternative. He slinks into himself, fiddling with his camera, ignoring her.

"Pick something or I'm picking for you."

He takes a photo of his feet.

She holds up a pair of black jeans and a gray sweatshirt. "Fine, we'll get these."

"I don't like those," he answers. "Stop choosing for me!"

"Then you choose!" his mother shoots back.

William lifts up the camera and fires off the flash in Catherine's face. Wide eyed, he looks at Peter as he does it, as if he can't believe the provocation he's made toward his mother. This one act of rebellion is all William has to combat the complete reordering of his life.

She lunges toward him. "What did I tell you about pointing that thing at me?"

William scampers deeper beneath the rack of sweatshirts.

Before she can take the camera, Peter intervenes. "What about these?"

William and Catherine freeze, and then cant their heads up toward Peter. He holds a pair of blue jeans and a red sweatshirt.

"I like those," says William.

Peter hands the clothes to Catherine.

"Let's try them on," she says, taking William by the wrist and guiding him out from beneath the rack of sweatshirts and toward the changing rooms.

"I want some privacy," he announces, tugging free from his mother's grip.

"Then go by yourself," she says.

He turns toward the back of the store but doesn't move.

Catherine glances over at Peter, who then leads William by the hand to the changing rooms, where they step into a stall and he pulls the curtain shut behind them. William strips off his pajama shirt and takes high-kneed marching steps out of the cuffs of his pajama pants while he asks, "How long are we going to stay with you?"

Peter tugs William's large feet through the jeans, while the boy leans on his shoulder to keep balance. "You should ask your mother," answers Peter.

"I don't think she knows."

"Well, I don't know either."

"We're not going home," says William.

Peter stops his work and straightens himself so that he looks directly at the boy. "What makes you say that?" Peter wonders about the night before, about Catherine's plans, and what has led William to conclude that returning home is no longer an option. William doesn't answer Peter's question. Instead he pulls away and finishes dressing on his own.

The two of them leave the changing rooms and find Catherine by the cash register. She jerks the plastic tags off the back of William's shirt and pants, handing them to the checkout girl. But when Catherine goes to pay, her card doesn't work. "Funny," she mutters, "try this one." It doesn't work either. The two other cards she presents are also declined. Peter offers to pay, but she refuses and then digs through her wallet and change purse. Her hand trembles slightly as she spreads the bills and coins across the counter until at last she realizes she doesn't have quite enough.

Peter passes the girl at the register his debit card.

"I'll find a cash machine and pay you back," Catherine insists.

Peter signs the receipt and hands Catherine the bag with the pajamas. William wears his new clothes out of the store. The three of them walk through the mall's gleaming corridors. William keeps a few paces ahead of Catherine and Peter. He makes a close inspection of each of the shop windows, pressing his nose right up to the glass. The jeans and sweatshirt had cost around ninety lira, or thirty dollars as Peter did the conversion. And it seems like such a bargain—not the jeans and sweatshirt—but rather the idea of it, the satisfaction it gave him. He had, after all, put clothes on this little boy's back.

When they pass a bank of cash machines, Catherine insists on stopping.

"Please, don't worry about the clothes," says Peter.

She ignores him, punching her PIN into the keypad. A minute passes, no cash. She tries again. Nothing. She won't say it, so Peter does: "He's frozen your accounts."

With the heel of her palm, she strikes the cash machine's keypad.

Peter grabs her by both shoulders. "Catherine."

She takes a breath and stands up straight. "I'm sorry," she says. Then she takes another breath and wipes her eyes once quickly with the back of her hand. "What now?"

Peter glances down at his watch. It is well past noon. The food court isn't far off. They continue their walk through the mall. The sun pours its light through the glass vestibule. Ahead of them, Peter sees the little girl from before, the one from the elevator. She rides her scooter through the mall, trailing after her parents, who have ducked into a restaurant. "Let's get a bite in there," suggests Peter.

"I don't want you to pay for anything else," says Catherine.

"Buy me lunch with what you've got left and we'll call it even."

She counts out a crumpled handful of bills. "Fifty lira," she says.

"I don't know if that'll be quite enough."

They walk a bit further. Then they come to the restaurant's front, where a menu is perched on a chalkboard easel. Fifty lira would be enough. They were offering a family special.

⌒

They had intended to meet for lunch. Lunch was casual. Yet Peter and Catherine wound up having dinner instead.

It was Kristin who had arranged everything. As soon as Peter had signed for the grant money and left her office at the consulate, she had followed up her email to Catherine with a phone call explaining that she had spoken with "a fantastic American photographer," and that she thought the two of them should meet. Catherine wasn't antisocial, but when it came to new acquaintances she had always been discerning. Her friendships were few and deep. Not long after Catherine adopted William, Kristin had come into her life. At first the relationship was professional, Kristin's duties in cultural affairs intersecting with Catherine's philanthropic interests. But their relationship soon migrated to the personal. The two women, both young mothers in a new and unfamiliar city, struggled with the role and this struggle became the basis of a friendship. Neither would call what they were experiencing depression—and never did to the other—but they could feel how through twice weekly lunches, or an afternoon coffee, or in certain instances a spontaneous phone call, the one was lifting the other out of the pit into which they had both fallen. In short, Catherine trusted

Kristin, and if Kristin thought she should meet this other American, then she should.

The initial plan was for her and Peter to have lunch at the terrace restaurant at the Istanbul Modern. However, that changed when William stayed home from kindergarten with the flu. Before Catherine could cancel the engagement, Murat volunteered to finish work early and care for William, so Catherine shifted her plan with Peter to that evening. Murat had, in recent months, closed on a number of highly profitable real estate deals in partnership with the government and, with the earnings from those deals secure in his account, he was, from time to time, curtailing his hours at the office. He had begun taking William to school once a week and, on Catherine's behalf, he had even made a sizable donation to the Istanbul Modern, financing both the planned construction of a new wing and exhibitions by well-known and lesser-known contemporary artists—a subject that may have once interested him, but no longer did. Most essentially, though, his donation had assured his wife a role at the museum. She had sporadically volunteered there for the last few years, but now became a trustee. Although Catherine had emerged from her depression, she knew how Murat worried about a relapse if she were not sufficiently occupied.

The night she met Peter, Catherine arrived at the terrace restaurant early, giving the hostess her name so that she might wander among the adjacent galleries. The museum was a cavernous, echoing space. The walls were insubstantial, no more than wood-framed partitions painted white. Above them the ceiling was a crosshatch of pipework, wiring, exposed air ducts, and halogen lights aimed at whatever assemblage of artwork the overworked curator had shotgunned into place. The museum was housed in a converted warehouse in Karaköy, a gentrifying neighborhood which had only a couple of years before been a deteriorating dockyard. Now its streets smelled like paint, wet concrete, sawdust, as construction companies like her husband's built cafés, artisanal bakeries and luxury apartments along the waterfront. The eastern face of the museum was partially constructed of glass and boasted an unobstructed view of the Bosphorus. It was a clear night, and winter. Outside the air was sharp and the boat and bridge lights reflected strongly off the chinked surface of the water, which glimmered like coins. The hills across the strait, in Asia, were pitch-dark along the folds, like dozing bodies ensconced under thick blankets.

"Catherine Yaşar . . . ?"

She startled.

Peter apologized and introduced himself. He stood regarding Catherine with eyes so dark and shining and alive, that she felt she had said something quite wonderful. He wore the one sports coat he owned, at least the only one he had brought with him when he moved to the city. It was brown corduroy, so didn't wrinkle easily. He had worn a tie also, but when he saw how Catherine was dressed—jeans, black silk blazer, white T-shirt—he loosened its knot and then took it off, affecting that he had come from some other, more formal engagement, and would now dress down, relax even.

"Karsh is one of my favorites," said Peter, as he pushed up his glasses and craned his neck toward the series of photographs hung against the wall. Catherine had been looking out the window, at the water and the city. She had hardly noticed the gallery she had wandered into. A placard also hung on the wall, summarizing the life and the portraiture of Yousuf Karsh: born during Ottoman times in Mardin, an ancient city in the Armenian southeast, Karsh grew up during the genocide; his sister died of starvation as the Turks drove his family from village to village, until, finally, at the age of sixteen he fled to Canada.

"He was an expatriate, like you," said Catherine.

"And like you," said Peter.

She laughed. "No, not like me, I think."

He then pointed to one of the portraits: a man in a three-piece suit who wore a thin set of spectacles, his arms crossed jauntily along the back of a leather-upholstered chair. The subject brimmed with an early-twentieth-century dignity, as if inviting the camera to look as deep as it wanted, confident that its lens could reveal nothing except what he had chosen to lay before it: an unshakable claim to wealth, empire, social standing. Peter read aloud from the placard, "Prince Bernhard of Lippe-Biesterfeld."

He glanced back at Catherine to gauge her reaction to the portrait, which she studied like a woman who understands all the answers to a work of art, or at least all the questions, first leaning back and then inching ever closer, as if searching for the correct angle from which to examine the photograph. She rested an index finger on her mouth and then smiled beneath it, but her lips were thin as thread.

"Do you see the hands?" said Peter, pointing into the portrait. "Karsh was an innovator. If you look at his photos, he lights the subject's hands and face separately. It's his trademark."

Catherine gazed down the row of frames, searching for what Peter referenced, the special lighting on each subject's hands. "I'm glad you like our exhibit," she said, feigning through her tone that she had, in some way, been part of putting the exhibit together.

"Has there been any controversy surrounding it?" asked Peter.

"None," answered Catherine, yet she felt herself on shaky intellectual ground. Why would an exhibit of twentieth-century portraiture by Karsh be controversial? Before she could answer Peter further, the hostess called their reservation from the entrance of the restaurant.

"I thought there might have been some anti-Armenian backlash around Karsh," explained Peter as he followed behind Catherine.

"Oh that," she said. "Usually when the government gets wrapped up around the Armenian issue, it's just posturing. How long have you been here?"

"About six months."

"Times are good now, the economy, security, everything is stable. When times get hard, that's when the Armenian question, or some other *question*, becomes relevant again." They had followed the hostess into the restaurant. She had found them a corner table in the back, one near the window. Peter offered Catherine the seat facing outside. She refused, saying, "I'm used to the view, tired of it even. You've got a fresh set of eyes."

※

They ordered three courses and the kitchen was slow. Behind Peter, on the wall of the restaurant, there was a clock. Catherine watched the time pass, not because she wanted to leave, but rather because she wanted to stay. She willed its hands to slow down, to allow her this night to sit and talk with him. He had produced a book of his work, setting it on the table. She then took it in her lap. He explained that his current project was a survey—thousands of photos—and that the book represented a sampling of the work he had gathered up to this point. Glancing through its pages she asked, "And what is the concept behind all these portraits?"

"There is an old political theory I'm interested in," explained Peter, "a holdover from the Cold War. The western powers called it the strategy of tension. They would at times support leftist terrorist attacks, propaganda and even radical politicians in order to keep their right-wing allies under threat. A society in crisis, one that is gripped by tension, can be more easily manipulated and controlled than one that's stable, or so the theory goes."

Catherine flipped through the images as Peter explained himself. The entire book was perhaps one hundred unfinished pages of black-and-white portraits, all shot on the street, and all shot from the shoulders up. Catherine found nothing remarkable in the photos themselves; rather, she was interested in their arrangement, the way each was juxtaposed to its pairing across the page—a homemaker in hijab buying groceries at the market set next to an uncovered female executive at a client luncheon, a politician campaigning through Beşiktaş district set next to an army officer waiting at Istanbul's Sirkeci Terminal for the train which would take him back to his front-line post in the restive southeast, a bar owner smoking a nargile off İstiklal Caddesi set next to a muezzin climbing his minaret in Ortaköy.

Peter leaned over the table to gauge Catherine's progress through his book. "The point of the survey is to take the portraits, but most importantly to arrange them against one another. It is basically a huge pairing exercise, not only are you seeing each person, but you are also seeing their contradiction."

"And that's the strategy of tension?" asked Catherine.

"The way two people suspend each other in place."

"What if they've never met that other person?"

"Doesn't matter, the idea of the other person is enough."

Catherine leafed through the pages, taking in the portraits one at a time. Peter watched her intently. He wasn't certain what Kristin had told Catherine about him, whether she knew that he was nearly ready to abandon the project altogether, that he was ready to return home. The question implied in each portrait was that the viewer also had a pairing, that they too existed in tension with another person, and in that tension resided their own fate. Peter felt the weight of this tension every time he opened the book, as if an invisible opposite was pulling him like gravity in a direction he didn't understand. He hoped that Catherine would feel that tension when she looked at the images. If Catherine felt nothing, Peter knew that he had failed, for what else was the point of art except emotional transference, the ability of the artist through some medium to transfer his understanding and what he felt to the stranger who viewed his work.

While Catherine continued to flip through Peter's book, a man wearing a dark double-breasted suit tailored snugly at the waist with a maroon turtleneck beneath tapped Catherine on the shoulder. "Wonderful to see you, Cat."

A relaxed smile blossomed across her face. She stood and kissed him on either cheek. "Deniz, meet Peter. He's a fantastic photographer, and I think we should talk about showing some of his work." Catherine, who was clutching Peter's book to her chest, offered it to Deniz.

"A pleasure," said Deniz. "I don't want to interrupt your dinner."

"Not at all," said Catherine, as she pulled up a chair from an adjacent table. Deniz sat, unhooking the single button of his coat so that its drape hung at his sides like a flag unfurled. Catherine spread Peter's book in front of him. "Deniz is our chief curator . . . and a complete genius."

"Not everyone thinks so," said Deniz. Without taking his concentrated gaze away from the photographs, he fished from his inside pocket a pack of Winstons, giving it a jerk so a single cigarette freed itself, and then he clutched its filter with his teeth, unsheathing a smoke, which he lit with the candle that served as the table's centerpiece.

An observant waiter crossed the restaurant and pointed to the No Smoking sign, which had only recently been affixed to the restaurant's far wall, beneath the clock, as part of a new and unexpected round of government provisions. The waiter and Deniz had a sharp exchange in Turkish, which resulted in the waiter eventually delivering an ashtray. "They won't let us smoke, soon they won't let us drink, and soon they'll shut this museum down."

"They approved the renovation plans," said Catherine. "Why would they shut us down?"

"They keep us open so as to claim credit when they shut us down," replied Deniz.

"Everything is a conspiracy with you," said Catherine.

Deniz rested his cigarette along the rim of the ashtray. Sensuous in his calm, he lazily turned the pages while shifting closer to Peter so that the two of them might comment together on the book. Their shoulders touched. Then their legs. Peter gradually leaned away as Deniz continued to flip through the photographs. Deniz then shut the book and glanced up at Peter, who was looking not at his work but rather at Deniz's cigarette smoldering in the ashtray. "Relax," said Deniz, noticing how Peter had awkwardly propped himself on his elbow to create some physical distance between them. "I'd take Cat home before you." Then Deniz began to laugh darkly over facts that seemed to amuse him alone.

"I'm not sure I understand?" said Peter.

"Oh, come now," said Deniz, who turned toward Catherine, as if she were his accomplice. "You Americans are suppressed bigots. In this country we are at least a bit more open about our prejudices. You pretend they don't exist. You say that when one person rules over ninety-nine people it is despotism, but when fifty-one rule over forty-nine it is democracy. If you're part of the minority, what's the difference?"

"Deniz set up the Karsh exhibit," interjected Catherine, trying to change the subject. "Peter is a great admirer of Karsh."

"I can see that," answered Deniz, as he glanced down his nose and resumed turning the pages of Peter's book. "Karsh can be controversial."

"Is it difficult to show an Armenian's work?" asked Peter.

Deniz returned a perplexed look. "No, that Armenian nonsense is not why he's controversial. The true controversy around Karsh is the criticism that his work is too static, whether his style—the absence of motion—is a reflection of his limitations as a photographer."

"He was a master of light," said Peter. "He would—"

Deniz interrupted. "Yes, yes, he would light the subject's hands and face separately so that one contrasted against the other. Does that make him a genius? It's a nice little trick, but aside from that all he did was photograph famous people. If he was alive today, he would be working as a paparazzo for *Posta,* or some other glossy gossip magazine."

"He could evoke the one shot that revealed his subject," Peter added.

"Or, perhaps Karsh only picked the photos that revealed the prejudices he brought to his subjects. Perhaps Karsh had already formed his opinions." Deniz rested Peter's book on the table.

"Why did you set up the exhibit if you don't like his work?" asked Peter.

"I don't have to like his work to think that it is important."

Catherine placed her hand on Peter's arm, catching his attention. "That's what holds Deniz apart from other curators," she said, speaking as though Deniz weren't sitting at the table with them. "Our collection is much broader because Deniz includes pieces that he might not like, but whose importance he recognizes."

"I also can't afford to buy the pieces that I really want," said Deniz, and then he glanced at Catherine. "But she keeps promising to help me with that."

"How long have you been at the Istanbul Modern?" asked Peter.

Deniz glanced subserviently at Catherine, volleying the response to this question over to her. "He's been here for several years now," she said. "He's risen very fast."

"Where were you before that?" added Peter.

Deniz again hesitated, looking once more to Catherine before speaking. "In Esenler," he said, "living a cheap life after being kicked out of university." The hardscrabble neighborhood was far from the Bosphorus, and thus far from the cultural, financial, and political forces that defined the city, and Peter struggled to imagine the conspiracy of events that had resulted in Deniz beating out his competition to ascend into the lead curatorial position at the Istanbul Modern. Far easier for Peter was imagining the circumstances that forced someone of Deniz's evidently omnivorous proclivities out of the city's conservative universities. To that question, all Deniz said was "I partied too hard . . . , or at least not in the acceptable ways." As the conversation continued, Catherine and Deniz divided and then answered Peter's questions as though they were a married couple being asked about a shared but complex history, each of them making quick determinations as to who was better suited to respond to certain chapters of their mutual story. Deniz added, "I consider Cat to be one of my oldest and closest friends."

"I was thinking," said Catherine, "that we could host an exhibit for Peter once we move out the Karsh portraits?"

Deniz, who had once again opened Peter's book, hardly seemed to hear her. He was deep in thought, as if for the first time considering the photographs Peter had presented and the manner in which each was juxtaposed against another. Deniz had begun to slowly stroke his radically smooth chin. Then in a single motion he clasped the pages shut with his one hand palming the spine. Like a mason setting a keystone, he rested the book on the table with great care and deliberation, but also as if he had completed his work.

"What do you think?" Catherine asked Deniz.

"You must have taken thousands of photos." There was a long pause. Both Peter and Catherine waited to see if he would say more.

Noon on that day

⌒〰

The restaurant is a kids' place and the vinyl tablecloths are sticky, so Peter keeps his hands in his lap. Their server has set out three menus. Catherine sits next to him while in the back corner by the kitchen a vintage arcade machine occupies William. He toggles the joystick and slaps the buttons, but he doesn't have any coins so only pretends to play, controlling nothing. Catherine and Peter sip their waters and poke at the bobbing lemon wedges with their straws while glancing down at the lunch specials. A frightening quiet settles between them. They have little to say to one another. Their relationship up until this point has been defined by a series of escalations: their first encounter at the Istanbul Modern, the night on the bridge when they talked about vertigo and she went home with him, the afternoons that followed in his apartment and, ultimately, her bringing William to meet him at last night's exhibit, hosted by Deniz. Each of these advances had fueled the one that proceeded, but they have now played to a standstill, to the silence between them.

A waiter arrives at their table, notepad and pen at the ready. Peter orders the köfte plate, so does Catherine. "And your son?" he asks. Catherine calls over to William, who, having given up on the arcade game, leans heavily over its controls, his chin notched on the crook of his elbow, watching the flashing screen. He doesn't reply. Pixelated aliens trickle down the display and he seems to have fallen into the grip of some interior awareness. A defending starship anchored to the screen's bottom shuffles back and forth repulsing the invaders, which, time and again, overwhelm its efforts.

Peter recognizes the game, which is a throwback to his own childhood and, watching William, he recalls himself at that age, when the exigencies of an adult's world couldn't be understood, but only felt. Peter can't help but wonder whether William's comprehension of the last day is deeper than his own.

Catherine orders her son a grilled cheese.

The waiter tucks his pad into his apron pocket and cradles the three menus beneath his arm. He hurries to the kitchen but stops as he passes by William. The waiter unclips a key chain from his belt loop. He bends down and unlocks the coin slot on the arcade game. After he jostles a switch deep inside the console, the game comes to life. William straightens himself up and returns to the controls.

While they wait for their food, William plays and Catherine researches flights from Atatürk International on her phone. "We're going back to the States," she announces. With those words, Peter recognizes that the question of who is included in this *we* has yet to be determined, along with so many other questions—airfare, passports, William's schooling, the logistics of what increasingly feels like an amateurish getaway.

Her purse lies open on the table. Spilling from it are the few credit cards linked to the accounts Murat has frozen, her little bit of cash, as well as a cigarette case Peter had given her many months before. After the night on the bridge, Peter had wanted to see Catherine again. He was concerned, however, about how she would perceive a direct invitation. Nevertheless, he asked her to dinner. They met at a restaurant built into the hillside overlooking Bebek, a neighborhood with a Riviera feel, twinkling reflections on the water, anchored yachts lulling on an esplanade crowded with fishermen who never seemed to catch anything. They sat out on a pine-board-slatted terrace painted white. The lighted apartments floated above, the crowded bars below, the parked cars washed with rain. It was early spring. The air had a snap to it. They huddled beneath a heat lamp among the small, closely spaced tables. By keeping this appointment with one another, they had crossed an illicit frontier far greater than the physical boundary they had crossed before. This meeting was deliberate. It couldn't be explained away as a single night's impulse.

When Peter had pulled a pack of American-blend Marlboro Lights from his shirt pocket, Catherine's eyes had lingered. He offered her one and then struck his lighter in a single practiced motion that began at his wrist. She glanced up at him gratefully. Her face had many possibilities. Looking at her, one could imagine many scenes. With the cigarette poised between her lips, she tilted her head like a thoughtful bird and dipped its tip into the flame, inhaling deeply, as if into some sensory memory. She never smoked at home, she explained, and didn't care for the local tobacco, which was too harsh. Her husband didn't approve of her habit, although he stole more than the occasional cigarette himself. Had Catherine confessed to Peter the deepest secret of her past, it couldn't have meant more to him than the way they sat out together on the terrace sharing his Marlboros. "Do you enjoy life as an expat?" she asked him. "Me too," she continued, "but it attracts a certain type. We come for the romance of a new place, but after some time the romance evaporates. So we leave. We expats are pretty faithless." An urge within Peter silently flared up. But that night they went home separately, neither of them finding adequate pretense to return to his apartment as they had done before.

Later that week they met at another restaurant, one block from where he lived. As they sat down, Catherine asked if he had brought his cigarettes. He had intentionally forgotten them at the apartment. They could just pop over and pick them up, if she wanted. After that day they abandoned all pretenses—they no longer met in cafés or in restaurants, they adopted their system of short and long knocks, they spent entire afternoons in the confines of his apartment.

They saw one another several times a week. They limited their communications, texting only when they would meet: usually four o'clock in the afternoon. In the hours before he saw her, Peter's work would come to a near standstill, distracted as he was. He would often lose the morning as he browsed the shop fronts around Cihangir and Galata, searching out some trifle for her, hoping that it might serve as an accelerant to her affection.

Wandering one morning, he discovered the cigarette case. It didn't cost much. He asked the engraver to chisel four little dashes into its back, a reminder of the usual time of their encounters. When Peter presented the gift to her that afternoon, she ran her finger along the case; a blue and black geodesic design was inlaid on its front, on its back she found the dashes. "What's this little hangman game?" she asked. Peter had shut the front door behind her and they were standing by the coatrack. "Are you asking me for a four-letter word?" she added. Then Catherine pressed her body against his. The time—four o'clock—didn't seem to be an adequate explanation for what those four dashes might mean.

Love? he had wondered.

"Fuck," she had whispered in his ear.

※

Catherine sets her phone on the menu so that Peter can see the price of a ticket back to the States. "How am I going to organize all of this?"

He glances back at William, who is hunched over the arcade game in a trance, working furiously at the joystick and buttons as he defends against a cascade of space invaders. His body contorts in a choreography of moves and countermoves. The little girl from before, with the red scooter and dark braid, has wandered over to him from the table where she had been sitting alongside her parents. She leans next to the controls, watching William as intently as he watches the screen. He ignores her, completely immersed in his game.

Catherine sits quietly next to Peter. Her eyes remain on her phone.

"You can pay me back," says Peter, and he hands her his credit card.

"It's not that. The passports are at the house."

"At the house?"

"Murat keeps them."

The starship on the arcade screen explodes in a pixelated cloud of smoke, dust and debris. The sound of a deflating chime comes from where William has lost at his game. His shoulders go slack over the controls. The little girl who had been watching him wanders away, back to her parents. William's eyes jealously follow her. On the screen, a timer counts down from ten. Above it is a question: CONTINUE?

PART III

2012 and 2013

March 8, 2012

⌐ ‿⌐

Kristin had received a text that morning from Catherine, asking if she was available for one of their lunches, "just to check in." Kristin already had plans, a meeting with a midlevel functionary at the Turkish Ministry of Culture and Tourism who needed help with a visa application and whose sister-in-law happened to be a member of parliament who sat on the Public Enterprise Committee. Nevertheless, Kristin canceled and arranged to meet Catherine instead at Kafe 6, a trendy restaurant in Cihangir which didn't accept reservations and had only a dozen or so tables. Kristin arrived a few minutes ahead of time, not only to ensure they got a table but also because she was anxious to hear about Catherine's dinner with Peter at the Istanbul Modern the night before. Kristin left her name with the hostess. She was told the wait would be about forty minutes, so she loitered out on the sidewalk among a gaggle of hopefuls who also aspired to lunch there.

Catherine soon appeared, ambling down the street in a black felt hat with a floppy brim. Her dark, bug-eyed sunglasses covered her face as though she'd selected them to conceal her features for a masquerade ball. She removed her hat and glasses at the door, kissed Kristin on both cheeks and then suggested they grab a table inside.

"I already left our name," offered Kristin. "They said forty minutes."

"Let me double-check," said Catherine. She wove gracefully through the crowd, which seemed to part owing to her demeanor alone. On approaching the hostess, she spoke in English, dropping the owner's name, and reiterated the request for a table. The hostess disappeared into the back of the restaurant and then emerged with a pair of menus cradled beneath her arm. "Right this way, Mrs. Yaşar," she said apologetically. "We'll open up the garden for you."

Catherine glanced over her shoulder at Kristin, as if asking whether the garden would be a suitable option. Kristin nodded, and the two women followed the hostess through the restaurant, where any number of Istanbul's cultural elites—media personalities, actors, politicians—sat elbow to elbow, preferring to be seen in each other's company among the closely packed tables, which felt like a galley, as opposed to eating in any of the more lavish but less trendy establishments in other parts of the city.

A sprinkling of freezing rain had passed through that morning and the hostess called over a server, who wiped down their seats and set up around their table a circle of space heaters as if they were the lights and audio equipment of a television studio where Kristin and Catherine were about to sit for an on-air interview. The hostess left them with their menus. A fountain bubbled in a far corner. Aside from this the garden was very quiet.

"It's nice back here," Kristin said. "So how are you? How's Murat?"

"We've been okay," said Catherine. "William's fallen behind a bit this semester at the lycée, so that's been stressful. His Turkish still isn't where it should be. What do you think of IICS?" she asked, referring to the Istanbul International Community School, where most members of the consulate sent their children and where Kristin's daughter had enrolled in pre-K that fall.

"How concerned are his teachers?" interjected Kristin, who'd always taken an interest in William.

"It isn't his teachers who are worried, it's Murat."

"Well, IICS is great, but the curriculum's only in English. They teach Turkish as a foreign language, so I doubt William would come out fluent. Do you think Murat would go for that?" asked Kristin, who knew full well the challenges Catherine had faced with her husband when first enrolling William in the lycée, which was less traditional than Murat preferred even though the majority of its curriculum was taught in Turkish. Then Kristin added, "What about a tutor? I could help you find one."

"Maybe," answered Catherine, noncommittally. "I'll figure it out." There was an awkward pause as she changed the subject. "I met your friend Peter," she added. "We had dinner."

"Oh," said Kristin, averting her eyes down at her menu. "And what do you think?"

"I wanted to tell you that I plan to help him."

"That's good news," said Kristin. "Thank you."

"And I was wondering what else you could tell me about him."

They both placed their menus on the table. Before Kristin could answer, their server appeared. Kristin ordered a salad and Catherine ordered the same but removed and then added enough ingredients that she might as well have ordered off menu. The server tucked his notepad into his apron and Kristin waited for him to leave before answering Catherine's question. Kristin then reviewed in greater detail what she knew about Peter: his East Coast education, the publications in which his journalistic work had appeared and his ambitions, as she understood them.

Catherine listened impatiently. She seemed to already know most of this.

Kristin, feeling obliged to offer up something more, began to list a few of the photographers and artists Peter had placed on his grant application as influences. "He likes the hyperrealist painter Taner Ceylan quite a bit," she said. "His work is being featured in a gallery opening next week. Fair warning, his paintings are—um—avant-garde. But you could *bump* into Peter there."

Catherine's attention fixed on this detail. She immediately removed her phone and Googled the opening. "This one, correct?"

Kristin glanced at the screen. "That's the one. The gallery is just on the far side of the First Bosphorus Bridge."

Catherine removed her calendar from her handbag and scribbled down the appointment. Having secured a time and place where she might see Peter again, she placed the calendar back into her bag and seemed to relax, as if she had achieved her objective and could now enjoy her lunch, which the server soon laid in front of them. The two women took the first bites of their food in awkward silence, until Catherine offered what else was on her mind. "I suggested Deniz show Peter's work at the Modern."

Kristin finished chewing her food. "And?"

"He doesn't seem convinced . . . Maybe you could help convince him?"

Kristin slowly shook her head. "That wouldn't be appropriate."

Catherine didn't quite understand what wasn't *appropriate* about Kristin putting in a word with Deniz. Promotion had come rapidly for Kristin, each rise coming with an approved tour-extension request, so that she was entering the seventh year of what should've been a two- or at most three-year posting. And although Catherine couldn't explain the reason for her friend's rapid ascent, it evidenced her influence within the consulate, a power Catherine had hoped to leverage to Peter's benefit, though it seemed she would be disappointed, so she began impatiently to tap her well-manicured fingers against the table. "Why would putting a word in with Deniz be inappropriate?" she asked, but received no answer, and so repeated herself. "What's inappropriate in this? I've always been a good wife and have never wandered far from Murat," she stated firmly, feeling the need to defend herself against an attack that Kristin hadn't initiated, or at least not directly. "The few men I've met along the way, like your friend Peter, they're all that's made things tolerable. And Peter—" she added, "well, he's special, isn't he?"

"Yes, he is," said Kristin. "You should go to the Taner Ceylan opening."

A slight smile pursed Catherine's lips, as if she were thinking of Peter and glad to have Kristin's blessing to see him again, even if Kristin wouldn't intervene with Deniz. "I'll be discreet," she said. "If I ever left Murat, the scandal would probably destroy his business. Who knows if I'd wind up with William . . ." She knew she was speaking dangerously now and allowed her voice to trail off while the chain reaction of events such a decision would precipitate played across her mind. Then she switched the subject back to Peter "And he's quite ambitious, too."

"I think he is completely invested in his career, which doesn't seem to be going anywhere at the moment," said Kristin. "I don't know if that makes him ambitious or not—"

"But he is talented," interjected Catherine.

Kristin nodded, not certain if Catherine was making a statement or asking a question, looking for an affirmation of Peter's artistic talent, which was by definition a subjective judgment. "He is one of those people who're capable of investing their entire identity into their careers," said Kristin. "So be careful."

"You make him sound like you."

"I'm not like that," said Kristin, leaning back in her chair.

Catherine shot her back an accusing glance.

Before Kristin could respond, Catherine explained that she would, of course, help Peter only to a point. Certain contacts of hers would not be on offer, at least not right away. Had she wanted to, she could have arranged for his work to be considered at venues like Art Basel or Paris Photo, or so she boasted. But she knew—or at least told Kristin she knew—that such high-level introductions would confuse whatever relationship she hoped to cultivate with Peter. First, she would work on convincing Deniz to show him at the Istanbul Modern.

Catherine's bluster was something Kristin hadn't observed before, as if there existed within her some latent and now manifesting insecurity. Kristin listened patiently, watching with wonder at the projections Catherine was able to make about Peter, someone whom at this moment she hardly knew. This was a woman, Kristin thought, whose equilibrium was held in delicate balance. What Kristin didn't know was that as Catherine thought of Peter, she felt grounded, rooted in a way she hadn't experienced in the many years since she'd come to this city. "Sounds like you'd make him a kept man," said Kristin, after listening to Catherine's proposed support of Peter's ambitions.

"That's an awful way to put it," said Catherine. "I prefer an ambitious man, one whose strength is huge, even at the risk of being broken by him."

"That's probably true of Peter, but don't you think your husband is strong?" asked Kristin. "You can't turn down a street in this city without seeing one of his buildings."

"He is," conceded Catherine. "But his is a different type of strength: it's the strength of one who is struggling not to drown."

Nine o'clock on that morning

⌒

Murat returns to the living room and lies down on the sofa. He can't bring himself to close the front door. The action feels too final, as if he would be shutting out all that had just walked away. He leaves it open and listens to the morning's gathering traffic. A draft blows from the driveway into the foyer. The crystal pendants on the chandelier glance against one another, the familiar noise of his empty house. He pulls a throw off a nearby chair and gathers it around his shoulders. As he attempts to sleep, his son's image appears against his lidded eyes. He tries to see himself or Catherine in the boy, yet he sees neither.

The tick-tock sound of heel strikes crosses the marble entry.

Murat sits up, retucking his shirt and smoothing out his crumpled suit pants. He straightens the sofa pillows. Kristin stands on the other side of the living room, hands planted on her hips. Her eyes dip toward Peter's book on the coffee table, as well as Catherine's unread magazines and the full ashtray, which she snatches away and brings into the kitchen. "Sit up," she calls over her shoulder as she empties it in the trash. The steady pitch in her voice is familiar to Murat. It refuses to indulge his weaknesses. It rejects the lesser parts of him. He's known it since shortly after he met her colleague from Cultural Affairs at the consulate. He believes it is the tone of a firm, unshakable love. It is a tone that reminds him of his father, and he hears it with equal parts reassurance and resentment.

Murat stands from the sofa. The two of them go to the kitchen to fix breakfast. When Murat had returned from work at around ten o'clock the evening before and realized that Catherine had taken William, he had immediately dialed Kristin. When she didn't pick up, he had texted her over and over until finally she replied, and Murat could imagine her pulling his phone from the bank of other phones he knew she kept on her desk.

From her wedding ring, Murat knows that Kristin has a husband, and from a photo saved to her phone's background screen, he knows that she has a daughter. He has met neither of them and he long ago realized that he never would. He has, on occasion, imagined their lives in one of the walled housing compounds leased by the consulate in nearby İstinye, a development no doubt chosen for its resemblance to America's pastures of prefab shopping malls and rambling bungalows. Based on the hours Kristin keeps, Murat has inferred that her husband doesn't work, for who else would be at home with their daughter, and Kristin, with her overbearing, controlling personality, doesn't seem like the sort who would entrust her child's care to a nanny. Kristin once let slip that she and her husband had endured a brief separation; perhaps this was the point when balancing two careers became too much. Murat doesn't know, he can only surmise. What he does know is that she has left her family this morning to be with him, and that she is now caring for him as though he were one of them.

Murat sits at the island in his kitchen while Kristin rummages through the cupboards with a frown etched to her face. She pulls down cereals high in sugar. She removes canned soups of questionable nutrition. Packets of cookies, bags of chips, she arrays the goods in complicit rows. "I work more than full-time," says Kristin, "and you won't find this junk in my house. How's William supposed to grow up strong eating this garbage?" She again opens the trash.

She then finds a cupboard stocked with expensive, imported health foods—kale chips, chia seeds, agave syrup—items that can't be bought at the local Migros supermarket. Each packet has Catherine's name written beneath the label with a black marker. Kristin reaches deep into a back shelf and removes a tin of raw oats. She fills a pot with milk and places it on the stove. She then measures out the oats. Murat and Kristin watch the burner's blue flame instead of looking at one another.

"I'm not surprised," she says.

Murat nods, unable to meet her gaze.

"Why didn't you stop them?" Kristin asks.

The milk comes to a boil. She flings the oats into the pot.

"How was I supposed to stop them?"

"She's your wife. He's your son. You could have figured something out."

Murat crosses the kitchen toward the trash. He opens the lid and quickly examines all that Kristin has discarded. What did she mean that she's not surprised? he wonders. She isn't surprised that Catherine has left with William? Or that he was unable to stop them? "I did try," Murat says, while a hard stone of regret sets in his stomach. He had built all of this for his wife and their son. Or so he had thought. Only when she threatened to leave him did he realize that he would never allow her to and that everything he had built he had built for himself alone.

"How is William's swimming coming along?"

"You know how it's coming along," says Murat.

❊

"I'm not trying to pry," she'd said when they first met, "but my colleague thought it was a little unusual that you and not your wife had come on your son's behalf."

Kristin had known that she was pushing him with this comment, but she thought that it was fair game. Murat had brought up these issues when he arrived at the consulate ten days before, seeking help. For purposes of discretion Kristin had a nominal assignment within the Cultural Affairs Section, the same as her subordinate, the blond-haired, well-attired gentleman whom Murat would never see again. However,

an essential component of her true work, which was within the State
Department's Bureau of Intelligence and Research, a group that took
on similar, albeit more anodyne assignments than their colleagues in
central intelligence, was understanding what, or who, was fair game. In
graduate school, she had taken a class on international negotiation and
elicitation techniques, and her professor—the one who later garnered
her this "special government job," as he'd put it—had spoken quite a bit
about how once an interlocutor brought up a topic it was fair game, or
on the table in any negotiation, though she wondered whether Murat
knew that he had entered into a negotiation with her.

They were sitting poolside at the Çırağan Palace Hotel, which
fronted the Bosphorus. Many of the hotels in the city had the word
palace in their names—the famous Pera Palace Hotel, the kitschy Sultan Palace Hotel—but the Çırağan, unlike the others, happened to
have been a palace. Murat had ordered a Coke. Kristin had ordered
a glass of rosé. A cascade of cool, pleasant wind came off the water, so
they faced toward it and not toward each other.

Murat's mind resided elsewhere, not concentrating on Kristin's com-
ments about his wife, his adopted son and the chain of events that had
brought him to the consulate. He was, in fact, daydreaming about the
rooms in the Çırağan Palace Hotel. The canopy beds built so tall that
you had to climb a footstool to get beneath the covers. The heated
marble floors in every bathroom. The east-facing terraces that looked
out on the strait and welcomed the sun. Terry-cloth bathrobes. A com-
plimentary box of chocolates left on the bed each night. Fruit left on
silver trays each morning. Folded laundry placed in a box. The cheapest
room was 1,076 Turkish lira per night. Dark-suited security men with
chest-holstered pistols lingered by reception. Membership to the hotel
club required three letters of reference. Even the most affluent families
booked weddings on the grounds two years in advance. Murat's father
had taught him to swim in the hotel's pool.

This is what he was thinking while Kristin continued to speak, her
face turned away from his, her every fourth or fifth word lost to the
wind. "The fact that your son was adopted in Turkey and registered

with the Central Authority does pose certain impediments. However, I could facilitate a reprocessing of his N-400 naturalization form, but this would require a special letter of dispensation from the ambassador in Ankara. With that letter in hand I could . . ."

Murat wondered if they still kept the pool open in the winter, as they had done when he was a boy. He recalled his footprints in the snow, and his father's alongside his as they approached the steaming water. The pool was almost a hundred meters long. To seal it with a cover in the winter would have created a tremendous eyesore, so they left it open and partially heated to keep it from freezing. His father had owned a majority share of the hotel in those days, so he could order the groundskeeper to turn the heat up on the pool. Shoddy management had plagued the Çırağan Palace under his father's tenure. The heating bill, the water bill, the salaries of the employees, all of it ran over budget. His father used to joke that no other guest in the hotel paid as high a room rate as he did.

The pool along the Bosphorus in the winter under a shroud of steam—Murat could remember it, he could almost see it, and he could feel the anxiety, the pressure on his chest, the cottony dryness in his mouth, his father's grip on his waist pulling him across the surface of the water trying to teach him to swim. "Kick your legs. Crawl with your arms. Keep your head up, boy." Murat would flail and when let go of he would sink. His father would heave him up. Murat would gasp the cold air. His father would repeat the commands. "Kick your legs. Crawl with your arms. Keep your head up, boy." Then his father would let go. Again Murat would sink, and on and on they went. This was how he had been taught to swim, by nearly drowning, over and over.

". . . a letter from the ambassador carries a great deal of weight, both with the authorities here and with our Immigration Services. As you can imagine, we can't just hand out these letters to anyone. Such a letter is usually reserved for those who have aided our diplomatic mission in some essential way . . ."

His father would eventually pull him out of the pool, he would wrap Murat in a towel, and then they would put their shoes on and cross back over the snow, into the warm confines of the hotel, where in the locker room they would change back into their clothes. If Murat hadn't complained too much, if he had been sufficiently brave with his crawling and kicking and if he'd kept his head up, then his father would take him into the hotel's restaurant. They would sit in the plush, silk-upholstered chairs among the guests, where his father would order a cup of strong black tea, served in an oblong glass on a porcelain saucer, the steam curling across its surface, while he would order his son a single glass of Coke on ice.

Kristin flagged down the poolside waiter. She had finished her rosé and ordered one more. "Would you like another Coke?" she asked Murat.

"One is enough," he said, as he emptied the warmish Coke into his glass.

The waiter nodded, cleared Murat's bottle and Kristin's glass and then disappeared through a service door that was discreetly built onto the north wing of the hotel. This entrance to the kitchen was used only in the summer. In the winter the kitchen staff kept it shut, as there was no poolside service.

The afternoon he had learned to swim, Murat's father had left him barefoot in the snow standing beneath that doorway. Murat had defied his father as they changed for the pool, telling him that he didn't want to swim in the cold. His father had ignored him at first, pulling off the boy's trousers and prodding his kicking legs into a pair of swim trunks. He had then wrapped Murat in a towel and lifted him up, carrying him outside, while repeating, "Now is the time to learn."

Murat cried. His body convulsed in his father's arms. When he tried to speak, his voice stuttered with hyperventilation. Unable to express himself—to speak, to bellow, to wail—in a way that would catch his father's attention, he instead wound up his arm and smacked him. The blow landed right on his father's temple. He calmly set down the boy near the locked doorway to the kitchen and out of sight from anyone in the hotel. "Why do I bother with you?" his father said. He tried to lift Murat and carry him inside. But Murat refused. So his father stared at him one last time with the sharp blue eyes that his son had not inherited and abandoned him out in the cold.

Watching the waiter depart with Kristin's empty glass, Murat estimated that perhaps thirty meters separated the pool and the doorway where his father had once left him. However, in his memory, that distance was a yawning chasm. He had stood in his swim trunks, his bare feet melting prints into the layer of snow beneath them, while his father returned inside, changed back into his business suit and then sat in the restaurant, sipping his black tea, waiting for the sense to return to his obstinate son.

Murat could remember the sensation of the melting snow gathering beneath his toes, his inability to act, the way his body betrayed him and froze as if he were again standing in snow, and the many times he had lain in bed with Catherine, feeling that same paralysis when a demand was placed on him to perform, the germ of which had appeared so long ago, perhaps not on this day he was now remembering, but through the many altercations with his father. He knew, as he remembered, that Kristin would soon make her demands of him. Murat would have to pay for the request he'd made for his son, and even if he wanted to refuse Kristin he felt that same chill of paralysis overtaking him as he sat next to her by the pool. He would do whatever she asked, not because he wanted to, but because he couldn't refuse.

After his father had left him, Murat decided that he would learn on his own and, not understanding the dangers of teaching yourself to swim, he ran across the snow and leapt into the pool. He could remember that moment in the air, the instant of the leap, how he hung suspended above the water while his father watched him through the restaurant's window. Then the water encased him. Murat clamped his eyes shut, not wanting to see. His body didn't float. He settled a few feet down, on the bottom of the shallow end, which, nonetheless, rose well above his head. A burning sensation spread through his lungs. He thought perhaps he would drown, teach his father a lesson, but the burning became too much. He braced his feet on the bottom of the pool and pushed, shuttling himself upward until he breached the surface.

His body rose out of the water, past his shoulders. He could see his father rushing toward him, sprinting down the steps and out into the snow. Once again the water enveloped Murat, but now he did as his father had instructed: he crawled and he kicked. His head was thrust back, his rhythmically gasping mouth sucking the air. He inhaled in the same hyperventilating cadence as when he had struck his father a few minutes before. However, this wasn't a tantrum—this was the struggle for breath, to evolve: to learn without being taught. This was the path Murat had decided to take when he entered the water alone.

His father leapt into the pool fully clothed while Murat flailed his arms, accidentally striking him across the temple, in the same place he had struck him before. His father continued to lunge after him, but he couldn't get a firm grip on his son, who jumped at him with his fists. Then he observed that Murat was, in fact, swimming. The stroke Murat had chosen didn't have a name or, perhaps, it could have been called panic. Nevertheless, he remained afloat. His father took a step back, the vent of his suit jacket billowing up in the water. With this little bit of distance, Murat now recognized that he clung to no one and to nothing, and that whatever he was doing it was that alone which kept him from sinking. He made it to the side of the pool. Exhausted, he rested his head by the drain and listened to his breath mix with the lapping sound of the water.

As he sat next to Kristin, Murat could hear the same rhythmic ebb and flow of the water lapping at the drain while she spoke without interruption, ". . . the good news is that in your case the entire process of naturalization is extremely complicated." Kristin's second glass of rosé had arrived and she was well into it.

Murat turned to face her. "I don't understand. How is that good news?"

"The more complex a bureaucratic matter is," Kristin said, "the more room exists for finesse."

"Finesse?"

"Favors that move things along," said Kristin.

Murat glanced at his Coke. The ice cubes had melted. He stirred them with his straw and took another sip. It had an unpleasant, watered-down taste. "Are you offering to do me a favor?" he asked.

"You're going to need one to get your son's naturalization sorted out."

"I don't know how I feel about taking a favor," Murat said.

"That's understandable." Kristin stood and took a few steps to the side of the pool, where she crouched, dipping her fingers in the water, making a swirling motion. "Perfect temperature," she said, while flicking her wet fingers toward the ground. From the small bottle of Purell she kept in her bag, she squirted a drop of hand sanitizer into her palm and then dried her hand on the back of her gray slacks. She returned to her seat next to Murat. "Your family used to own a large share of this property, didn't they?"

Murat reluctantly nodded.

"The consulate used to host receptions here," Kristin said. "I once even stayed the night. The mattresses are so thick that they have these little footstools on either side of the bed so that you can climb into it. Did you know that?"

Again, Murat nodded.

Kristin finished off her rosé, and before she had a chance to set the glass down, a waiter appeared to offer her another, which she refused, asking for a bottle of mineral water instead. "I read an old news clipping about the hotel's sale to a Japanese company, in the nineties, when the Japanese were buying everything up. Who owns the property now?"

"A group of Saudi investors," said Murat, but as soon as he spoke he regretted having answered, which only offered Kristin a framework to continue this thread of conversation.

"Don't you think it should be held by a Turkish family?" she continued.

Murat pointed to the pool. "That's where I learned to swim."

Kristin lowered her sunglasses, raising a palm to shield her eyes from the glare that came off the tract of water. "It's a beautiful place to learn to swim," she said.

Murat thought that perhaps he would tell her about the snow, about the day he'd jumped into the pool alone and how he'd struck his father, and about how his father had left him in the cold only to then leap into the water after him, and about how once they'd stepped from the pool the two of them sat in the locker room, Murat with a dry change of clothes and his father without one, his business suit ruined, and about how the hotel staff had brought his father a robe and slippers to wear home and the way his father had cradled his wet clothes in a dripping bundle as he crossed the lobby toward the bellman, who had a taxi waiting.

"If you'd like your son to swim here," she said, "I could help."

"I learned to swim here in winter," said Murat. "Do you know why?"

Kristin turned away from the pool and faced Murat, sensing, perhaps, that she had made some miscalculation about the significance of this place in his memory. If she had made such a miscalculation, the outcome was the same: he had a visceral attachment to the property, one which she could leverage.

"My father already knew that he would have to sell his share in the hotel," Murat explained. "He had only the one winter left to teach me how to swim and, instead of not teaching me at all, he chose to do it in the cold. I wouldn't have learned otherwise. But, to your question, yes, I would like to teach my son to swim in this pool. And I would prefer to teach him in the summer."

Murat's stare was fixed on Kristin as he spoke and her mouth was tense with the grin she endeavored to suppress. Whatever concession she sought from him, she now had. She began to explain that the U.S. diplomatic mission struggled to understand the real estate market, where many of the country's elites allocated their wealth. It was a market, that, to use her words, required a great deal of finesse. "There is no Turkey," Kristin explained. "There are only Turkish elites. To understand this country's economy and politics, our embassy always needs deeper insights into their decisions, especially their investment decisions. If you could provide us with discreet, nonpublic information, we would be more than willing to assure some of your own deals, not as business partners, of course, but rather as a favor."

"Meaning what?" asked Murat.

"Meaning I could provide you access to a network of accounts with, all told, a value approaching three hundred million lira, not to draw funds from, but rather accounts you could reference to the banks as proof of collateral. This would allow you to take out greater loans than they would ever approve in the normal course."

Murat hesitated, and Kristin wasn't certain whether he was processing her proposal or whether he was about to reject it outright. Instead of offering more specifics, she asked Murat a few questions, ones she knew he had no answers for. "If you wanted to buy this hotel, how would you finance the purchase? Who would secure you the loan? How would you keep the local authorities from demanding kickbacks? Where would the operating cash come from? If you want your son to swim in this pool—when it's warm, not freezing as you experienced—you need answers to these questions. But that's just for starters. You also need answers to questions you haven't even anticipated. I can help with that, too."

Murat finished the mix of melted ice and Coke in his glass.

"Are you sure I can't get you another?" asked Kristin.

He shook his head no.

"I'd be concerned if you didn't want to think about it," she said, and then raised her hand in the air, making a motion like she was scribbling out a check on her palm. The waiter brought her the bill. "But I'd also be concerned if you didn't see the wisdom in this. I'd be concerned if you didn't say yes."

Murat detected the slightest threat in her last remark but left it alone.

They crossed through the lobby, and for the first time Murat became aware of everyone who saw them together, how each of those strangers could implicate him in the relationship he might enter into with Kristin, as if suddenly the rules of his life—of who he could and could not be seen with and what those relationships meant—had shifted from the moment he had entered the Çırağan Palace Hotel to when he now left it. He had felt the same way that day many years ago, when he and his father traveled through the lobby together, the relationship between them also changing faster than Murat could understand.

Finesse, thought Murat. It was a good word. Like the way you turn a key to a lock that doesn't work properly: you finesse it. His business required these discreet manipulations. Had his father engaged in manipulations similar to those Kristin suggested? Murat couldn't say. The dwindling family holdings that Murat had inherited did, however, prove that his father had possessed little finesse.

Kristin allowed Murat to climb into the first taxi. She tipped the bellman for him as he settled into the backseat. He gave the driver directions to his office. His mind again turned to the day he had learned to swim and his father. On the drive home neither of them had spoken and his father had sat next to him with his wet clothes heaped in his lap, fishing out his wallet, keys and other valuables from his suit's pockets. His father had also removed his watch, the Patek Philippe. He wound and rewound its mechanism, holding it to his ear, listening for the *tick, tick, tick* of its internal gears working tirelessly against one another. But it was a sound that in his lifetime would never return.

❉

His ambition, the same ambition that had allowed him to agree to Kristin's proposal at the Çırağan Palace seven years before, had caused him to neglect his family, to set into place the conditions that would cause him to lose them. He had, in all that time, never once taken William swimming.

"He's going to learn about this one day," says Kristin, standing by the stove in his kitchen. "He'll know that you allowed him to be taken from you." She calmly stirs the oats, turning them over in the milk with a wooden spoon. The more deliberate her movements, the thicker the oats become. Murat knows that she is right: William would learn, one day. He had failed his son, his wife, himself. He hadn't known what combination of words he needed to say in order to keep them from leaving.

"Where do you think she would go?" asks Kristin.

The question humiliates Murat. Kristin knows the answer. He also suspects that she asks only because she wants to hear him say it, if for no other reason than to chasten him, to prove the control she's exercised since their meeting at the Çırağan Palace those years before. Perhaps she also wants to hear him speak Peter's name, so that he will acknowledge what's been taken, so that he might muster the will to take it back.

Murat pivots away from the counter. He leaves Kristin in the kitchen and climbs the stairs to his bedroom, where he takes off his shoes and pauses in the doorway of the walk-in-closet he shares with Catherine. His toes clutch the plush cream-colored wall-to-wall carpet she had picked nearly ten years before. Strong light rebounds off the Bosphorus, refracting into shards that angle inside through a pair of grand bay windows. Staring into the closet he is confronted by rows of his pressed suits, shirts, ties, and the sheen of polish on the black leather lace-ups he wears each day.

He wanders inside. Ranks of her shoes are arranged in racks by height, flats to stilettos. Dresses and evening gowns hang along one wall. Slacks and blouses hang along another. From floor to ceiling an entire wall is made of cabinets. He opens them, rifling through her drawers. He begins slowly, lifting the folded jeans, T-shirts, her socks. What he is looking for isn't here, but the pretense of a search allows him to violate her personal space. He empties the drawers and now tugs her clothes from their hangers. He stands in a pile of bright, expensive fabrics. He tosses her jewelry, too. He counts the pieces, each one given on an anniversary, a birthday, a holiday. An accounting of their years of marriage spills across the carpet.

"Why don't you come eat something?"

Kristin stands behind him, surveying what he's done. She steps into his side of the closet and unhooks a charcoal gray suit, a white shirt, and she takes a pair of socks out of a drawer. She lays them across the foot of his bed. Clutching a bouquet of his ties, she stands over the outfit.

"There's no shame in your wife leaving," she says as she slides the shirt beneath the lapel of the jacket. "My husband left me once." She holds a tie to the collar, rotating them one by one for a sense of which color will match best. "When I was first assigned here, he refused to come. He hated the idea of following me from posting to posting. He hated this city. And I came to hate him for that. Which led to an episode, one which was my fault. Eventually, though, we put it behind us. And he moved here. This will work itself out, too." She settles on a conservative burgundy. "Get dressed," she says, her back turned toward Murat as she rehangs the remaining ties. "You're going into work today."

She leaves his bedroom and he dresses in the closet, stepping into his sharply creased trousers before reaching deep into a drawer. Long ago, he had hidden a manila envelope among his shirts. Clean-shaven, hair combed, wearing the suit Kristin has picked for him, Murat returns to the kitchen, where she sits at the counter. He clutches the envelope at his side. Then he places it in front of her.

"What's in that?" she asks.

He dumps the contents: a red passport and two blue ones.

Kristin glances at the inside pages, her fingers manipulating the documents with the precision of a veteran bureaucrat. Two of the passports are William's. The third passport, the second blue American one, is Catherine's. Kristin gathers them. "I guess they won't get far."

Murat looks away from her, toward a photo of William that sits on the end of the counter. He was not much more than four years old. He and Murat stood at the Kabataş ferry terminal. A storm had ruined a beach day they had planned to the Princes' Islands, an hour's boat ride away. A fine-beaded rain drizzled down, so airy that it diffused to almost a mist. The pavement was slick. Behind them a flock of hovering seagulls surveyed the fishermen who snatched sardines from the Bosphorus with their long poles threaded with a dozen or more pin-size hooks. William sat on his shoulders, looking skyward, through a transparent plastic umbrella. But Murat wasn't holding the umbrella, his son was. He was the one who protected them from the weather.

April 30, 2012

⌒

The Istanbul Modern's renovation was far from complete. Murat's firm had drawn up conceptual sketches that envisioned a sleek restructuring in glass, plus a new administrative annex to house all of the museum's back office. During construction the museum staff had been housed in a series of trailers along the Karaköy dockyard next to the visitor parking lot. The construction crews housed in the adjoining trailers made erratic progress based upon the delivery of materials, the status of labor negotiations and renegotiations, and the restrictions on noise pollution enforced by the municipality. In recent months work on the annex had come to a standstill, the labor crews ceased arriving at their trailers and the museum's administrative staff was forced to settle into offices whose electricity was run by chugging diesel generators that they needed to refill twice daily from large red jerricans in the parking lot.

Nearly two months after her dinner in the museum's restaurant with Peter, Catherine found herself standing next to a stable of those jerricans as she searched for the door to Deniz's office. She had seldom wandered around the ad hoc administrative annex for fear that a member of the museum staff might question her about the renovation, probing to see if she had some information through her husband on its progress, or lack thereof. Murat rarely spoke to her about his business, most of what she knew came from reports in the papers, so whatever answers she had for her colleagues—this is how she wanted to think of her relationship to them—were unsatisfying, segregating her further from them, for she was, after all, in her position at the museum only by dint of her husband's largesse.

As she waited, Catherine heard a whistle from across the parking lot, a sharp catcall. Her eyes fell to the ground on reflex. She then searched a bit more desperately for Deniz's office, tugging on a locked doorknob. The whistle repeated. When she glanced up, her scowl instantly relaxed: it was Deniz. He approached her with a broad smile that revealed the slot between his two front teeth, which were bound by a nearly invisible picket of braces, an extravagance which had not been available to him in childhood and which he had only recently been able to afford due to his rapid ascent through the museum's administrative hierarchy.

"Cat," he said, as he glided up alongside her. "To what do I owe the pleasure?" Before she could answer, he continued boisterously, "And why did you scowl at my whistle? Aren't I allowed to appreciate a beautiful woman?" The day was muggy and overcast, prematurely warm after a cold winter, and the stale taste of the night before still lingered in the air. Deniz wore a pair of sunglasses despite the lack of sun, and he wore a calf-length trench coat despite the stifling heat. Catherine noted his jeans, which peeked from beneath the coat's hem: they were an eccentric red. Several months before, after his promotion to curatorial director, Deniz had moved from his rented apartment in Esenler to a place off İstiklal Caddesi. The new apartment needed work, but he now owned it, an idea that had yet to settle in. The trench coat was a habit from his old commute, when he had needed to hide his peacocking appearance as he took two buses and then a train through the more conservative parts of the city. The fact that he no longer needed to hide, or at least needed to hide less, also had yet to settle in.

"Could we speak inside?" Catherine asked.

Deniz unlocked the flimsy door to his trailer. A steel foldout chair sat behind a plastic desk and in front of it was another chair. Deniz swiveled the rod on the blinds, releasing a ladder of light into the shadowy confines of the office, which was completely bare except for the wall behind the desk, where a poster hung, a Rothko, entitled *No. 3, 1967*, taken from the gift shop, a hazy cube of orange balanced on an equally hazy cube of red. Even on a poster the paint looked heavy and textured. Deniz draped his coat over a steel hanger on the back of the door. In the far corner a stand-up fan kicked up motes of dust as it circulated the thick, soupy air. His shirt was orange linen and its several unfastened top buttons exposed his chest and its hair, a masculinity he expressed in tandem with his other eccentricities, which read so feminine. Worn with his red jeans, the orange shirt replicated the color scheme of the Rothko, which Deniz noticed as he crossed the room. "Clearly, I've been in this trailer too long," he said. Deniz then tossed his sunglasses on the desk, revealing his eyes, which were crowded with red fissures. He sighed heavily as he settled into his uncomfortable chair. On his desk were two neat stacks of paper. He began to review the one on his left.

"Late night?" asked Catherine.

"Out late, up early, that seems to be my rhythm." Deniz raised his stare from the forms. "These are complaints against our exhibits," he said, holding up a sheet of paper from the largest stack. He then gestured to the other stack. "And those are portfolio samples from new artists whose work we're considering."

"Daunting," replied Catherine.

Deniz returned to his stacks of paper.

"Remember my friend Peter," she added. "What did you think of his work?"

"Perhaps he should submit a portfolio," Deniz answered.

"How many new artists have you shown?"

"Not one yet."

"So . . ."

"So perhaps he should submit a portfolio," said Deniz.

Catherine stepped next to Deniz, her body bent at the waist so she could read over his shoulder. "If you say no to all of them," she asked, "then why do you review their portfolios? Why not show only established artists?"

"Because that wouldn't be fair. Even if I never take one of these, the process of rejection is fair. If we shut that down, what do we have? A museum that closes out certain people instead of inviting them in, even if they never get in." Deniz drummed his fingers against the desk, each one hitting with an impatient thud. His hands were large, like a strangler's hands. His knuckles were crosshatched with scars. Both of his pinkies bent out at slightly obtuse angles, the products of dozens of neighborhood brawls. And now that he was grown, no matter how he dressed, or what work he did, or what interests he developed, from Caravaggio to Jasper Johns, nothing could conceal those hands, which had carried him through his youth and which, from time to time, he still relied upon. "You have never been much for process, have you, Cat?" he added.

"And how is your new apartment?" she asked.

He turned over his shoulder to where Catherine ominously lingered. He offered her a sharp, reproachful look. "Fine," he said, allowing the word's single syllable to depart in one suspicious breath.

"And the job?" she added.

"Also fine," he said. "And how is William?"

She didn't reply, but now fixed her gaze on Deniz.

"Are we threatening one another?" he asked.

"Are we?" she asked, pausing for a beat before answering her own question. "We're not, but I need your help."

"If we show Peter's work, it is my reputation, not yours. It's no small favor."

"You owe me this favor."

Deniz went back to his forms, considering the claim she made. An account of favors exchanged did exist between the two of them, yet the balance of who was in debt to the other lay in dispute. Sitting across the desk from Deniz, Catherine began to speak, reiterating the history between them and the terms upon which they had first met in Esenler, six years before. "I gave your son a home," said Catherine. "I found you a first job. How is it that I'm in your debt?" But even as Catherine laid out her argument, she knew that it was only one half of the ledger.

※

Catherine had traveled to Esenler alone on the afternoon she first met Deniz. Her secrecy was born not from her shame about adopting a child, but from Murat's shame at not being able to conceive one. In those days she had wanted to protect her husband. She knew that Murat would've come with her had she asked, but she hadn't wanted to ask. She had wanted the child just to appear, like an immaculate conception, and she thought that if Murat were exposed to none of the back-and-forth concerning the adoption, the child might eventually feel as if it had been theirs all along.

The house Catherine had arrived at in Esenler wasn't really a house but a gecekondu, a shanty with two cinder-block walls, two plywood walls and a corrugated tin roof. The gecekondu didn't have an address. All Catherine had was a road intersection and a cellphone number with a name. "Call when you arrive," she'd been told by an intermediary with vague connections to the U.S. consulate. "He will come to meet you." It had taken her nearly two hours to cross the city. It would have been half that time had she driven in a taxi, but she hadn't wanted anyone, not even a cabdriver, to know about the trip.

After two transfers on the metro and one on the bus, she had arrived. The streets were wet with filth. The residents would take their plastic garbage bags and empty them into the choked gutters simply to save the expense of another bag. Staged next to one empty lot she found stacks of building materials—boxes of nails, scraps of plastic roofing, paper sacks of unmixed cement, a wooden door painted red on one side for luck—all lined up in preparation for a frantic night of building, for *gece* meant "at night" and *kondu* meant "settled," and this warren of hastily built homes existed due to a legal loophole that stipulated if one starts building after dusk and moves into a completed home before dawn the next day without having been noticed by the authorities, then the structure cannot be torn down without a proceeding being registered in court—a difficult thing to do—and in this way entire neighborhoods had been populated.

She called Deniz's cellphone and then waited for him in the street. She had dressed modestly in a hijab and abaya tailored in the Turkish style so it looked more like an ankle-length trench coat. Her eyes were hidden by the only set of sunglasses she owned, made by Versace. As much as she had tried to fit in, she stuck out, and knew it. Yet he stuck out, too. She placed him immediately. This wasn't due to anything Deniz wore, but rather the manner in which he carried himself, his demeanor. He was powerfully built but also effete, with strong arms, those strangler's hands and a mouth shaped like a kiss. When he approached, she could feel the foot traffic around them slowing as his neighbors or even an anonymous passerby brushed them with an extended gaze, as if she and Deniz had entered a film where they moved at one frame speed and the rest of the world moved at another.

In a single evening at his home they had agreed on the terms of the adoption. They had sipped tea at a simple wooden farmer's table in one corner of the gecekondu, which was partitioned in half by a bedsheet slung across a wash line. On one side were the kitchen and table, on the other Deniz's bed and a wicker bassinet for the newborn, who slept peaceably through the night. Stacked in the kitchen were tins of formula. Two empty bottles lolled in the half-filled washbasin. A jute rug covered the floor and at its edges the floor was dirt. An electric camping lantern hung from a bent nail in the ceiling.

"I don't want to give him up," Deniz had told Catherine.

The next morning, she would register his son as her son with the Central Authority. In return she would find Deniz some steady work and from time to time she would permit him to see the child.

"We didn't give him a name," Deniz said. "We thought whoever took him would want to do that."

"Who is *we*?"

"*We* is no one now. Just me." He stepped to a small burner in the kitchen. Its flame sputtered erratically as the gas seeped through a snaking hose fastened onto a propane tank. The kettle had come to a boil. He reached for the handle and at that moment an uneven surge of gas caused the flame to leap over his wrist before it snuck away. Deniz dropped the kettle back onto the burner and cursed, clutching his hand to his chest.

Catherine found a dish towel and dipped it into the sudsy washbasin with the two bottles. "Let me see that," she said, reaching for Deniz, who slowly unhinged his arm toward her. The dark hair around his wrist had been singed and a finger-length welt already spread across a strip of burnt skin that was turning translucent. She wrapped and then tied the wet dish towel around his wrist while he gritted a single curse as she cinched it down.

Catherine shushed Deniz, glancing toward the wicker bassinet. "You'll wake him. Keep that cloth pressed there." The kettle steamed heavily and she carefully lifted it from the burner and poured them both their cups of tea. They returned to the table.

Deniz cast his eyes toward his son, who had begun to stir but was now settling back to sleep. "Already you're taking care of him."

Catherine nodded.

"You don't have to worry about his mother . . ." Deniz said and paused, searching for a sufficient explanation. "It's my fault. I allowed her to think I was one way when clearly I am another. I never meant for this to end so badly." Deniz sipped his tea, his stare shifting from Catherine to the infant who slept in the corner. "If a man trapped on a sinking ship handed off his son to a stranger, you wouldn't judge him, would you?"

Catherine shook her head no. But she wasn't certain he believed her.

"And you? You want this child because . . . ?"

"We can't have children," answered Catherine, recognizing that her misfortune had promised to rescue Deniz from his, and when she caught him glancing at her stomach, Catherine felt an impulse to immediately correct his assumption that she was the barren one, but loyalty to her husband prevented this and left her with a spike of resentment that she would once again have to assume Murat's frailties as her own.

"I think that we can help one another," she added, and then reached across the table, pulling Deniz's arm toward her. She removed the wet dish towel and examined his burn. It would heal in a few days. Perhaps it would leave a scar but nothing more.

They spoke late into the night. Catherine missed the last bus. The first bus would run out of Esenler at just after three o'clock in the morning, taking the janitors, laundresses, busboys and day laborers to their stations in the eastern, affluent reaches of the city. Deniz thought that Catherine should be on the first bus with the child. "Do you have a name picked out for him?" Deniz had asked.

Catherine said that she didn't, that she would talk it over with her husband.

"Do you think it will be an American or a Turkish name?"

Catherine said that she wasn't sure.

"You'll have to pick before we go to the Central Authority," said Deniz.

Catherine nodded.

"So you'll have to pick by tomorrow," he added.

"Yes, by tomorrow," answered Catherine.

"And will I meet your husband then?"

"I don't think he'll be coming."

Deniz's gaze shifted around the room, to the kettle on the now cold burner and to the washbasin and to the carpet, which didn't quite cover the dirt floor, and, last, to the infant, who still slept in the corner. "It is better if your husband doesn't know much about where his son came from . . . or maybe nothing."

Catherine crossed the room and swaddled the sleeping infant in an extra blanket before taking him outside. She and Deniz arranged a time to meet in front of the Central Authority the following morning and then Catherine stepped into the street. The half-moon was up and it was reflected in the puddles of filth that pooled in the clogged gutters. The road was slick and Catherine walked unsteadily, getting turned around almost as soon as she left. The alleyways all looked the same, an endless congestion of ramshackle gecekondus. She was eager to get to the seat on the bus that would take her home.

But she was lost. She remembered that she had passed an empty lot with a pile of building materials staged nearby, but she couldn't find it as a reference point—those materials had disappeared. After doubling back several times, she had even become confused about where Deniz's home had been. She retraced her steps, but only became more disoriented. It was then—not the next day when they signed the papers but then, when she was lost and alone—that she realized the irreversibility of her choice. The child was hers.

In the clutch of this fear, she heard a noise from behind the shut door of one of the gecekondus: it was a hammering. Then the door swung open; its backside was red and beyond it a man was jointing together the crossbeams of a wooden frame while another stepped outside for a cigarette. In the corner of the nearly completed gecekondu, a woman and her two sons slept on a rug laid across a dirt floor. From the empty lot earlier that day, she remembered the red door—red for luck.

She now knew where she was going. As she walked toward the bus stop, she thought how remarkable it was that a home could be built in a single night.

※

That morning in his office Deniz had refused her. No matter her approach—whether it was pointing out the merits in Peter's work or asking for a personal favor on his behalf—Catherine had made no headway. "What is the debt you believe I'm obliged to repay you?" Deniz had said. Without Catherine, Deniz would still be living in the gecekondu. Without Deniz, Catherine would be childless. There was no debt between them, quite the opposite: they were even.

Catherine understood this. But she also understood that they weren't free from one another. Her mind turned to the book Peter had given to her at their first meeting, the paired photographs and their premise. She wondered if Deniz's ambivalence toward Peter's work was, perhaps, not indicative of something Peter's photographs failed to reveal, but indicative of something that they did reveal: an uncomfortable truth that Deniz would rather ignore.

Catherine had plans to meet Peter at his apartment at the usual time that afternoon. She had hoped to arrive with the good news. She had wanted to triumphantly announce that the Istanbul Modern had, with some persuading by her, decided to exhibit his work. She had, of course, not told Peter ahead of time that she would be meeting with Deniz. This was to guard Peter against disappointment in the event that Deniz said no. And now that Deniz had said no, the disappointment was hers alone.

Peter had left the key beneath the mat and she had let herself in. When he knocked on the door—one short, two long—she immediately offered herself up to him, without speaking, without asking him about where he had been that morning, so that, she hoped, he would not ask her the same. She reached into her pocket and removed the cigarette case he had given her, pointing to the four dashes on its back, showing him a wry, seductive smile.

"Fuck," he whispered back.

She wished that she had chosen a different word.

But with her silent, consenting nod they moved quickly into the living room, their steps tangling one on top of another. They undressed awkwardly. She had yet to master how the buckle came off his belt. He could not find the tiny zipper on the side of her trousers. She helped him and he helped her, but such help wasn't an affirmation of increasing intimacy, instead it was a negative affirmation of the unfamiliarity that still existed between them. They exchanged whispered instructions as they undressed. Once naked, they proceeded in silence.

They spoke again only when they had finished.

Peter lay on the sofa with the elbow of one arm thrown back and his hand wedged behind his head. His other arm draped heavily over Catherine's shoulder. "How long can you stay for?" he asked. Catherine was nestled against the side of his warm body, her head tucked just beneath his chin and her leg draped over his thigh. Her instep had a lovely fleshy curve, which cradled his calf. He could feel the length of her against his arm. "What time is it?" she asked.

Peter lifted her watch off the floor, where it had rested among the folds of their mussed clothing. She knew that she needed to get home and didn't have to know the time to understand how it had passed, but she wanted Peter to believe there was a possibility that she might linger. It was a little before six. William would be returning from school and Murat from work. The light that crossed the rooftops came into the living room and cast long shadows, and the view from the window out to the city looked directly into the sun, which heated their pale skin.

"I'm exhausted," Peter said. "I was out all morning."

She tugged up the small zipper on the side of her pants with pinched fingers.

"I walked from Sultanahmet up to Ortaköy," he added.

She reached her arms behind her, her elbows bent awkwardly as she fastened her bra clasp.

"I got some good new stuff. I'm making progress every day." He had opened his eyes and was glancing at her from their corners. "What's going on with your friend Deniz?"

Catherine had finished dressing. She perched on the edge of the sofa and combed her fingers through Peter's hair. She hoped that he would close his eyes again. She hoped that he would allow her to leave. His gaze remained fixed on hers. "Nothing much, he enjoyed meeting you," she said.

"He didn't seem particularly interested in my work."

"Why do you care what he thinks?" she asked.

He leaned his head back, raised his eyes to the ceiling and then closed them.

"I shouldn't care," he said.

She stood to leave.

". . . But I do, Catherine. I'm trying to make my life here work."

"What would you have me do?"

"Maybe he'd do you a favor?" His eyes were still shut.

She noticed that he wouldn't look at her while he asked. She would have said yes, or tried again with Deniz, had Peter simply looked at her. Whatever Peter hid beneath his lidded eyes was enough for Catherine to hold back that last measure of herself.

"I already tried," she answered.

"What did he say?" Peter was looking at her now, his eyes fastened to hers. She felt close to him, but not because she loved or admired him, rather because she recognized in him the same desperation she had so often felt. Her closeness with Peter, she realized, was more akin to self-pity.

"He says no," she answered.

When she left, Peter sat up from the sofa. She had taken her watch with her. He looked out his window. From the sun's orientation against the rooftops, he could tell that it was exactly six o'clock.

January 27, 2012

The foundations of the five buildings had been set along a diagonal so that each would have a view. The hillside was terraced with large man-made plateaus cut and then leveled out of its side. Half a dozen excavators sat in the darkness with cakes of wet earth clutching the teeth of their blades. Three months before, the hillside had been crowded with several dozen gecekondus. Anytime he displaced someone from their home—even if those homes were gecekondus—Murat risked arousing undue attention, perhaps a story in a newspaper or an inquiry by a local magistrate, even though he always offered generous buyouts to the families he removed, enough to pay rent for at least a year in one of his soon-to-be-completed glass residences. But if that wasn't enough to silence their complaints, hush money could always be paid to an overzealous official or journalist. He resorted to those methods with reluctance, however, and only on occasion.

He harbored few misgivings when forcing people out of their old, rickety homes. In fact, he had thought that it was progress: you start out in a gecekondu and you end up in a glass residence. How come a newspaper never took an interest in that story? How come the magistrates never took note of the service he provided to the city? But no positive stories made it to print and no official ever recognized his contributions. This bothered him, but also only on occasion.

The five diagonal buildings were in the development Yaşar Zeytinburnu 4. Since Kristin and her colleagues—for this was how she referred to that invisible cohort toiling at the consulate—had helped Murat acquire a majority share of the Çırağan Palace Hotel six years before, they had gone on to help him finance an elaborate constellation of other projects in the same way—by allowing him to post their network of accounts as collateral so that he could secure loans worth tens of millions of lira from the banks. This included the first three developments in Zeytinburnu, a burgeoning outgrowth of the city by the airport. But this, the fourth development, he had financed himself, guaranteeing his loans against his already purchased properties.

When they had texted to arrange this meeting, Kristin had at first been confused. She sat at her desk, staring at the coded message Murat had sent: YZ4-3-13 0200. YZ, she knew that: Yaşar Zeytinburnu. They had met at this series of developments before, although not for several months. The digit 4, this was what didn't make sense to her. Usually this was the development number. Kristin wasn't aware of the fourth Yaşar Zeytinburnu project. To her recollection only three had been built. The next three digits she did recognize: third building in the development, thirteenth floor of that building.

The two of them met as infrequently as possible, which over the years had averaged approximately once every three months, or quarterly as Kristin referred to it, keeping their encounters to a schedule that Murat never entirely understood. Early on, they had met in restaurants, cafés or perhaps a museum, including the Istanbul Modern when Murat was considering the size and scope of the donation he would later endow and had wanted Kristin's opinion. Soon, however, Kristin moved their meetings to more discreet and less scenic locations: an anonymous studio apartment, the back of a car, once in an alley off Taksim Square when Murat had lifted a handwritten ledger of payouts to government officials from a visiting foreign developer's hotel suite, a document of such sensitivity that he'd had to pay off a maid in order to get it returned unnoticed within an hour. When Kristin realized the risks he'd taken to do this, she'd scolded him, explaining that he was more important than any one bit of information. She often encouraged Murat to bring William to their meetings, the logic being that a child would reduce suspicion. Murat relented and brought the boy, but he noticed they got virtually no work done as Kristin doted endlessly on William. She had later sheepishly explained to Murat that she'd always wanted a son.

Murat had expressed the occasional frustration to Kristin that no results ever seemed to come from the information he provided. "What results are you looking for?" she would ask. He realized that he didn't know. "You can quit whenever you want," she would also say, though he never believed her. Although he had been naïve enough to start working with Kristin, he wasn't naïve enough to think that he could divest himself of her.

It was one minute after two a.m. Murat stood on the thirteenth floor of the skeletal Yaşar Zeytinburnu 4 building, his lazy eyes browsing the city, a terrain of lit and darkened diagrams. Kristin had instructed him early on about the four-minute window for their meetings. You could be two minutes early or two minutes late. Never arrive any earlier. Never stay any later waiting. Glancing at the clock on his cellphone, Murat thought that perhaps tonight she would miss her window, an unsettling first for Kristin.

A chill, steady breeze whistled through the building. The workmen had yet to install the fourteen-foot-high panes of glass that would encase each floor. The night air played through the open, cavernous spaces and it howled like wind blown through an enormous hollow instrument. Murat had always enjoyed touring an unfinished building. It was an exercise in vision. His father had taken him on construction sites as a boy, pointing out various corners of a project: of a concrete shaft he would say, "Twin glass elevators will go here"; of an empty floor he would offer, "Four separate suites." Murat could still hear his father's voice in the sound of the wind passing through empty spaces.

A pair of headlights twisted up the dirt road where the excavators had been parked. Halogen bulbs peppered the job site, though most of them were switched off. The project was currently ahead of schedule and would likely reach completion without relying on night shifts or overtime. The workers would then receive a bonus. Murat came a step closer to the edge of the building, inching his way forward so that he stood between two load-bearing pillars. He recalled the first time he'd brought his wife to one of his construction sites—though she never came anymore—and what she'd said about heights, that vertigo was caused not by one's fear of falling, but rather by one's desire to jump.

He allowed himself to take a step closer, but as he did, the hem of his trousers caught on the teeth of a handsaw, which had been carelessly abandoned on the floor. The work crews knew better than to leave their tools out. Perhaps they were taking shortcuts in order to finish ahead of schedule. "Inspect what you expect on the job site," his father had taught him. Murat had in recent days caught himself saying the same to his son.

Murat tidied up the mess left by the workmen as if his father were watching, or as if Kristin might comment on the general disarray. He heard the elevator gate slam shut on the ground floor. He checked the time: 0205. He should have left three minutes before. He stepped even closer to the edge. Glancing down the thirteen stories, he felt his stomach turn and a slight spell of dizziness. Yes, vertigo, he thought.

The elevator door opened behind him. Before he could see Kristin, he heard her hurried steps echo across the open floor plan. "I'm five minutes late," she announced. Murat stood with his back to the expanse of skyline. His silhouette was all that she could see, but she could have recognized him from behind at a hundred paces in a crowd: the way he slumped forward with his hands in his pockets, the width of his shoulders, the length of his arms. He turned toward her as she glanced down at her triathlete's watch and pressed the function button on its side. An emerald luminescence confirmed the time. "You waited for me," she added, "when you should have left."

"You shouldn't have shown up," he said.

They had both breached a protocol that each had assured the other they would always keep. When Murat was a boy, his father once pulled him out of school with a fake doctor's appointment so that he could join him at a groundbreaking ceremony one afternoon. "What if one of my friends sees me?" Murat had asked. "Then you'll see him," his father had answered.

Kristin stepped alongside Murat, who remained perched near the edge of the thirteenth floor of Yaşar Zeytinburnu 4, just where he'd said he would be. She apologized for being late, admitting that she'd misplaced her car keys, which was a first for her. Then she popped up the collar of her rain jacket and tugged it tight around her neck. "It's freezing up here," she complained.

A snatch of wind carried off her voice.

She spoke louder. "I had a hard time finding this place."

Murat pointed out to the city, to the headlights which threaded an east-west-running highway. "Probably fastest to come in on the O-3 and then drive south," he said. "Did you pass the seaside road on the way here?"

She ignored his question about directions, taking it for the diversion that it was. "I didn't know you were building a fourth development in Zeytinburnu."

"You didn't?"

"No, I didn't."

"Perhaps I didn't mention it."

"Why wouldn't you mention it?" Kristin replied.

"I haven't asked for your help," said Murat. "I financed the entire project."

"By taking on debt against properties that are already in debt," she said. "You should have at least let me know."

"If I do some projects with you and some on my own, what business is it of yours?" Murat reached to the floor and continued to gather up the workers' scattered hand tools, carefully placing them in a nearby chest. "You always said that we were partners."

"We are," replied Kristin. "That's why between us we can't have any misunderstandings." She picked this last word carefully. The word that had first come to mind was *secrets*, but she had chosen otherwise. She recognized Murat's selection of this meeting place for what it was: a signal of his desire to become independent of her. This wasn't the first time he had equivocated about their relationship. After she had helped him finance his purchase of the Çırağan Palace, he had collateralized his share to take out another loan and buy another hotel, which had failed. She had bailed him out of that loss and helped finance his initial developments in İstinye, where the consulate was, and in Kadıköy, on the Asian side of the city. These had both been modest successes, so too had the Zeytinburnu developments one through three. Now there was this fourth development. Murat needed to hint no further about his intentions to end his relationship with Kristin. That he'd financed this development on his own was indication enough.

"How is William?" Kristin asked.

"I haven't seen much of him recently," Murat confessed. He then finished straightening up the scattered workmen's tools in the dark.

"You should bring him to more of our meetings. We look more natural with him around. And he's such a smart boy," Kristin said wistfully. "But it sounds like your days have been busy."

"They have, and that's what I wanted to discuss with you," said Murat. "An opportunity has come up." He explained how officials from the Ministry of Interior had approached him about putting in a bid for a new football stadium in Beşiktaş. "The government will be my partner in the financing," he said. "It's part of a much larger development initiative revitalizing the city. All of the political leadership—the Kemalists, the Gülenists, the Islamists—every one of them is profiting in their own way. It would be helpful for you to have inside information on all of this development, right?"

Cautiously, Kristin nodded. "Yes," she said, "that would be helpful."

Murat pursed his lips, as if he had tasted something bitter. "It's always difficult to partner with a government, any government." He had begun to stroke his chin. Kristin had long ago learned that when living a double life, the person who could be hurt the most by the truth was oneself and so Murat's concern about working for a government seemed sincere, as if he had deluded himself to the point of believing that his work with Kristin, for her government, fell into some other category, that it wasn't government work at all.

"I'm sure you'll figure out how to navigate it," she said.

He nodded and continued to stroke his chin. "You and I will do a side deal," said Murat, "and then I'll let the ministry know that I plan to put in a bid for the stadium."

"I'm not sure what you mean by *side deal*."

Murat elongated his neck, making a face like he was sniffing the air, and then he looked out over the city. In every direction new towers rose from similar construction sites. Enormous, T-shaped cranes bristling with lights picketed the horizon. The national flag—a red banner with a white crescent moon pinching a five-sided star—hung from the crossbeams of the crane arms. The wind rippled through them. There was a patriotic fervor to all of this construction, as if it wasn't just buildings but an entire people that were sprinting skyward from the great, gaping concrete-lined holes in the ground. But like any sprint, it was unsustainable. Murat needed to draw a profit while he could. As he looked at the city, he didn't see progress. He didn't see the development as distance traveled forward. Rather, he saw this progress as the distance they would all travel backward when the inevitable happened: the collapse.

"This Zeytinburnu Four project is on schedule but over budget." Murat stared at the clutter of handsaws and screwdrivers littering the floor. He picked up a hammer. "Each wasted nail costs me a cent," he complained. "These sloppy workmen have their hands in my pockets."

"So the side deal is we help you get the money to break even?" asked Kristin.

Murat told her that he couldn't afford to have this project fail. Such an embarrassment would be ruinous. He then approached a wooden joist braced against an internal wall. With pinched fingers he held the point of one of the nails against the bare side of the timber. "Do you know the secret to hammering a nail in with a single stroke?" he asked.

"Hit the nail hard?" she said.

He was taking long practice strokes with the hammer. One eye closed as he lined up his strike. He glanced back at her, dissatisfied by her answer. "Unfortunately, it's more complicated than brute strength," he said. "To get the nail all the way through on the first try you don't need to hit it hard, what you need is to have perfect follow-through. You need a vision of the nail buried into the wood. If you can see it, then the nail will slide right in."

She stood quietly next to him.

He took a couple of deep breaths, winding up and then decelerating the hammer just as it came close to striking. He then cocked his arm all the way back. His body was coiled, the entirety of its energy focused on the three-millimeter surface of the nail head. His hand darted forward. It moved with speed instead of strength, as if he were grasping a hot coal from a fire. The nail entered the wood not with a *thud,* but with a sharp *pop.* Murat dropped the hammer to the floor. He bent over at the waist, clutching his hand to his chest.

He cursed, and then jabbed his index finger and thumb into his mouth.

"You all right?" Kristin asked.

He winced, gazed up and then ran his uninjured fingers over the wood, which was completely flush from where his single stroke had pounded the nail all the way into the joist, splitting the grain. "See," he said, his fingers still in his mouth. "One stroke."

She again asked if he was okay.

He held out his hand. His thumb was bleeding from underneath the fingernail. "You have to envision the nail buried into the wood," repeated Murat.

"And keep your fingers out of the way," added Kristin.

"So what about our side deal?" he asked.

"How am I supposed to justify helping you get that money?" replied Kristin. "You got involved in this fourth Zeytinburnu project without consulting us. Now you want us to underwrite the rest so that you can finish it without embarrassing yourself. That's a lousy deal."

"If this project fails, maybe I lose the football stadium?" said Murat. "People are saying the government is overreaching with so much new construction. They are building in Eminönü, İstinye, Levent. I've even heard they're going to dig up Gezi Park for a shopping mall. When this whole system collapses, when the construction boom is over, I'm going to be very helpful as you try to decipher what remains."

"What makes you so certain that it's all going to collapse?"

"Too many people in this country have gotten rich," he said.

"There's nothing wrong with that," said Kristin.

"Ministers, deputy ministers, party officials, their sons, their nephews, too many of the wrong people have gotten rich. Everyone is taking a cut. Those cuts have already sliced off the head of this whole economy. It has been a gradual decapitation, so gradual that no one has noticed. And they won't notice until we walk into a wall."

"How much do you need?" asked Kristin.

He told her.

She ran her finger over the joist where he'd pounded in the nail. "That's a lot of money," she said. "How did you get that deep into debt?"

Murat didn't answer her. The wind had died down. The thirteenth floor was very quiet now. He didn't want to explain himself further. His pride wouldn't allow it. He looked past Kristin, out to the jagged skyline and its many incomplete and hollow buildings. The flags affixed to the crane arms hung limp. The air no longer moved them. The collapse was coming, Murat thought. She could believe him or not.

He picked up another nail and placed it against the joist.

"What are you doing?" asked Kristin.

He gripped the hammer and again began with his long, overarticulated practice swings. He sighted down the wooden handle, taking aim, breathing slowly. "This time I'm going to do it without my own hand getting in the way."

Kristin turned in the other direction. She couldn't watch.

One o'clock on that afternoon

⌐⌐

The three of them wander out of the restaurant and into the gleaming corridors of Akmerkez. Having slept no more than a few hours the night before, they stumble dazedly among the other shoppers. Catherine loops her arm through Peter's. William walks on his own. To pass the time they stop and browse the occasional storefront. William asks for nothing, except to be left alone to look at whatever he pleases and to fiddle with Peter's camera, which hangs heavily from his neck. Catherine and Peter linger behind him, speaking in hushed tones.

"You can stay at my apartment as long as you need," says Peter, choosing to focus on a problem he can solve as opposed to the crucial problem of the passports.

Catherine nods.

"Could someone from your family wire you a bit of money?" he asks. But Peter knows little about Catherine's family, just what he's learned from the occasional offhand remark, that she's an only child and had gone to five different schools growing up, that her father had made and lost his fortune about the same number of times, and that her mother, a socialite and homemaker, had managed to weather these upheavals while running their household, raising Catherine and even remaining beautiful well into her later years, always suspecting that when her husband finally lost everything she'd be forced to fend for herself and that her looks alone would have to sustain her. The secret of those youthful looks, Catherine had once explained, was a daily ice bath, a practice she planned to take up herself. Where her parents are now, whether they are still in good health, she has never volunteered. The parts of Catherine's life and of Peter's which fell outside the scope of their affair had mostly gone unmentioned. Certain boundaries existed.

In the confines of his apartment on those many afternoons in his bed, they had hardly spoken of such things. What had he learned of her? That as a girl she had once successfully auditioned for a summer program at the School of American Ballet, that as a young woman she had left home with Murat to escape her family, who were critical of her unfulfilled ambitions, even though leaving with Murat meant she turned her back on those very same ambitions. When she left, she hadn't cut ties with her family, or at least she hadn't wanted to. Her mother and father had visited only once, though it hadn't really been a visit, rather an intervention, just before she married Murat. And after they married, her parents never returned. They had wanted to support her, money was no issue, but they would do so only on their terms, if she crafted a life acceptable to them. When she refused their support, she refused their vision of her life. Peter learned that she had continued to write them and that they had never responded, and that when she had written with news of William and they still didn't respond, she wrote a final letter, and then stopped writing altogether.

When Peter had asked what that letter said, she had waved her hand dismissively and mentioned something about Cortés burning his ships while she smiled, and when he looked into her eyes, they were wide as empty plates and endlessly sad so he couldn't smile back. She had then kissed him, relieving him of the pressure to say something reassuring. Often they said very little, cocooning themselves in silence. During their lovemaking she fitted herself to him and afterward they would lie in his bed, reposed in whatever raw sunlight came through the windows, or they would end up in the living room, watching television, reruns mostly. Lately, they had developed an affinity for the reality show *Survivor*.

When Catherine doesn't respond, Peter again asks if someone in her family might wire her a bit of money. She tells him that she wants nothing from them, that she will take nothing from them and that if she returns home she will refuse to see them, just as they have refused to see her since she's left.

"What about calling Kristin at the consulate?" Peter asks.

"It takes two weeks to issue a new passport," Catherine replies.

William scrambles over to them from the pet store. He grasps Catherine by the wrist, leading her to a partition of stalls at the window, each filled with a litter of two or three puppies. Nestled in a bed of shredded newspapers and spilled food pellets is a terrier. The dog's white coat is feathered with grime. Filth cakes around his black nose. His rheumy gray eyes focus on nothing in particular, not even William, who now shows Peter a couple of photographs that he has taken of the dog.

The shop owner steps out from the store. He crouches to eye level with William and beckons him inside with a wave. William looks to his mother, who in turn looks to Peter. There is something very dangerous about allowing a boy to play with a dog that he can never have, thinks Peter.

The insistent shop owner waves to them again.

"Why not," says Catherine, unable to say otherwise to her son.

As they come through the door, the shop owner proudly hooks his thumbs beneath a set of suspenders that bow outward where his gut hangs heavily over his belt. A pair of spectacles balance on the bridge of his bulbous nose. When he peers over their rims at Peter, he grins, having successfully persuaded them inside. But there is something insidious in his jolly affectation, like that of a fairy-tale villain who lures children away from their homes.

The store is a maze of chirping birds, gurgling aquariums and sacks of vitamin-enriched pet foods. The choking animal-scented air smells like too much creation in too small a place. William seems to notice none of this. He hands Peter back his camera and follows the shop owner toward the dogs. William can't see over the partition, so Peter lifts him beneath the arms. The sound of the yipping dogs grows louder as William looks down at them and they vie for his attention. He points toward the terrier, his original pick, which he had seen through the window. Peter sets William back on the floor. The shop owner nods and then shouts after a young woman in hijab and jeans, who appears from a storeroom office. He points out the little terrier to the girl. She leans deeply over the partition to pick him up, a maneuver the owner can't perform himself, inhibited as he is by his girth.

She places the squirming white terrier in William's cradled arms.

The shop owner claps Peter on the shoulder. "You good, baba," he says.

The compliment rings hollow to Peter as he isn't William's father, and he has no intention of buying William the dog.

The terrier gives William a quick sniff and then begins to lick his face, faster and faster, as if the more he tastes the greater appetite he has. With both of her hands resting on William's shoulders, the girl in the hijab steers him to a sofa beneath a display of aquariums, where Catherine has installed herself among the cushions, continuing to scroll through airline flights on her phone. Clutching the puppy to his chest, William sits alongside his mother. Deep as the sofa is, his legs extend straight out in front of him and his feet dangle above the floor. The terrier soon scrambles free from his grip, making a play for Catherine's lap. William lunges after him but loses his balance. Both he and the little dog topple over, swallowed by the cushions.

Catherine helps William up and places the dog back in his arms, but the terrier isn't content to stay there and continues to lunge toward her lap, his front paws pedaling in that direction while William clutches the dog's body. The shop owner then reaches into a brown paper bag beneath the cash register. He palms William a fistful of greasy dog treats. The terrier calms, content to eat from William's cupped hand.

The shop owner stands shoulder to shoulder with Peter in the center of the store. "Boy, dog, make good friend," he says. Peter glances over at

Catherine, who remains immersed in her phone, searching out a solution to the myriad problems presented to her on its screen.

William kneads the terrier's white coat. "Can he come home with us?" His eyes rebound between his mother and Peter as if he is uncertain who in this new situation possesses the authority of that home. Peter hesitates to speak, hoping that Catherine might refuse her son. But she says nothing, and instead only leans more deeply toward her screen.

Peter gently explains to William that this isn't the right time for him to have a dog. The terrier finishes the last treat, licks William's palm and once again breaks away from the boy's grip and makes for his mother's lap. The shop owner waves over the girl in the hijab, who had returned to her office in the back room. He recites a paragraph to her in a clipped, barely audible mutter. Intermittently, his eyes fix on Peter. Each of these looks is like a punctuation mark as he speaks. Peter understands none of it.

The shop owner finishes his speech. He lifts the dog from William's lap and helps the boy from the sofa to his feet. He guides William to a display where they sell collars. Before Peter can protest further, the girl explains that William can take the terrier home on a trial basis and that if things don't work out the dog can always be returned. "Keep him for two weeks," she says. "If he's too much trouble, bring him back." But she must know the impracticality of this because she speaks with a sour, guilty look, as if her words are a piece of fruit she has bitten into only to discover it spoiled when it passes into her mouth.

Catherine stands from the sofa and tucks her phone into her pocket. "Two weeks?" she asks.

The shopgirl nods, but the question isn't aimed at her. Catherine clasps Peter by the elbow, gently guiding him into a corner. They stand beneath a high shelf lined with birds chirping in their cages. "We could keep him at your place," she says.

"You're not serious?"

"It would be a good distraction for William."

"And when you leave?" he asks.

"We'll bring him back here. It's a two-week wait for new passports anyway."

"So now you're getting new passports?"

"Peter—"

"It's not fair to get him a dog when you know that it can't work out."

"Fair?" she says in a single exhaled breath.

She clutches Peter's hand and laces her fingers through his. Her hair still smells faintly like the cigarettes she smoked at Deniz's apartment last night. Before Peter can pull Catherine closer to him—or choose not to—she lifts her head so that her eyes affix to his. She then releases her grip on his hand and turns down the next aisle, finding her son and the shop owner. William holds a little red collar. Catherine takes it from him, kneels down and fastens it around the neck of the terrier. The shop owner lifts the dog and places him on the counter next to the cash register. The girl in the hijab touches the bar code scanner to the collar and rings up the price. She offers Peter the receipt for him to review. He is hesitant to know how much all of this will cost. So without reading the receipt he hands over his debit card.

※

The shop owner had tried to sell them more things: a dog bed, an enormous sack of food, inflatable chew toys, but Peter refused to buy anything else, much to William's and Catherine's disappointment. They have wandered back out into the mall, where they still quibble about it. "We didn't need all that stuff," Peter insists. They meander toward the escalator that will take them to the first floor and then out to a taxi stand.

"He at least needs a tag," says Catherine.

"No, he doesn't."

"We need to put his name and address on it, in case he gets lost."

"He doesn't have a name and address," says Peter.

Catherine grasps William by the hand. The two of them—and the dog—take a few quick steps and distance themselves from Peter. Catherine searches the mall for a place to purchase the tag. She soon stops in front of a window filled with cheap curiosities: copper lockets, tarnished music boxes, chipped porcelain statuettes, the junky paraphernalia of a thousand attics. Catherine disappears inside with William and the dog. Peter trails after them but stops for a moment before he enters, examining the handwritten prices stickered to each item. The tinny brass bell affixed to the doorframe jingles as the door closes behind Peter. He soon finds Catherine in the back of the store, where she and the proprietress wander among the merchandise searching for some trinket they could engrave for the dog. Catherine then stops her search. She fixes herself above one of the black-felt-lined display cases, staring at the contents.

Peter steps beside her. "What did you find?" he asks.

She startles at his words and then averts her eyes to the floor. Catherine scoops up the dog and takes William by the hand, leaving the store. "This wasn't a good idea," she says to no one in particular as she exits, the bell once again jingling against the doorframe.

Peter gazes down at the display. Laid out among the trinkets is the same model cigarette case he bought her when they began their affair. Beneath it is the price, written on a small tag. The thing is worthless, which, of course, he had known all along.

May 28, 2013

⟳

He watched the dawn with sleepless eyes. Peter lay on the sofa in his living room. A seam of light expanded over the hilltops and dissolved when it reached the Bosphorus, which was filled with mist and shadows and a relentless parade of ships, their stern lights and bow lights faintly visible as some traveled north to the Black Sea and others traveled south to the Mediterranean. Occasionally he heard the long mournful blow of a foghorn. Seagulls circled the ships, disappearing into the grainy mist as they scavenged scraps of food from the idle deckhands who gazed landward, catching glimpses of the city and civilization for the hour or so it took to transit the strait before they would once again return to the vast, roiling emptiness of the open sea.

Peter turned over so he faced away from the window. The grant money he had received from Kristin nearly a year before had almost run out. He had nothing to show for that time. He had taken a year's worth of photographs but had ceased to see how they fit together. The concept at his project's heart—the idea of a strategy of tension—no longer made sense to him. Hundreds of black-and-white portraits, each one indexed, then re-indexed and eventually altogether unindexed lay strewn across his kitchen table. He had stopped believing in his theories, which is to say he had stopped believing in his work. He had taken to sleeping on the sofa because that was where the television was, and he watched it most nights until he fell asleep, or didn't.

He checked his phone. There was a missed text from Catherine. She would be coming by at their usual time. He hoped that she'd stay for dinner but doubted she would. Out on his windowsill a few birds landed and took off, heading between the hillside apartments with their damp laundry hanging from the lines and the ships that passed along the strait, plying their enormous frothing wakes through the water. He lifted his camera from the coffee table and practiced shooting the birds just before they landed or right after they took off. It was a drill he had learned years before to help improve reaction time. The impulse he still felt to take photographs had kept him from despairing entirely in his work. After a few minutes he had ten perfectly captured frames of birds transitioning in and out of flight. He deleted all of them.

His trousers were folded over the arm of the sofa. He stepped into them while watching the television. The morning news, which was in Turkish and thus barely intelligible to him, showed images of what looked like a hobo encampment. The newscaster was commenting on a live feed, in which the cameraman had placed himself behind an advancing phalanx of baton-wielding police officers. He held his camera above their navy blue, practically black, helmets. There were perhaps two dozen tents—some of them just tarps strung between the trees—with university-age students splayed beneath them in congregations of brightly colored sleeping bags. Peter recognized the location immediately—the thick-trunked elms, the surrounding office buildings and five-star hotels, the concrete footpaths hemmed in by weeds, the haphazardly planted flower beds and the fountain anchored at one end: it was Gezi Park.

Peter turned up the volume. He could hear a popping noise, and then in the corner of the television he could see wispy trails of smoke spiraling through the air as the police launched arcing salvos of tear gas. The protesters fled, wheezing into their bent elbows and tripping over one another and their brightly colored sleeping bags, which tangled around their feet as they ran through the thick, noxious clouds.

The police trampled over their encampment, enthusiastically hacking down the tents with their batons as if they were carving a machete path through deepest, darkest jungle. The cameraman fell away. The live feed filled with the sound of him choking on the tear gas, for which he had come unprepared, while the police had donned their gas masks, which transformed them into a faceless singularity of navy blue uniforms, plastic riot shields and glossy black leather boots.

Peter shut off the television. He checked his watch. It was just after seven o'clock. He had nothing to do that day, except to see Catherine in the afternoon, which he felt he could miss. Their encounters had come to feel routine, a series of continuing no-things. He sat on the edge of the sofa, his eyes fixed on the television. In its blank screen he soon perceived his own reflection, and not wanting to stare at himself he looked down at his bare feet. The sound of foghorns resumed outside his window. He stood. The birds that had perched on his window-sill minutes before had all gone elsewhere. The noise of the foghorns picked up. There were two of them, dueling with one another. A pair of lights, one green and the other red, sliced through the mist, which was still thick in the strait. The red light hardly moved. The green light approached it relentlessly.

Watching the lights, Peter recalled a story he'd heard as a boy. It was about a ship off the Atlantic coast, a behemoth oil tanker, one of those steel-bellied monsters that with a single navigational error could spill its contents and destroy an entire coastline. The tanker had been blown off course in a storm and had become shrouded in a dense fog when a light appeared off its bow. Up on the tanker's bridge the look-out handed a set of binoculars to the captain, who peered through them and then grasped the radio. "Approaching vessel, adjust your course twenty degrees northwest." A moment passed and a sleepy voice replied, "Negative, adjust your course twenty degrees southeast." The captain snatched up the radio's handset again. "Approaching vessel, this is the SS *North Cape*. Adjust your course twenty degrees northwest." Again the sleepy voice replied, "Negative, adjust your course twenty degrees southeast." The captain glanced around the quarterdeck, at his

first mate, at his radio officer, at the various members of his crew, who
in their time together at sea had always thought their captain to be able
and had never seen his authority openly questioned. Once more the
captain spoke into the radio. "Approaching vessel, this is the SS *North
Cape*, supertanker with over two million barrels of crude aboard and a
crew of one hundred and thirty-seven souls. I repeat, you are to adjust
your course twenty degrees northwest!" For a moment there was silence.
The captain glanced out of the corner of his eye to his crew, who continued unquestioningly with their duties on the bridge. The radio crackled
back to life. "Understood, SS *North Cape*," came the sleepy voice. "But
this is a lighthouse. Adjust your course twenty degrees southeast."

Peter stood at his window. He watched the determined green light
approaching the small, immovable red light. He took his camera and
bounded down the stairs of his building, out into the street, where he
would find a taxi to Gezi Park. Although he didn't see it, about the
time he left his front door the green light shifted its course. Had Peter
been watching, he would have seen a break in the mist reveal the large,
hulking ship and, directly in front of it, the red light affixed to the
insignificant yet immovable Kız Kulesi, or Maiden's Tower, built on an
islet that was inconveniently located at the mouth of the strait.

Peter saw none of it, however. To know the outcome, he hadn't
needed to.

※

The first two taxi drivers Peter stopped refused to take him to Gezi
Park. The third agreed, but insisted that Peter pay double the normal
fare, and that he pay up front. With his depleted funds, this was a not
insignificant expense. Peter accepted the terms, however. He fished a
billfold of cash out of his pocket and paid the driver nearly all of it.
The two of them then rushed along Cevdet Paşa Caddesi, the driver
grasping the wheel in both hands as though it was a jackhammer's T-bar
and he was tearing up the ancient pavement. They sped through chic
waterfront neighborhoods such as Arnavutköy and Ortaköy, which in
Ottoman times had been sleepy fishing villages, and they soon passed

the beautiful yet ominous stretch of road that abutted Dolmabahçe Palace with its unscalable limestone walls built by the sultanate with the single purpose of protecting the royalty that had once lived in opulent seclusion inside, isolated from the populace—the same populace which now defied the current authorities in Gezi Park.

Past the palace, two police cruisers had parked herringboned across the road, their siren lights turning orbits. The officers leaned against the hoods of their cars. Holstered pistols brooded at their sides, as they commented on the passersby and exchanged risky grins. Across from them was the new, incomplete stadium for Beşiktaş football club. A placard staked into the ground touted the project as a public-private endeavor, sponsored by both the government and Yaşar Enterprises. As much as the police officers manned their roadblock in order to regulate traffic heading toward the protests, it also seemed as if they'd taken up this position to ensure that no one disrupted construction on the new stadium, which from the lack of building equipment or materials on-site appeared beset by an indefinite delay.

When Peter's taxi approached the roadblock, one of the officers glanced up and flicked his wrist in the opposite direction. Needing no further instruction, the driver immediately turned around. He double-parked adjacent to the football stadium and motioned for Peter to get out. This was as far as he would take his taxi. Peter leaned over the gearshift and gestured through the windshield to a couple of narrow, unblocked alleyways, which could likely get them all the way to Gezi Park unnoticed. The driver responded by removing his key from the ignition and stepping onto the curb. He then opened Peter's door and stood, impatiently waiting.

Peter gathered his camera bag and walked in the opposite direction from the police, who rerouted traffic while they continued to chatter idly with the heels of their palms resting on their pistol grips. Although the seaside road had been cordoned off, dozens of tributary passages unspooled toward Gezi Park. Some were just wide enough for two people to pass shoulder to shoulder, while others could accommodate a single car. It was impossible for the police to block all of these. Most of the shop fronts had been shuttered, but housewives and children who'd been kept home from school because of the turmoil throughout the city filled the apartment windows from the second floor up. Leaning over window boxes or out toward the wash lines stretched between the buildings, they kept vigil above their streets.

Peter made a quick survey of what would be the quickest route to the city's interior. As he glanced to the heights and the park, he could smell the faint chemical scent of tear gas tumbling toward the waterfront. The trace of it in the air excited him and he could feel his stride lengthening as he passed around the back of the football stadium in the direction of an access road that would—he thought—deliver him to Gezi Park undetected.

Halfway up the access road he came across a pair of excavators poised to dig out a new foundation although they had not yet begun; the teeth of their steel shovel blades remained clean. Crouching by the treads of one of the excavators, a pair of men sipped tea from paper cups. One was smoking. The other was not. The one without the cigarette, who was tall and slim with the lean sunken cheeks of a distance runner, shouted for Peter to stop. He had spoken in Turkish, but he could have issued the command in any of two dozen languages and Peter would have understood him by inflection alone.

Upon noticing Peter's camera and fair complexion, the other man, the one who smoked and was of a normal height and handsome, or at least appeared comparatively handsome next to his companion, called after Peter in English, "Come here!"

Peter stood motionless on the dirt path he had been following, which curved around the back of the stadium. A hundred meters up, the path would fork in a half dozen directions, leading him into a labyrinth of neighborhoods where he could, likely, get away. He considered the option of running for an instant and in that same instant surveyed the pair of men who'd called after him. They were dressed shabbily, in old jeans and nearly identical fake leather jackets. Neither had shaved for a few days and Peter could see the traces of gray in their stubble. If they were thugs out to profit from the morning's chaos, they appeared about a decade too old. Peter also noticed their identical black leather boots, which were shined to the same mirrored gloss as those worn by the uniformed police.

Peter followed their instructions and approached.

"The roads up to Gezi are closed," said the shorter of the two as he exhaled a plume from the nub of his cigarette, which he'd smoked nearly to the filter. He flicked it on the ground, where it drizzled a cascade of embers at Peter's feet. "What are you doing back here?" The man had meat-flavored breath, a dog's breath, and one solid gold tooth, an incisor, which gnawed fang-like on his lower lip as he spoke from the corner of his mouth. The rest of his teeth were clean and straight. Peter wondered how he'd lost the tooth and imagined it had been punched out in a brawl.

The taller man, the lean one, pointed to Peter's camera bag. He raised his dark eyes, which contained no expression, and then muttered something to his friend in Turkish, which Peter couldn't understand.

"What have you got there?" The man with the gold incisor cocked his head and gave a lopsided smile. "Are you a journalist?" Before Peter could answer, the taller man took a step toward him, grasping after the bag. Peter tugged away.

"I don't have to show you anything."

As soon as Peter issued this challenge, both men reached into their pockets and removed their wallets, inside of which they carried police badges that they now brandished like a winning hand of cards, one that they had held through several rounds of betting, knowing all along that they'd collect from anyone foolish enough to gamble against them.

They ordered Peter to hand over his bag.

The prospect of losing his camera sent Peter into a mild panic. He didn't have the several thousand dollars he would need to replace it and without the camera there would be no reason for him to continue with his project. And so no reason for him to stay in the city. It would be the perfect excuse to abandon the work he'd invested himself in.

He couldn't be blamed for a crime perpetrated by the authorities. He would be a victim, not a failure, and could go home as such. His panic strangely began to feel like relief.

Peter reached into his bag. Next to his camera was his wallet. Inside the wallet was Kristin's business card with the phone number she had given him. He could call her. Perhaps she could use the weight of her diplomatic position to clear this up. Whatever temptation he felt to hand over his camera was immediately overruled by his desire to avoid the humiliation of a robbery. Whether it was a survival instinct or self-pride, Peter couldn't say. Perhaps, he thought, there wasn't much of a difference between the two. The reason didn't matter. He was not handing over his camera.

Peter pulled Kristin's business card out of his bag. "I am with the U.S. consulate," he said. "You can call that number for a reference." He pointed to Kristin's handwritten scrawl from many months before, which was smudged, and the edges of the card were worn and dog-eared. As far as credentials went, what Peter had presented was a poor offering and he imagined Kristin sitting at her desk, the ranks of cellphones arrayed in front of her. What were the chances that she'd even answer? And if she didn't answer? Peter imagined himself disappearing into a holding cell in the bowels of the local precinct until he could contact someone who would vouch for him, which might be never.

Holding out the business card to the two men, Peter wished that he had never volunteered it. But there was nothing he could do about that now. He had placed his fate in their hands, and in Kristin's. He'd never known that he could feel such precise regret.

The taller man snatched the card. He held it at arm's length as he read, offering a slight grimace. Whatever I'm selling, they aren't buying, thought Peter. Next it was time for the man with the gold incisor to examine the card. He took it from his colleague, rotating it between his fingers before he held it steadily in front of him and began to read. Then he glanced up. "Cultural Affairs Section?" he said gravely.

"That's right," answered Peter.

"You expect us to believe that you are with the Cultural Affairs Section?"

Peter explained that he was a photographer on an artistic grant from the consulate and that his work dealt with "cross-cultural dialogue." The two men exchanged blank, confused stares. Peter described in greater detail the nature of his project, his theories about how societies are held in place by invisible yet binding constructs, his method of categorizing photos to reveal this, the manner in which an image conveys one impression when displayed on its own but another impression entirely when it's paired with a different image. "It's a matter of context," Peter said.

They both began to laugh at him.

The taller man then said something to his partner in Turkish. They turned serious, determining what they should do with Peter. They kneaded their stubbled chins. They kicked at the dirt with the toes of their shined boots. Pondering his fate was a form of torture and they chose to torture him. Once or twice each of them glanced directly at Peter. They even offered smiles.

The day was heating up. The sun had burnt off most of the mist, which had stalled so thick along the strait that morning. The wind came steadily now, blowing down the hillside and carrying an increasing measure of tear gas, an indication that it was being administered in more liberal doses further up the path.

Peter began to sneeze.

"God bless you," said the man with the gold incisor.

Peter couldn't stop sneezing. He'd broken into a fit, bending over at the waist. The taller man reached into his pocket and handed Peter a somewhat used handkerchief, which Peter took, not wanting to appear impolite. He blew his nose and wiped his eyes and soon recomposed himself. "Give her a call," he said, pointing toward the business card. "She'll sort this out for us." He struggled to speak confidently as he imagined either of the two dialing the number, holding the phone to his ear while they all listened to its empty ringing when no one answered. Peter also imagined the phone on Kristin's desk and her ignoring it as she spoke to someone of greater importance, or answered emails, or did any number of things except for the one thing that Peter needed her to do, which was to help him.

Peter waited to see what they'd say.

"We don't want any problems with Cultural Affairs," concluded the man with the incisor. "You can go. But if you're determined to spend the day in Gezi Park, you should try to get a gas mask." He returned Kristin's tattered business card, holding it with both hands as if it deserved at least this much deference. Peter felt he had managed to capitalize on the reliable strain of paranoia which ran among the Turks. Cultural Affairs, he thought, almost speaking the two words. Then a half dozen menacing three-letter acronyms of U.S. government agencies flashed through his mind. Peter couldn't help but find it amusing—even empowering—that someone would presume his affiliation with such dark, conspiratorial forces.

He set off toward Gezi Park, climbing a web of alleys that ran in switchbacks up the hillside and toward the city's heart. Belief in conspiracy theories was a form of paralysis, he thought. To be unable to look at a person, or a series of events, and take them at face value, to see manipulations and lies everywhere, it must cripple a society, make it incapable of progress, vulnerable to an unbearable hysteria.

He glanced over his shoulder, struck by an unsettling premonition that the police officers had chosen to follow him. The path behind was empty, as if proving that they were hidden somewhere on it, for surely they weren't amateur enough to be discovered with a simple turn of the head. And if they were back there, unseen, what could he do? He could forget them, as if that were possible. Once he had climbed a bit further up the path, Peter surveyed the congested traffic on the seaside road beneath him. The pair of uniformed officers still leaned against the hoods of their cars with their hands resting on their holstered pistols. He then looked beyond the traffic, to Dolmabahçe Palace. From his elevated vantage, he could see behind its walls and into those once forbidden grounds.

He could see the football stadium too, just beneath him. It was an
enormous hole in the earth. Before construction stalled, work crews
had levered thick wooden stanchions temporarily into place to keep the
sides from collapsing in on themselves so that a new foundation could be
poured. Peter recalled the placard he had seen outside. The government
and Yaşar Enterprises had partnered on the project, yet this partnership
made no sense. The government had never worked with a private sports
team and Beşiktaş hadn't won a championship in decades. The two were
unlikely collaborators for a new, subsidized stadium. How much would
this all cost? he wondered. And who, ultimately, would pay for it?

Peter continued his ascent toward Gezi Park, threading his way
through the crooked lanes where the pavement was a bit uncertain.
What concern was the stadium to him? He kept his back to it as he
climbed. He could have constructed any number of conspiracy theories
around this unusual project, but there was little point. So he didn't
waste his time. Such theories could paralyze a mind, he told himself as
he traveled steadily upward.

❋

The street was empty and Peter hiked along its center. The mist had
slickened the cobblestones and asphalt. The grade was steep. He lost
his footing once or twice. The wind smelled like the sea. The birds that
circled the ships in the strait also circled the treetops, some of which
were beneath him. The leaves on the trees were full and green and the
birds landed inside them. In places the leaves rustled and Peter could
not tell if the rustling was from the wind or from the many invisible
birds jockeying for space within the crowded branches.

The air became still again. Peter watched the moving trees and
thought they must be very full of birds. The higher he climbed, the
more the sound of the leaves mixed with the sounds from up the hill,
from inside Gezi Park. He could hear the murmur of the chanting
crowd, whose voices rose and rose as he approached, until they were
dispersed by the pneumatic *pops* of discharging tear-gas canisters. He

had begun to sweat as he climbed, and he could feel the residual tear gas seeding its menthol tinge into his pores and the corners of his eyes when he blinked.

He felt very awake.

The alley he had climbed emptied onto Sıraselviler Caddesi, an avenue in the European quarter of the city. The shuttered café façades gave off an early-morning atmosphere, as if at any moment the owners would sweep the sidewalks, set out their tables and scour the streets for customers. Adjacent to one of these cafés was the German Hospital, a relic that had long ago been turned over to local administration. Four men and a doctor stood at the front gate. They had gathered around a green, military-style stretcher. A woman was sitting up on the stretcher. She wore a red dress and carried a white canvas tote bag. Her hair was black and she was bleeding from behind her ear. The blood had traveled down her neck and mixed invisibly into the left strap of her red dress. Her arms were crossed over her knees. She looked confused.

All four of the men argued with the doctor. They had carried the woman down from Gezi Park and the doctor didn't want her in his hospital, lest there be trouble with the authorities. The men were muscular, athletic types. Their shoulders were rounded, their waists were trim and their arms hung low at their sides, their knuckles practically brushing at their knees as if they were perpetually carrying a stretcher.

Peter thought that the woman had been lucky. Four physically fit men had been nearby in the crowd and ready to help her when she was struck. Peter then realized that this was no accident. Someone had decided that these four men should be stretcher-bearers—the protesters had begun to organize.

While the argument around her continued, the woman stood and began to walk back up Sıraselviler Caddesi, toward Gezi Park. She wore a pair of heels and as she stepped on the cobblestones she wobbled a bit. She had likely been on her way to work and, like Peter, had seen the morning news and been curious about the protest. Unlike Peter, she had gotten caught up in these events and now, seemingly, she wished to rejoin them.

The four stretcher-bearers and doctor came after her. They took her by both arms and began to help her back to the hospital's front gate and her stretcher.

She swatted them away with her open palms.

Had she known how to make a fist, how to deliver a punch, she likely would have. But she didn't know how to fight. She'd never had a reason to know. That morning she had been a woman in a red dress on her way to work, nothing more, and now blood spilled from a gash on her head. Life had had an order before that morning, tenuous and strained though it may have been. The woman had known her place within it. And now she didn't. Whatever dignity had been taken away from her, she didn't seem to understand how to recover, so she appeared determined to return to the spot where it had been taken, to go back to Gezi Park, as if she might reclaim it there.

Her open-fisted blows landed on the uplifted arms of the men, who blocked their faces as they tried to lead her away. Peter lifted his camera and got off four shots. Then the woman came after him, her arms cartwheeling with suddenly clenched fists. She cursed at Peter in Turkish and he thought to run away but didn't. He had done nothing wrong. It was his right to take these pictures—for this was how he thought about such matters, in terms of his rights and the sanctity of those rights. He stood in the street with his camera clutched to his chest.

She switched over to English. "Get that thing out of my face."

Peter affixed his lens cap. This seemed to satisfy the woman. The doctor had slunk up behind and again grabbed her arm above the elbow. "Okay," he said, relenting. "Let's do a quick examination. But for the time being I don't want you going up to the protests." He faced the stretcher-bearers and explained further. "She needs help. I can examine her, but I can't do it inside the hospital."

The woman in the red dress paused. Her mouth was slightly agape. This was the first time Peter had had a chance to look at her eyes. They were brown and of the normal sort, but the whites had reddened at the corners and it was difficult to say whether or not this effect was solely the result of the unavoidable tear gas or was perhaps a by-product of other, hidden emotions, or hidden injuries of the sort the doctor now searched for.

The doctor helped her walk back down Sıraselviler Caddesi, to the stretcher laid adjacent to the wrought-iron gate at the German Hospital's entrance. She perched on the stretcher's edge. The doctor reached into the pocket of his clean white jacket, which seemed out of place in the street. He tugged on a pair of turquoise rubber gloves, the latex snapping at his wrists, and then he began his examination, standing over the woman, glancing down at the back of her head while he combed apart her hair with his fingers like one primate grooming another.

Peter sat next to the woman on the curb.

She gave him a sidelong glance, and then winced as the doctor pressed the gash on the back of her head. A fresh trickle of blood crept down her shoulder and was absorbed into her dress's left strap. The doctor made a quick call on his cellphone, asking an orderly inside the hospital to bring a few supplies to the front gate.

The four stretcher-bearers excused themselves. They had other work to do. The morning was pressing on and they returned up the road, toward the police barricades and the chanting protesters, toward the sailing canisters of tear gas and the sound of batons smacking against riot shields. Taking a bend in the road, they disappeared.

Watching them go, Peter couldn't help but ask the woman why she hadn't gone into her office that morning, why she'd come to the protests instead. When she glanced up at him, her eyes twitched a bit, as if they couldn't hold focus.

"I was curious," she said.

An orderly rushed up to the front gate in a pair of scrubs. She carried the doctor's medical bag, an old leather satchel with a brass clasp and hinged opening. The doctor removed a hooked needle and thread, a bottle of rubbing alcohol and cotton swabs from the bag's ample interior. He doused one of the swabs in the alcohol and then picked apart the woman's hair as he'd done before, looking for the gash.

"Is this going to hurt?" she asked.

The doctor applied a liberal dose of the alcohol to the exposed wound. The woman in the red dress gasped and then her voice choked off. She reached up, as if she was going to punch the doctor, but instead she clenched her fist and placed it firmly in her mouth, where she bit down on her knuckles, releasing a breathy whimper. Her eyes were already red and weepy from the morning's events, so her expression changed little while all the pain mixed together. Except she was crying.

Soon the doctor had threaded her wound and bound the stitches tightly, leaving them to heal. After making a last cut with his scissors he placed a compress at the base of her skull. The woman stood and rolled her head on her shoulders, stretching out her neck.

The doctor bent over his bag and put away his instruments.

The woman looked at Peter and her eyes seemed clear for the first time. The noise of the protests up the road was still very loud and the sun had burnt off all the mist which had lingered so stubbornly through the morning so that the air was again easy to breathe.

"Would you like to take my photo now?" she asked.

Peter removed the lens cap. He helped the woman in the red dress to her feet and guided her by both shoulders to stand in front of the German Hospital's half-open gate with its intricate geodesic pattern. When Peter brought her image into focus, the garden courtyard beyond the gate was also visible. He could make out the bright flower beds and a birdbath with sunlight-varnished waters. But this background was blurred in the frame. He glanced up from his viewfinder. He stepped forward and adjusted the woman's chin, lifting it slightly, which gave her a defiant air, but also turned it just a bit more in profile so that the compress on the base of her skull showed clearly.

Peter stepped back, reexamined his viewfinder and snapped the portrait.

The doctor presented a handful of hospital forms to the woman and gave her a pen. She leafed through them, and after examining a half dozen she began to rub the aching wound on the back of her head. The doctor offered to help her with the forms and the two of them sat on the curb. When it came time to enter her personal information, the woman handed the doctor her identity card, which contained her full name and address.

The woman in the red dress returned her identity card to her purse. The doctor finished the last of the forms and placed them in a paper folder he'd brought along. "You should go home," he said, glancing up the road. "That goes for you, too," he added, looking at Peter. The woman and Peter stared down Sıraselviler Caddesi, away from Gezi Park and in the direction that the doctor suggested they depart.

Turning a bend in the road, a column of protesters advanced toward them, headed in the opposite direction. They walked three across and maybe ten deep, with military precision. They had the confidence of veterans. Each of them wore a white hard hat while a housepainter's gas mask and a chemist's set of protective goggles hung from elastic straps around each of their necks. The noise of their jangling equipment and footfalls echoed down the cobblestones, as if carried by its own momentum.

The woman in the red dress had seen enough. She began to walk in the opposite direction, away from Gezi Park. Peter wasn't ready to join her, but he wasn't certain if he should venture any further. Then he heard his name called out.

Near the front of the column, a man took off his hard hat. It was Deniz.

"It is Peter, right?" he said. "What are you doing here?"

Peter held up his camera and wagged it in the air.

"You should come with us," said Deniz.

And Peter did.

Twelve-thirty on that afternoon

Murat knows where Peter lives. Kristin has told him that he needs to go and wait for his wife and son there, but he doesn't want to go. He has their passports, so Murat imagines that Catherine will have to bring William home eventually. If they show up at the consulate requesting new passports, Kristin can have her colleagues turn them away, or so Murat assumes. There is no need for him to wait in front of Peter's apartment. There is no need for him to endure the humiliation that such a confrontation will surely entail. Kristin insists, though. "You have to head this thing off," she says. "Otherwise I can't guarantee that I'll be able to keep her from leaving the country."

The admission takes Murat by surprise.

Kristin stands in the kitchen, explaining herself. "Your wife has certain rights."

"And my rights?" he asks.

Kristin removes her bag from the counter. She digs through its contents, checking for her identification badge and cellphone as she prepares to head into work. Murat's crisis has consumed her entire morning.

"What about my rights?" he repeats.

Kristin holds up her badge by its lanyard. "Do you see Turkish

Ministry of Interior on this thing? I can't help the fact that she and your son are American," she answers. She shoulders her bag. "I have done and will do everything that I can to stop them from leaving. That's why I'm telling you to go wait for them at Peter's apartment. They have to head back there."

"William wouldn't be an American if it wasn't for you," says Murat.

"Need I remind you that you asked for my help?" answers Kristin.

She exits the kitchen and passes through the foyer, with its grand marble floor and white orchids in the vase by the door. For a moment, Murat thinks that he might try to stop her, just as he had tried to stop Catherine. That had been a spectacular failure. If he hadn't been able to think of anything to say that would keep his wife from leaving, he knows there is nothing he can say to keep Kristin from doing the same. However, he possesses an instinct that Kristin won't abandon him, at least not yet, though he can't say why.

The door shuts behind her.

He sits at the kitchen counter. He is left staring at the photograph of him and William at the Kabataş ferry terminal, with William holding the umbrella over both of their heads when their excursion to the Princes' Islands had been rained out. They had managed to make the trip a couple of weeks later, just the two of them. It had been an unmitigated disaster. William had gotten seasick on the transit, vomiting over the railing into the water. When they'd arrived, the beach had been closed. Unbeknownst to Murat, who hardly ever vacationed, the season had finished the week before. The father-son excursion fell short of expectations. Perhaps this is why Murat looks at the photo of their aborted trip with such nostalgia, even though he would rather forget the day itself. When it comes to his family, he loves the idea of them while, at times, he isn't certain if he's capable of actually loving them.

He recognizes this as the challenge Kristin has put before him. Were he truly a family man, he would already be parked in front of Peter's apartment willing to say and do anything to get his wife and child back. If the humiliation of waiting at Peter's apartment is Kristin's way of testing his fidelity, Murat knows that his fidelity to her has already been proven in other matters. He was the one who had helped Kristin—and by that measure the entire U.S. diplomatic mission—navigate the treacherous days around the Gezi Park protests.

Kristin's genius wasn't that she understood the intricate web of regulations and relationships that proved essential to interpreting the uproar around Gezi Park, but rather that she understood months before anyone else that she would need someone who could decipher those intricacies on her behalf. Throughout that entire summer of protests across the city and then across the country, Murat had delivered to her the information she needed so that the U.S. diplomatic mission never compromised its interests by misbalancing its nominal support for both the government and the protesters. Murat had provided the information required for American diplomats to do what they did best in crisis: keep each side in a state of tension—which is to say, equilibrium—with the other.

Kristin had been prepared for that summer. Murat had not been. His collected real estate holdings had since lost more than fifty percent of their value and the government had reneged on supporting the new football stadium in Beşiktaş, leaving him to support a ruinous debt on that property. Murat had inadequately anticipated the change that was coming. And he had paid dearly for it.

This is also the case now. Kristin must have intuited that Catherine would leave him. She might not have known the exact moment, but if Kristin possessed the foresight to predict the Gezi Park protests, she surely possessed the foresight to know that Catherine would inevitably try to escape. Now that Catherine has acted, Murat recognizes that he should begin listening to Kristin. She has already told him what to do and, reluctantly, he will do it.

Murat climbs into the black Mercedes sedan parked in his garage. The cream-colored leather interior creaks pleasantly as he sits down, releasing a luxurious new car scent. He had bought the Mercedes only the year before, after the last of the contracts had been signed on the Yaşar Zeytinburnu 3 development and before his more precarious investment in Yaşar Zeytinburnu 4 had failed to pay out. He searches the glove box for the keys; that is where his driver usually leaves them. He readjusts the motorized seat controls to cater to his slightly longer legs.

He turns over the ignition and sits for a moment in the garage with his hands resting on the steering wheel while the engine idles. He will drive across town, into Cihangir, and he will wait outside Peter's apartment in the parked car. He will know what to say to Peter and Catherine when he finds them. He will also figure out how to say those things in front of William and in such a way that William might someday forget about the entire episode. His mind churns through the sequence of events, which will likely take all afternoon. He hopes it won't take into the evening; otherwise he will have to call the office and cancel a business dinner. Murat feels irritated, and in this moment of maximum crisis he is struggling against the idea that his family is, at its core, one massive inconvenience.

This is what he's thinking as he pulls out of the garage and this is what he is still thinking as he sits in traffic nearly an hour later, cranking at the gearshift as he ekes his way across the city. When he finally pulls up in front of Peter's apartment, he is confronted with a contingency he hasn't planned for, and neither has Kristin: there is no place to park. He can't wait out front if he doesn't have a parking spot. So he circles the block. It is all that he can think to do.

May 28, 2013

Deniz suggested that Peter take a photograph of the sunset. After they'd bumped into one another along Sıraselviler Caddesi, Peter had followed him up through Taksim Square and then on into Gezi Park, which brimmed with tens of thousands of chanting, flag-waving protesters. It was late afternoon. The two of them sat among dozens of others at the base of the Statue of the Republic, a boastful bronze replica of Atatürk and his companions advancing against the great imperial powers—the British and French—to found their democratic nation. Peter had brought Deniz a cup of bitter tea from an old man with a steel samovar fastened to his back on a makeshift aluminum frame. The old man brewed and sold his tea in the same manner it had always been done, from the time of Constantine to the present day, a reminder that some things didn't change, or couldn't be improved upon.

"The sun will set right there," said Deniz, pointing down İstiklal Caddesi. The wide boulevard gleamed in the fading light, curving in and out like a sheet of iron. Belle epoque façades and kitschy, shuttered tourist shops lined the way. The protesters congregated in Gezi Park and overflowed into the adjacent Taksim Square, readying themselves for the night and the chaos that the darkness would inevitably bring when the police advanced on their encampments, attempting again to disband them. "The police will come from that direction, with the sun at their backs so we can't see them in the glare. Before they do you should get a photo."

"Sunrises and sunsets never come out right," said Peter, placing the lens cap on his camera. A soft, orangish end of day touched the rooftops and slowly spread into the streets. He could feel a last, extra bit of warmth on his face. "My apartment has an amazing view at sunrise, one of the best in the city, so I've tried."

"The best view in the city at sunrise is from a suite in the Çırağan."

"When were you in a suite at the Çırağan?"

"Many times," Deniz said casually. "The concierge used to be a friend of mine. If one of the suites wasn't occupied, he'd let me stay for free."

"That's some friend."

"Let's just say he couldn't have that job and be open about who he was. I never would've outed him, but he was always worried that I might. I had nothing in those days, living in a gecekondu in Esenler after I was kicked out of school. But a few nights a month I'd show up at reception having dressed the part and he would check me in. When I met someone in the lobby, or in the restaurant—man or woman—and told them I was staying in the suite . . . well, it wasn't as hard as you'd think to convince them to come up, 'just to see,' they'd insist. And once they came up, they always stayed. Watching the sunrise from the suite in the Çırağan after a night like those is the best view in the city."

"And your friend, the concierge?"

"Eventually, the police found him in a hammam in Çukurcuma," said Deniz, slowly shaking his head. "They beat him so badly he couldn't return to work. Do you know what they call us?"

Peter grew silent.

"Do you?"

"I can imagine."

"*Ibne* . . . it means faggot," said Deniz. "That woman you helped earlier, the one with the red dress, how many times do you think she's squared off with the police?"

Peter shrugged.

"Never, I would bet." Deniz then pointed out to the crowd.

Professional women and men milled about in their business suits, clutching their briefcases as if they'd gotten lost on the way to work. Students had brought out guitars and stereos that they danced around as if they'd transplanted their dormitory common areas into the midst of this protest. "The police are going to try to clear out the square. We *ibneles* have seen how ugly this can get. All of them"—and Deniz once again gestured to the other protesters—"all of them have not."

Peter's phone vibrated in his pocket. It was Catherine. That afternoon he hadn't shown up to their scheduled time at his apartment. He didn't want to explain where he was, lest she worry. He also had an instinct not to tell her whom he was with. Peter had spent the day with Deniz, staying within an arm's length of him among the sea of protesters. Taksim Square's Gezi Park had the energy of a rock festival, one fueled by the danger of impending violence instead of music and drugs. The police lingered among the tributary roads, which fed into the demonstrations. Some of the roads they had closed, others they had left open. When they shut a road, they sealed it with a span of chain-link fence and a sawhorse painted powder blue with POLIZ stenciled across its length in white, or they parked one of their armored buses across the road's width. Water cannons were fitted on the rooftops of the armored buses. Chicken wire spanned their windshields. Black steel I beams that could be used as battering rams were welded across their fenders. The protesters danced, turning circles in place as they sang with their mouths wide open and their heads tossed back. They took over one of the excavators that would have been used to break ground on the shopping mall, the construction of which they had at this moment successfully brought to a standstill. They had spray-painted the excavator pink. They drove it in figure eights into Gezi Park and out through Taksim Square, waving a Turkish flag from its cab. Peter took photographs. He locked arms with the protesters when they chanted and danced. But always he watched as the police rearranged their barricades and parked and then reparked their armored buses.

The band of men Deniz had arrived with milled about the park and the square. They hung their hard hats, gas masks and goggles from their belts as they joined in with the most enthusiastic of the protesters, who counterintuitively weren't the young but the old, the septuagenarians with their smokers' coughs, who hacked and laughed as they danced, giddy with the idea that they had survived long enough to deliver a final word to the State. When the old kissed one another, the young cheered. The hours of the day passed across a wide spectrum of embrace. The music played on.

But the day was over now. Deniz crumpled his empty paper teacup. "Are you curious about why I didn't choose to show your work?" he asked Peter.

"I assume you didn't think that it was good enough."

"Good has nothing to do with it. What's shown is largely a political decision."

Had his work in some way been deemed politically subversive? This idea intrigued Peter. Perhaps the grant he had taken from Kristin disqualified him from an exhibit at the Istanbul Modern. Or, better yet, perhaps he had made a bold statement, one that even he didn't fully comprehend. He suddenly felt himself to be at the center of an intrigue. "I don't want to cause any problems for you," he said. "I could always tighten up or reimagine the project—"

"I'm not asking you to tighten up or reimagine anything," interrupted Deniz. He exhaled a long, impatient breath. "When I say that it's political, I mean that there is a rift between Catherine and me. I'm not comfortable with her dictating what gets shown in the gallery and, because she and I share a history, she increasingly tries to influence decisions that aren't hers to make. I don't mean to offend. I know that the two of you are"—his voice wandered off and then he resumed—"that she is your friend."

"I understand," answered Peter, though he didn't quite.

"I did like what you showed me," said Deniz. "Have you tried reaching out to the consulate to see if they could help you?"

Peter nodded but said nothing. He had no intention of bringing up the grant he'd already received. Deniz fished a pack of Winstons from his shirt pocket. He offered one to Peter and then lit both of their cigarettes.

"So now that I can't help you, what's your plan?" asked Deniz.

Peter appreciated the honesty, though he had no answer. Instead he stood, stretched his limbs and faced down İstiklal Caddesi in the direction Deniz had told him the riot police would enter the square. He thumbed at his camera, scrolling through the viewfinder and examining the photos he'd taken throughout the day: the triumphant crowd standing atop the excavator, the old couple kissing one another as they danced, the boy who had climbed onto the Statue of the Republic and shrouded the likeness of Atatürk with the national flag and the portrait of the woman in the red dress. Peter had documented these moments but added nothing to them. What he had produced memorialized the day but went no further. With night setting in, he felt as though an opportunity had escaped him.

Peter allowed his camera to hang heavily around his neck.

The old man with the samovar circled the Statue of the Republic one last time as he tried to corral a final bit of business, his eyes flitting anxiously up toward the few unbarricaded streets, which were the only avenues of escape into the adjacent neighborhoods. "Bir chai," said a thirsty university student, holding up one finger. His voice was hoarse from chanting in the square. A winsome pane of black hair fell across his forehead.

The old man poured out his cup of tea. "Iki lira," he said, extending his palm.

The student knifed his hands into the pockets of his slim-fitting designer jeans. He fished out a carelessly folded wad of bills and a couple of coins, which tumbled to the ground. As the student picked up the coins, the old man held the cup of tea in front of him and continued to cast his eyes nervously toward the few open roads exiting the square. To the north, to the south and to the east, in every direction except the west, the police had begun to congregate. They weren't blocking the way, not yet. Their assembly signaled a grace period to the protesters: Now is your chance to leave.

From their knees to their ankles the police wore greaves, and from their wrists to their elbows they wore gauntlets; they covered their torsos with breastplates, and all of it was made of a black carbon fiber that was tough as steel yet light as plastic. They tilted their weapons on their hips and cradled their white helmets in their overdeveloped biceps while they opened and closed the transparent visors on their face guards. With their chest-high riot shields leaning against them, they appeared like modern-day hoplites, men who were well practiced in old forms of violence. They smoked cigarettes and laughed among themselves. Their superiors handed out fistfuls of tear-gas cartridges and bandoliers of rubber bullets from plywood crates. The sound of their easy conversation rose up, hardly matching the pitch of the demonstrators' chants, but serving as an ominous undertone for anyone who chose to listen.

The thirsty student didn't have enough change, just a twenty-lira note. The old man with the samovar nervously asked if he had anything smaller while his gaze hardly moved from the gathering ranks of police. The student apologized. With the cup of tea already poured and the night setting in, he assumed that he would be given it for free. The old man refused and demanded that the student find change among the crowd. Halfheartedly, the student asked a few of the others who were standing nearby, including Peter, who checked his pockets for the meager sum, but he had already handed over his change to the old man for the tea he'd bought earlier for him and Deniz. When the student said that he couldn't find the two lira, the old man made a libation of the tea by pouring the full cup onto the pavement. It splattered against the student's shoes and expensive jeans.

"What good did that do!" said the student, squaring off with the old man. The crowd constricted as they sensed the conflict stirring.

"Why not give him the tea?" came a voice.

"We're all in this together," came another.

In the name of unity, and for a cause no greater than a cup of tea, they seemed ready to tear the old man apart. As they shoved him, the old man explained himself. "He's a rich university boy. Why should I give him something for free simply because he doesn't have a coin small enough to pay me?"

A pair of students reached behind the old man and opened the spigot on his samovar. The hot tea poured onto the backs of his legs. At first he ran in a circle to the sound of their jeers. Surrounded by these youths, he didn't dare come out of his shoulder straps and stop the flow. He soon changed course and fled toward the police. The taunting students followed after him for a few steps, laughing as he trailed a long brackish thread of tea across the pavement stones of Taksim Square. Then they stopped, recognizing that they had come within striking distance of the police, who, upon seeing the old man sprinting toward them, took the opportunity to don their helmets and form into ranks.

The sun was setting.

The police had blocked all of the roads in and out of the square, except for İstiklal Caddesi to the west. The dancing and singing stopped. A low hum of conversation reverberated among the police and among the protesters. But it wasn't a sound. It was like the absence of sound after a period of unsustainable noise. It was like a ringing in the ears. Peter could hear it everywhere. His eyes shifted to the barricades and the immovable police. The fading light fell upon them very clearly. Their helmets were on. Their face masks were down.

The first tear-gas canister sailed upward, its tail whinnying across the sky.

Peter followed its arc and then he lost it in the low sun.

He stared down İstiklal Caddesi, blinded by the end of day. His phone began to vibrate again in his pocket—Cat. He could hear rhythmic footsteps marching in time, but he could see nothing. He silenced his phone and then lifted his camera in the direction of the noise and allowed his shutter to release. Later, after the events of that night and the next morning, he would look at these photos. The exposure would develop as a brilliant ring, like a shot of an eclipse, but on the circumference's periphery he would be able to make out the dark, ominous figures of the police—nearly one thousand of them—advancing through the glare.

Deniz and his companions began to assemble around the Statue of the Republic. They donned their gas masks, their protective glasses and their hard hats. These were the *ibneles,* as Deniz referred to them. The disorganized masses filed in behind them. Clouds of tear gas wafted up from the sputtering canisters that now littered the ground. The front rank of protesters punted them like sport. Above the crowd a haze gathered with silent fatalism. Someone blew a metal whistle. Everyone advanced, shoulders forward, heads down, as if into a diagonal rain. Peter followed. He didn't know what else to do. Holding his hand like a visor along his forehead, he squinted upward. He stayed shoulder to shoulder with Deniz. Catching Peter's eyes, Deniz began to laugh. From his pocket he removed a pair of dark glasses, and with Peter close behind, the two of them headed off in the direction of the sun.

One-thirty on that afternoon

He drives in circles. It takes Murat less than a minute to lap Peter's block. There is little traffic. Most people have left for work or already dropped their children at school. Older, heavy-chested women emerge from the windows. They cradle their heaps of bed linens and laundry in plastic mesh baskets beneath their arms. Their waists press to the windowsills as they lean outside, clothespins clamped between fleshy lips, while they hang the wash from lines suspended apartment to apartment.

From behind the steering wheel Murat wonders which window is Peter's and about the extent of the plan that Catherine has set in motion. And he tries to imagine Catherine living with Peter and being reduced to one of these neighborhood women, yet he cannot see it. Murat knows she would never be satisfied with such a quotidian life, hanging out her husband's clothes to dry and locking up her days with domestic chores, and he wonders how Catherine could have deluded herself into thinking otherwise and if Peter knew her so little as to believe that he could ever make her happy with such a life.

When Murat had asked Catherine to marry him, she had added one distinct caveat to their engagement. "Family," Catherine had said, "should be the center of who you are, not the circumference." This had made good sense to Murat. He hadn't wanted to be limited in his ambitions, which Catherine had always supported. When they'd been younger, she used to steal her favorites of his architectural drawings, only to return them a day or two later in frames. "That's where they belong," she had insisted. "Never forget, they aren't your *work*. They're your *art*." As for Catherine's dreams, Murat felt no desire to curtail them by becoming her circumference. Though, in truth, he no longer knew what his wife's dreams might be. Whether Catherine had an obligation to articulate these dreams to Murat—so he might understand and support them—who could say? Murat had understood them when they first met, at least partially. Aside from her onstage ambitions, she had wanted to leave home, in effect to run from that center of who she had been. Murat had once enabled that. Now Peter did.

Murat tries to imagine his confrontation with his wife and Peter. He will double-park the car, which will ensure that the altercation can't last for too long. With the engine idling, he will tell Catherine to load William into the backseat. He plans to be quiet yet firm, and he will focus his demands on his son as opposed to on her. His rights as a husband could be questioned. She could lay claim to her emotions and insist that she doesn't love him. She could also point out his many failings. His rights as a father, however, don't require her approval. William is as much his son as hers.

Murat continues to drive. With his shoulders hunched over the steering wheel, he scans the sidewalks around Peter's apartment building. Hunting for his son, he notices how his vision has become clearer. At a hundred meters he can catch the details of someone's face as surely as if they had sat next to him at a dinner party. While Murat doubts any physical harm has come to William, he knows that he is no longer in control of his son's fate. That uncertainty sends a jolt of fear through him. He can feel it in his fingertips as he grips the steering wheel, maneuvering the car through the narrow streets. He can see it in the way his vision has momentarily sharpened. He loves the boy.

Murat's urge to recover his son is a primal one, like that of a parent discovering the strength to lift a car when their child is pinned beneath it. How lucky Murat would have been to find himself in those circumstances. But he has no car to lift. His child has been taken from him. Did Catherine understand the cruelty of this?

Of course she did.

He had taken something from her, after all. Had he forgotten what he never gave her, what he couldn't give her? And now, she had taken away his son. Because of his inadequacies, he had always made allowances for Catherine, even turning the other way when she took the occasional lover, men she seemed to select by a criterion of vapidity, in deference to her husband, so that they would never threaten him. But those allowances had come with the promise that she wouldn't leave. Or worse, that she wouldn't separate him from William. Each loop Murat makes around the block is like a spring winding itself tighter and tighter inside of him.

What she has done—in its way—is obvious.

She has the power when it comes to their son. Custody always goes to the mother. This isn't America or Western Europe. He is now at her mercy. She is exploiting his vulnerability, a reprisal of sorts for what he could never give her. It makes perfect sense to Murat. If a man's wife denies him physical affection, the husband might choose to take that affection by force. But for a woman? A woman cannot take in the same way. As Murat realizes Catherine's method, he almost admires her subtle genius. It might not have been one for one, but what Catherine has done is a near-equivalent revenge.

His inability, and the freedom it afforded her, had worked in their marriage for many years. She had understood his limitation from the outset and although he had managed better when he was a student, it had always been there and only grew debilitatingly worse once they left her country and returned to his home, which was the center of his angst. Then there was no course to run except to make allowances for one another: her occasional infidelities, an adopted child, but not much else. If she wanted to take William, to make him and him alone the center of who she was, could he justify denying her when he'd already denied her so much?

Murat continues to drive, retracing his path, but also searching for the answer to how it had all gone wrong. How he had done this to his wife. And how his wife had done this to him. He keeps returning to what she had told him those many years ago: *Family should be the center of who you are, not the circumference.* Thinking of that circumference, he scans up and down the sidewalks, looking for his son, as he circles and then re-circles the block.

※

The digital clock on the dash reads 13:47. He has been in the car for nearing an hour. The fuel gauge hovers around a quarter of a tank. This gives him an hour more until he will need to find a gas station, which he is loath to do. Having settled into his vigil, he doesn't want to break it and miss Peter, Catherine and William when they enter or exit the apartment. He has switched the radio on, tuning in to a political talk show. The subject is the faltering economy. Since Gezi Park, the lira has lost a third of its value. It threatens to depreciate further. Foreign investment has dried up. Internal threats (discontent at home, Kurdish separatists) and external threats (Syrian radicals) have destabilized the nation. The radio host and his guests argue about who is to blame.

As Murat listens, he catches himself nodding in support of certain points and shaking his head to refute others. He continues around the block, leaning slightly to the right, over the gearshift, in the direction of his turns.

A police cruiser pulls up behind him.

Murat at first doesn't notice the wheeling rack of lights in his rear-view mirror, immersed as he is in the radio program and his driving. The cruiser lets out a single blare from its siren. Murat doesn't pull over right away. He needs to take one last turn so that he can still see the front door of Peter's apartment when he stops. The road is narrow so Murat pulls two of his wheels up along the curb, allowing traffic to pass. The police cruiser behind him does the same. Glancing into his rear and side mirrors, Murat can see the officer checking and rechecking a computer screen bolted to a console on the dashboard. The door to the police cruiser swings open.

The officer steps into the street in no great hurry, stretching some stiffness from his lower back as he bends his torso frontward, rearward and side to side, as if in salutation to the four cardinal directions. He is a man with a curious figure, which tapers upward and gives him the look of a bowling pin. The paunch around his middle appears to be the product of decades of daylong shifts in his patrol car and, as such, this rim of fat doesn't bespeak laziness or neglect, but rather years of fidelity to his job.

The officer walks from his door to Murat's in a near waddle. His proud white hair is combed back from his forehead, while a healthy amount of black remains in his thick eyebrows and ample scrolled mustache. He knocks on Murat's window, and Murat, glancing into the officer's mirrored sunglasses, notices both his reflection and the thin line which segments the lenses into bifocals.

"What are you doing out here?"

"Waiting for some friends," answers Murat.

"How long have you been waiting?" the officer asks.

"About an hour."

"Someone in the neighborhood called about a suspicious vehicle. Do you usually circle the block for an hour waiting for your friends?" The officer glances inside the Mercedes's cream interior. Black piping lines the leather seats. Mahogany paneling inlays the dashboard. Each morning Murat's driver lightly perfumes the interior, and that scent, which is unmistakably foreign and expensive, wafts up as if to answer the officer's inquiry about whether this vehicle is suspicious.

"In this neighborhood," the officer continues, "they don't see many cars like this." His eyes cast along the street and then dart up for a moment, catching the residents at their chores through the open windows. He seems to hold them in contempt, even though with a policeman's wages and the promise of nothing more than a civil servant's pension he can never hope to rise any further in stature than the husbands of the working-class women who flog their area rugs with paddles and hang their tangled wash above the street.

The officer leans into Murat's lowered window, reaches across his body and turns up the radio. "I was listening to the same thing before I pulled you over," he says. A beat of silence passes between them and the broadcast pours into that vacuum. The commentators discuss Berkin Elvan, a fourteen-year-old boy who hovers near death after a canister of tear gas struck him in the head when his parents sent him to the grocer for a loaf of bread during the demonstrations around Taksim's Gezi Park. For six months doctors have sustained him in a coma while protesters have demanded justice against the police who shot him. The radio blares on:

"His parents should face charges for the damage from these latest protests," says one of the commentators. "This tragedy is their fault."

"But it is the police who shot him," says the other.

"His parents sent him to buy bread during a riot, but you blame the police?"

Leaning against Murat's door, the officer glances over his shoulder and down the street behind him, to where two or three cars have now backed up. The drivers idle, not daring to honk at the police. The officer stands straight and waves them past, allowing himself to be drawn out of the radio program and its arguments. The cars timidly accelerate by. The officer gives each of the drivers a long, disdainful gaze, for no particular reason, except, perhaps, that he can.

Observing the manner in which the cars submissively pass, with their drivers riding the brakes, Murat can't help but think about the changes that have occurred across the country in the months since Gezi Park. Two or three years before, a police officer would have been cursed at for needlessly blocking a road. After the protests of that summer, the government had reasserted itself like a parent who had long been too lenient with a petulant child. The people could bang their drums, chant their chants, they could howl in all the public squares of the world, but unless they could topple the State, and unless they could build a new state in its place, their optimistic visions would remain delusions and these delusional children would be the architects of their own prison. When Murat imagines that prison, he knows it to be a place where an aging traffic cop in an ill-fitting uniform inspires fear.

After the last of the cars eases past them, Murat feels that fear in the next question the officer asks: "You're Murat Yaşar, aren't you?" Murat keeps both his hands planted on the steering wheel. He stares straight ahead. The radio program fills the silence. The two commentators continue their debate about Berkin Elvan and who is to blame for this latest spate of violence. "Your license plate number came up immediately," the officer explains. "I wouldn't have expected to find you in this part of the city?"

"I'm here on business."

"Business?"

"Scouting out development opportunities," Murat answers in a meek voice that escapes his mouth in almost a whisper, as if he needs a drink of water.

The officer smirks.

Murat grips the steering wheel more tightly.

"Why would you build anything in this part of the city?" asks the officer. "Regardless, the charge is loitering. Unless you'd like me to do you a favor?"

"Loitering?" asks Murat. "Are you threatening me?"

"Why should you feel threatened?" asks the officer. "Listen, I could simply write you the ticket but I've offered to do you a favor." He leans a bit closer to Murat. "You could call the precinct captain, or even the police commissioner and ask for a favor, correct? They would, of course, drop this charge for you. You're an important man. But asking that favor of them would require a bit of explaining, don't you think? Whereas I could let you go now. Would you rather owe a favor to powerful men like them, or to an inconsequential one like me?"

Murat recognizes the officer's logic. He also recognizes that a person is only as powerful as the favors he is owed. He can't afford to have this episode with his unfaithful wife play out in any public way. The charge, "loitering," has become a catchall by which an investigation into any number of areas could begin. The officer stands with his bent arm thrown jauntily on top of the car door as he awaits Murat's answer. Of all the negative feelings Murat harbors in this moment, the most pronounced is envy. Yes, he envies the officer. He reluctantly admits it to himself. For his entire life Murat has invested in a series of assets—his father's business, his marriage, his adopted son—and he has watched as each transformed into a liability. Murat wants what the officer has: the freedom of possessing nothing. It is that freedom that has always allowed the powerless to challenge the powerful, or, put another way, that freedom has allowed the unencumbered to outmaneuver those weighted down by their own successes.

Murat reaches into the silk lining of his suit jacket. He removes his billfold. "How much do you want?" he asks.

"I don't think you understand," says the officer. He holds out his palm toward Murat, refusing him. "I'm not interested in your money."

Confused by this, Murat awkwardly inquires whether there is a policemen's association, or some other benevolent organization where the officer could proffer a contribution on his behalf. For what seems to be his amusement alone, the officer allows Murat to struggle with the appropriate method to offer a bribe. But the officer has no intention of taking a bribe, which only confuses Murat further. "Then give me my ticket for loitering and let me go on my way," he says.

"What's the real reason you're down here?"

Had the officer been willing to take a bribe, Murat would have happily explained everything, knowing that the officer would be vulnerable to him for having accepted money just as he would be vulnerable to the officer for having revealed the disarray in his personal life. But to reveal a vulnerability without the other person making themselves equally vulnerable, Murat knows the power he'd be granting this man. He grows very quiet.

The officer reaches into his pocket and removes his pad of tickets and a pen. He begins to fill out a citation while speaking to Murat. "You will see in the bottom right corner I am putting down a date. That is the deadline for protesting this citation, otherwise . . ." The officer doesn't need to go further. Murat knows that an official recording of the ticket would be registered, that he would then have to take up the matter at a court summons and, hopefully, he could get the entire issue dropped before any further inquiry. He hasn't committed a crime, far from it, but he has foolishly allowed himself to come under suspicion. He knows all too well that, just like guilt, suspicion carries its own sentence.

"You see that building." Murat raises his finger.

The officer stops writing. He squints upward.

"My wife's lover lives there."

"So that's your explanation," says the officer.

Murat nods.

The officer flips closed his citation pad. He slides it into his pocket. "Good enough for me" is all he says and walks back to his cruiser.

Murat's admission is done. His hands grip the steering wheel. His eyes shift nearly imperceptibly into the rearview mirror. The police cruiser pulls out from behind him. Its lights are off. As the officer drives past Murat's window, he stops so that their cars are alongside one another. The officer removes his sunglasses. His eyes are gray and dull, like unpolished silver, or a day without sun, or any other neglected and disappointing thing. "Drive safely, Mr. Yaşar," he says. "Maybe I will see you around."

❋

Murat still circles the block. The two commentators on the radio continue their debate about who is to blame for the tragedy of Berkin Elvan. "Blame rests with the person who committed the original crime," says one of the commentators, "and that is the government."

"The demonstrators began this chaos, not the government."

"The Gezi Park protests were the inevitable reaction to corrupt policies."

Murat wonders how much longer they can volley inconclusive arguments at one another. The fuel gauge on his dash nears empty. He hasn't seen another car on the road for at least a quarter of an hour.

Then, up ahead, he glimpses a taxi. He can make out the silhouettes of three people in the backseat. The taxi's blinker signals its turn in the direction of Peter's apartment.

"Ultimately everyone is to blame or no one is to blame," announces the radio commentator, as if such a sweeping statement might settle the matter.

"Why do you say that?"

"Because this circular argument has no use."

"Circular argument? Ridiculous. You're missing the point."

Murat mutes the program. He is hunched forward over his steering wheel, peering up the road at the taxi. Then its blinker switches off. Changing its course, the taxi doesn't take the turn but continues straight ahead. Murat considers following after, but he isn't sure. They'll have to return here eventually, he concludes, so it's best to keep on looping the block. And this is what he does. But he leaves the radio off. His mood is such that he prefers to drive in silence.

May 28, 2013

There was no wind. Clouds of tear gas obscured İstiklal Caddesi. Peter couldn't breathe. He stood shoulder to shoulder with Deniz, who had removed his gas mask so the two could share it. They hacked and wheezed between inhalations with their heads hung toward their feet. The front rank of protesters pressed their heaving bodies against the riot shields of the police, while the back rank pressed against the front rank. Peter and Deniz stood in the front rank, and when a spiraling canister fell at Peter's feet and spurted a thick white cloud of tear gas from its end, he wound up huffing a mouthful, which left him choking, his torso bent so far forward that he nearly toppled headfirst onto the pavement.

Deniz scooped Peter up beneath the arms. He cupped his gas mask to Peter's mouth and nose. "Stay on your feet," he yelled at Peter, but shouts from the crowd carried off the sound of his voice so it registered as barely a whisper. Peter gasped into the mask, catching his breath from what felt like the brink of suffocation. Then Deniz yanked the mask away, taking a breath for himself. One of the protesters held a bullhorn over his head. Its siren blared and blared. The man holding the bullhorn shouted, but his voice was also lost in the crowd and his open mouth became nothing but a silent hole in his face.

Soon it was night.

When one of the many protesters was struck in the head by a police baton, or asphyxiated by tear gas, or simply collapsed from fatigue, the crowd would lift them up and without instruction pass them from the front rank to the rear. Bottles of water were shuttled forward. Protesters doused their heads, cleansing their burning skin and eyes, or they drank in unrestrained mouthfuls, exhausted as they were by their efforts.

And on it went, until, inexplicably, the police stepped away, opening a seam in the center of their tightly formed ranks. The throng of protesters in the back now pushed the front rank forward. Peter watched as all around him people lost their footing. A woman fell facedown on the ground. Her long black hair tumbled against the sidewalk. Unable to lift her head, she struggled to stand as the advancing crowd trampled over her hair, pinning her to the cobblestones.

The police lined the İstiklal in two parallel ranks. With rubber bullets, they took potshots at the protesters who advanced past them into the open boulevard. Each bullet left its muzzle with a hollow exhalation, an apathetic *hiss* that was somewhere between a sigh and a laugh. At such close range the potshots easily found their marks and escalated into a steady fusillade. More protesters fell to the ground, clutching at invisible wounds. Their ranks thinned, and having successfully broken through the police lines, they lost all form. Flags appeared among them, waving in cautious triumph. Peter and Deniz milled about in the confusion beneath the flags. A halfhearted cheer rose up from a few perplexed voices. It soon cut off.

Turning a bend on İstiklal Caddesi, three armored buses lumbered forward. Like the fingers of a reaching hand, their headlights cast eerie shadows in the darkness. The water cannons on their rooftops sprayed out in lazy, rhythmic arcs. The bone-crushing pressure couldn't be seen, only heard. The sound of shattered glass as the water struck a shop window. The crush of metal as the water hit a shuttered kiosk. And the tide of that water, which descended the slight downhill grade and pooled at Peter's and Deniz's feet as they both realized the trap into which they had fallen.

"Get on your stomach," shouted Deniz. He pancaked onto the sidewalk and reached after Peter, jerking him down by the front of his shirt and pulling him to the ground, where they both lay in a prone position. "Cover your head."

Peter could already feel the mist from the water cannons against the back of his neck. A dull pain stabbed at his chin. He wiped his face and raised his hand in front of him. A trickle of blood smeared across his fingertips. He had cut himself on the jagged cobblestones. His eyes then focused past his hand and up ahead, to where a lone protester stood in the center of the İstiklal, stubbornly waving the national flag in front of the advancing armored buses. Even the police were hunkered down behind their riot shields as a precaution against an errant blast from the water cannons. But this lone protester refused.

Peter fumbled for his camera, which was pinned beneath his stomach in its case. The flag-waving protester leaned forward, bracing herself. The indifferent cannon continued to sweep the crowd, not even bothering to aim at this one specific target. It traversed and caught the tip of the protester's flag, snatching it and then cartwheeling it down the İstiklal. The protester's entire body jolted as if a single electric shock had struck her. This reaction wasn't because of the impact, but rather in anticipation. When the flag was torn from her hand, she must have felt the power of the blast that was about to strike her. Like many others who had allowed the police to lure them deeper into the confined İstiklal, she had underestimated the force of water. Peter watched her. He imagined that the protester would have turned and run away if given the chance to reconsider the stand she had chosen to make. It was now too late. It would take a fraction of a second for the cannon to find the flagless protester again.

The jet of water struck her center-chest. Deflected spray toppled onto Peter. The woman was lifted from her feet. Her body bent at the waist into a right angle. She traveled ten yards or so in the air, as if an invisible tether yanked her back in the direction from which she had marched, flinging her cartoonishly toward Taksim Square and the Statue of the Republic, where they had all gathered hours before in the end of the day, dancing, chanting and extolling the merits of their grievances.

The protester landed on her back. She whiplashed, her head striking the jagged cobblestones which had so easily split Peter's chin. She wasn't moving. The armored buses continued their advance. Peter rose into a half push-up like a sprinter's start. Before he could run off, Deniz grabbed him once again. "Stay down, you idiot."

As he was pulled to the ground, Peter glimpsed from his periphery a half dozen other protesters who now stood from the rows where they had lain flat. Panicked, they also had turned to run. The lazy arc from the water cannons caught them from behind, upending their legs and popping them skyward as effortlessly as bottle corks. These dazed few lay writhing on the ground when the police flanking the İstiklal peeked from beneath their riot shields and then lunged after them, falling onto their bodies like carrion birds as they bound their wrists with plastic zip ties and dragged them into their ranks.

The armored buses parked. They continued to sweep their cannons over the heads of the crowd. The effect was an artificial rainstorm. The powerful headlights refracted through the falling droplets of water. In a few places, Peter caught the forms of little, curious rainbows being cast in a violent night.

The police broke ranks. They fanned out across the İstiklal, working in pairs, one wielding a baton and the other a canister of pepper spray. To ensure a compliant arrest, the pepper spray was administered liberally. The officer would depress the nozzle in the protester's face, dispensing a steady stream until the other officer could administer a pair of zip-tie handcuffs, or a few blows from his baton—this last measure depending on how he assessed compliance.

The roundup had commenced. Peter was soaked. His shirt stuck to his shoulders and his pants clung to the backs of his thighs. He was now shivering. But he didn't dare move. The pepper spray had begun to mix with the water. The solution pooled among the cobblestones. Diluted, it tasted like bitter medicine, the sort he remembered his mother spooning into his mouth when he was a boy. It also stung his eyes and particularly the cut on his chin. He lay stomach down with his head craned upward.

He couldn't see much. The shimmering flash of black leather boots. An occasional frightened glance from a stranger who, like him, was lying flat on their stomach waiting to be cuffed, sprayed and dragged off by the authorities. And Deniz. He could see Deniz, who had turned his head away from Peter. Deniz had crossed his legs at the ankles, a signal that he wouldn't run off. He had also placed his wrists together behind his back, so that they could be easily cuffed when his turn came. The two gestures conveyed defeat as clearly as any white flag, and, so defeated, Peter recognized that Deniz didn't want to exchange looks with him.

A pair of officers stood over Deniz, whose shoulder blades pinched together as he offered up his wrists. The officer with the pepper spray tucked his canister into a holster on his black mesh utility belt. With a gloved hand he raised the visor on his riot helmet. The other officer, the one with the baton, nimbly cinched Deniz's wrists together. Deniz came to his feet. Scum from the loose grouting in the cobblestones clung to the side of his face which had been pressed to the ground. The two officers stood behind him, leading him away as each clasped one of his elbows, which were bent so his hands pressed into the small of his back. Deniz accepted his defeat with a resignation that bordered on dignity.

Lying in the street, in that instant before the police would take him away, Peter felt outside of himself, as if he surveyed the protest from a stratospheric vantage, one that could contextualize the day's events and his role within them. He also felt a comradeship with the police who had just taken Deniz. Although they found themselves on opposite sides of a dispute, it was the dispute of their time and it was time itself which bound them together more surely than any particular political disagreement divided them. Prostrate on the street, Peter was filled with this impulse.

He came up to his elbows. He wanted to look around. He didn't want to forget all that had happened that day and this night. Peter glanced behind him. His gaze caught the limp, inert form of the protester who had been hit squarely in the chest by the water cannon. Having assumed that she would have by now returned to her feet, Peter was surprised to see her in the same place on the ground. But the protester still wasn't moving. Her lifeless body had come to rest within just an arm's length of her flag.

The generous impulse Peter had felt a moment before evaporated, replaced by crystalline fear. Deniz had understood what could happen in these streets. The way he surrendered himself wasn't due to dignity, but rather to an equally powerful and Darwinian impulse for self-preservation. Before Peter could follow Deniz's example—cross his wrists behind him and his legs at the ankles—he felt a knee on his back and a man's entire weight crushing his spine. A helmeted officer, visor down, held a nozzle right at Peter's face.

It was the last thing he saw.

Two o'clock on that afternoon

⌒

They are four now: Peter, Catherine, William and the white terrier. On the way back to his apartment Peter sits in the taxi's front seat. The window is rolled down a crack. The driver slowly inhales a cigarette while frigid air creeps into the taxi. The smoke is sweet, rotten, rich and forms a stirring foulness. Peter asks the driver to roll up the window and toss his cigarette. The driver ignores the request. His arm hangs lazily outside between drags and the wind traces swirls through the thinning black wisps of hair atop the driver's head.

"Onun adı ne?" The driver points at the dog, asking its name.

Catherine cradles the terrier in her arms. She has taken to stroking its coat and liberally kissing its head so that a tinge of pink lipstick has formed on the white, fleecy puppy fur.

"He doesn't have a name," says Peter. "We're just taking care of him for a bit."

"No name?" says the driver, switching into heavily accented English. He shakes his head disapprovingly and tosses what remains of his cigarette through the window, which he then finally shuts. With his free hand he reaches back and kneads the fur on the dog's head.

They inch through traffic. The driver turns on the radio and drums his fingers along the steering wheel, listening to what sounds like Turk-ish house music. A compact disc on a string dangles from the rear-view mirror, revolving like a disco ball as it catches and then throws off shards of light. The music, the occasional flash from the disc, the acrid smell of cigarettes trapped in the seat cushions, plus the jostling stop-and-start of traffic flushes the color from William's face. He has turned a greenish, sickly pale.

Peter catches a glimpse of him in the rearview mirror. "Are you all right?"

The boy looks up, doe-eyed. Cool beads of sweat are collecting on his forehead and in the dimple of his chin.

"Pull over," says Peter to their driver, who glances into his rearview mirror and recognizes immediately what Peter has recognized, whereas Catherine is busy with the dog, running her fingers through its coat and soothing herself as much as anything else. She hasn't noticed that her son is about to vomit.

Before the taxi has rolled to a stop, Peter bounds out of his seat, nearly tripping over his steps. He flings open William's door and lifts him beneath the arms, hoisting him into the street. William retches his grilled cheese onto the curb. Peter hooks his arms beneath William's, holding him up. He can feel the boy's entire body convulsing. Cath-erine now rushes around the back of the taxi. She cradles the dog in her arms, but then sets him on the curb so that she too can support her son. Peter steps away as Catherine begins to rub her palm on William's back in wide clockwise circles.

William remains bent over at the waist. He continues to heave, shaking all over, only now he isn't just sick; mixed in with the heaving is the occasional repressed sob. Catherine moves her hand up to his head, where she runs her fingers through William's black hair. The boy continues to whimper, as if frustrated at his empty stomach, frustrated that there isn't some other part of himself that he can retch up onto the street.

The taxi driver offers William a few tissues and a bottle of water to rinse out his mouth, both of which he reluctantly takes. Catherine helps

William clean up, wiping his face. "Feeling better?" she asks him. He nods, but the color hasn't yet returned. Unsteadily, his mother and the driver help him back into the cab. This leaves Peter standing alone in the street, except for the dog, which Catherine has already forgotten, and which, to Peter's further displeasure, has begun to sniff at all that William emptied up onto the curb.

※

Catherine and William fall asleep, his head rests on her shoulder and her cheek rests on his head, they have collapsed one onto the other. Traffic is at a standstill. Had they been awake, Peter would have recommended they all walk. But they need to rest, so he says nothing. "Maybe twenty minutes more," the taxi driver whispers to Peter, who checks his watch and examines the road ahead of them, which leads toward his apartment.

"How old is your son?" asks the driver.

"He's not my son," answers Peter. There is a dip in the conversation. It is unclear who's supposed to speak next. The driver allows Peter this space, which he soon fills. "His mother is my girlfriend." Peter has never referred to Catherine in those terms. He feels an impulse to offer more, as if he is confessing himself. The driver continues to drive, saying nothing, which is in effect his invitation for Peter to say more, if he chooses. "His father is a problem," Peter adds. "So they're staying with me."

The driver glances in his rearview mirror, his reflection only a pair of watching eyes. He makes a quick examination of Catherine and William. Perhaps in their sleeping faces, a clue exists as to the problem Peter has referenced, but if a deeper examination might reveal some concealed history, the driver seems to quickly lose interest. Within an instant his stare has returned to the road.

Like a burden being shifted uncomfortably back onto his shoulders, Peter resumes his silence. He is alone next to the driver. Searching for something to do he rolls down his window. The driver shoots over an irritated look.

"Do you mind if I smoke?" Peter asks.

✳

Catherine jolts awake the moment they take the final turn toward Peter's apartment. While she straightens her clothes and hair, William continues to doze with his head propped against her shoulder. His color hasn't completely returned. Nevertheless, he appears refreshed, for he is still young enough that his face bears few signs of last night's and this morning's ordeals. His mother, however, wears the evidence of that strain in her puffy eyes, and the faint wrinkles etched around both her mouth and forehead like fine handwriting, and in her silence.

Catherine continues to adjust herself—retucking her shirt, straightening her jacket—taking care not to dislodge William's cheek, which remains on her shoulder as he sleeps. She glances outside. A heavy lid of clouds continues to hover at the tops of the tallest buildings. The sun has yet to burn through the morning overcast and by the early afternoon it seems as if it never will. Rows of apartments crowd the narrow street. They reach skyward, like inadequate columns built to support a vast ceiling. Without color, shading or halftones, a gloom of simple light follows their return.

"Almost home," says Peter, hooking his arm behind his headrest so that he faces Catherine in the backseat. He offers an easy smile as he turns toward her, but now that smile vanishes and in its wake a blank stare forms—confusion turning to fear—when his eyes focus out of the rear window.

A black Mercedes has taken a right turn, following behind them.

"Keep straight," Peter snaps at their driver, and then faces forward.

Murat's silhouette appears in the rearview mirror. Like when a shark appears in a wave with its unmistakable outline shooting darkly through the aquamarine, Murat's menacing silhouette proves unmistakable. Then, just like the shark in the wave, and just as quickly, Murat disappears. His Mercedes breaks right, looping the block in the opposite direction as Catherine and Peter's taxi, which continues straight on.

Peter slinks down in his seat. The slackening in his body is equal parts relief and disappointment, for he feels a reluctant draw toward

Murat, as if he wants to park the taxi so that he can step onto the curb, flag down his rival and, perhaps, clear the air between them.

Catherine has seen the Mercedes too. "Wake up," she says, shaking William by the shoulders.

The boy whimpers, pleading for his mother to leave him in peace.

"Where do you want me to drop you?" asks the taxi driver.

Peter glances at Catherine through the rearview mirror. Her uncertain gaze matches his own. He resents her silence, her lack of a plan. She has imposed herself on him, first by bringing William to his exhibit the night before, and now by luring Murat to his apartment. Peter can't return home. She has placed him in the exact same position she is in, upending his life. She could redeem herself somewhat by offering an idea of what they should do now. But he knows that she has none. The entire contour of their affair—that first night on the bridge, sharing cigarettes on the terrace at dinner, the afternoons at his apartment— none of it has been thought out. It has been a series of ill-considered impulses. None of it deliberate. None of it with meaning.

"Stop the cab," he says.

The driver presses hastily on the brakes.

"Where are you going?" asks Catherine.

"I'm going to talk with him."

"You can't do that."

"He's your husband," says Peter. The door is open and his foot is planted on the pavement, though he has yet to transfer his weight onto it. "Come with me. We'll do it together." Her eyes shift toward the street in a flash of consideration, but then her gaze freezes. She stares straight ahead, at the road.

He steps from the taxi.

Catherine reacts to his departure by placing her arm around her son, who glances from the backseat upward at Peter. William has listened to their exchange, but if he feels any concern that he might not see Peter again he doesn't show it. With both hands William clutches the camera Peter lent him, which he wears around his neck. Peter can't bring himself to ask for his camera back. He also can't bring himself to abandon

Catherine entirely. Had theirs been a normal, casual romance, he would have left. But it hasn't been. They have become entangled within one another's lives. From her son, to his work, to her volatile husband, she has encumbered him. And Peter can feel the weight of those tethers holding him in place as he attempts to leave her.

Then a thought comes to him very clearly: Perhaps she has been deliberate. Perhaps she had known all along what she was doing with me, how she has held me in place.

Before he shuts the door behind him, Peter dips his head into the taxi's open front window. "Drop her at Bebek Park," he tells the driver, pressing a few bills into his hand. He turns to Catherine. "I'll meet you there within the hour."

"And if you don't?" she asks.

Peter straightens himself. He glances up the empty road.

"In an hour."

Before she can respond, he pounds once on the roof. The taxi eases into gear and quickly makes a turn, descending toward the Bosphorus. Then it disappears. Peter walks to his apartment. He can hear the scrape of his shoes on the wet asphalt. He can feel the wind on the back of his neck. The air is damp and the clouds above him are heavy with rain.

The black Mercedes reappears, making a turn, easing onto the road directly ahead of him. Peter continues in its direction, taking unrushed and measured steps. He places his hands in his pockets. He notices a parking space which hadn't been there before. The Mercedes drives past it. Murat double-parks instead. He opens his door, one foot in his car and one foot on the street, waiting for Peter.

May 29, 2013

⌒

Kristin had spent that entire night at her desk answering questions from her superiors in northern Virginia and their superiors in Washington, D.C. A muted television on a wheeled stand in the corner played the news. She had watched the live footage of the armored buses lurching along İstiklal Caddesi. When their water cannons tossed a person down the street, she wasn't surprised by the harm water could do. She had seen it before, not here, but in other postings. She had also seen crowds mowed down by rubber bullets, choked by tear gas, blinded by pepper spray. Violent images had little resonance with her. Although they might be shocking, such images did nothing to place that violence in its political context, which was what interested Kristin.

After midnight her husband sent her a series of text messages. He was going to sleep. He had left her dinner warming on the stove. She thanked him, for the dinner. No problem, he replied. She told him that she didn't know when she'd be home. He didn't answer. She wrote that she loved him. He still didn't answer. She figured that he had already gone to bed. At least this is what she hoped. The alternative, that her relentless hours at the office might have disrupted the delicate equilibrium of their marriage unsettled Kristin. Although her work supported their family, his patience was the essential adhesive binding the two of them together, and marooned at her desk on nights like this, she wondered if that patience had turned cold, and into his resignation.

She considered sending him a last text in case he hadn't seen the other two. But she thought better of it. He was asleep, not ignoring her. She assured herself of this and then set her phone down amid the chimes and flashing lights of the many other phones she kept strewn across her desk with their dozens of unanswered calls and texts. Over the last two days her scattered network of contacts had reached out to her in a singular panic. She couldn't process all of the calls and messages, so in a nearly subconscious attempt at fairness she responded to no one.

Kristin leaned back in her chair, trying to make sense of the protests and what appeared to be their relative spontaneity. Murat had warned about corruption within the government's massive urban development initiatives. Although she didn't doubt the truth of his reports, she hadn't figured that it would amount to this popular eruption that choked the city. She struggled to understand why repurposing a dilapidated patch of earth like Gezi Park into a shopping mall would result in citywide and what now seemed to be nationwide protests.

A photograph taken earlier that day was circulating on the cable news channels. A woman in a red dress stood on the park's grass in front of a rank of police shields. An officer in a gas mask had stepped from the pavement onto the grass to confront her. He cradled a metal cylinder and from it he released a gust of pepper spray, which tossed a wave of the woman's curly black hair skyward. Slung over her shoulder was a white canvas tote bag.

Kristin switched stations.

The photo had begun to run on nearly every news channel. Kristin could see why it resonated. The colors: a red dress, a white tote bag. These were the colors of the national flag. Contrasting with them was the sickly mustard-colored stream of pepper spray directed at the woman's face. And she was pretty, not beautiful, but familiar. Any person watching the television could see her as whatever they chose, their daughter, sister or wife.

The next morning the photograph ran in the papers on the front page. By midday it was sketchily painted on banners that would be unfurled in the park and in the square and held by dozens of hands while they marched. That night at her desk, Kristin wondered if perhaps Peter had taken the photograph. She doubted it, but imagined that he could have headed down to the square. She wondered if he had gotten caught up in the protests. She had no idea that he had met the woman in the red dress and that he had taken a different picture of her, one that few people would care about, one that revealed far less.

She wondered whether Catherine would convince Deniz to show Peter's work at the Istanbul Modern. She understood how important this was to Peter and that he might leave if nothing came of his project. She could always circumvent Catherine and take the matter up directly with Deniz, though her instincts told her this wouldn't go well. Deniz's rise through the museum's hierarchy had been improbable, and Kristin's intervention would only play on his insecurities, reminding Deniz of her familiarity with the poverty and obscurity from which he came. No, thought Kristin, going directly to Deniz is sure to backfire. You know too much about him. A second thought percolated in her mind. Before it could assume a shape, she snuffed it out like a tic she had long ago learned to suppress. That idea, had it formed entirely, was: He knows too much about you.

Early in the morning, in that part of it that was still night and not long after her thoughts had turned to him, the phone she had assigned to Peter began to ring. Of all the calls that had come in, it was the only one she would choose to take. And when she answered, it wasn't his voice on the other end of the line.

※

"How long has it been now?" Peter asked.

Deniz sat next to him on a concrete bench cantilevered to the wall.

Pockets of darkness lingered in the corners and beneath the steel bunks strewn haphazardly about their dimly lit cell. He angled his watch toward a single two-inch-thick plexiglass window, which admitted a rectangle of orangish light from the streetlamps outside. "Two hours," Deniz said.

Peter raised his head from his cradled arms. He blinked tentatively upward, his eyelids breaking apart the tears that had crusted around the lashes. The final thing he had seen was the nozzle thrust in his face before the police doused him with pepper spray. Although he knew that pepper spray didn't blind, it was a hypothetical knowledge, one that didn't correspond to the pain he felt, which suggested permanent injury in its intensity, and he was in a near panic to regain his vision, no matter how excruciating it was when he tried to pry apart his tender eyelids. He grimaced in an attempt to open them, drawing his lips together tightly.

"Just leave it," said Deniz. "You'll be fine in another hour or two."

Peter again lowered his head into his arms. The small of his back pressed against the cold concrete wall. He was listening carefully. All around him he could hear the heavy breathing of those who slept and the murmured conversations of those who didn't. These sounds were punctuated by disagreements, the predictable bickering between those who wanted to rest and those who wished to talk. They had arrived soaked from the water cannons, and to keep them from freezing in the night the police had handed them each a wool blanket, which trapped the residual scent of tear gas from their clothes as effectively as it trapped a damp second-rate warmth.

"I need to make a call," Peter muttered.

"With this on my record, I'll lose my position at the museum," said Deniz.

"Will you flag down an officer and ask about the phone for me?" said Peter.

"Without work, I'll have to return to Esenler." Deniz collapsed his head into his arms. "I can't return to Esenler." He spoke to himself alone, his imagination casting a spell of paralyzing outcomes. Peter could hear the desperation in Deniz's voice, but he needed his help, even if Deniz believed himself to be beyond help. Peter raised his head and with scissored fingers made another attempt to peel apart his eyelids. The world blurred as if submerged underwater.

"I need to make a call," Peter repeated.

Deniz lifted his head. His bottom lip had been split open and bled badly from where his braces had cut into it. The blood that pooled in the ridges of his gums outlined his teeth in red. The white of one of his eyes had also been stained red from a blow to the temple. His hair was mussed in such a way that it revealed a slight bald spot, which with his hampered vision Peter managed to notice even though he had never noticed it before.

"Who are you going to call?" Deniz asked. "The consulate? Are you going to call Kristin?" A look of surprise registered across Peter's face. Deniz continued, "You thought I didn't know her? I was one of the first people she met in this city when she was newly assigned to the consulate, newly married . . . she was newly everything back then. She was newly posted to Cultural Affairs, too. They sponsored a reception at the Çırağan, that's where we met." Deniz smiled serenely as he thought of Kristin. "Cultural affairs," he said, rolling the word around his mouth like a peppermint. "That's one way to put it. Yes, I'm all too familiar with her."

Deniz gathered himself. He wiped his mouth with his sleeve, swallowed and then smoothed down his hair. Straightening, he approached the cell bars and hooked his arms through them, stuffing his index and ring fingers into his mouth, releasing a piercing whistle as though he were hailing a cab, or catcalling a woman. A commotion began among those who were trying to sleep in the steel bunks, a chorus of voices pleading for him to shut up, and then they began to offer threats of their own, pledging an assortment of ways in which they would soon silence him. Rising above the growing commotion, someone called him an *ibne.*

Nearly half those in the cell sat up. "What'd you say?" came a voice. "*Ibne.*"

Peter couldn't see who had said the word, but beneath the rectangular window one of the bunks came crashing down. Whoever had offered the insult had been swiftly pulled to the ground. Sides quickly formed. Among stomps and cocked fists, those who wished to offer this homophobe a beating paired off against those who wished to defend him. And like that, their ranks once again devolved into a mob.

The mêlée instigated by Deniz's whistling didn't last long. Tucked in a corner of the cell was a camera, a menacing black orb that held a view of everything. Half a dozen officers materialized down a long corridor as if from nowhere. They didn't enter the cell, not at first. Instead they rattled their unsheathed batons across the bars. This did nothing to silence the prisoners, who exhibited little concern at the prospect of receiving a further beating by the police.

Peter and Deniz didn't participate in the brawl. With his severely hampered vision, Peter could hardly protect himself, so he and Deniz hunkered alongside one another near the cell door. One of the officers had begun to blow a steel whistle, which some of the prisoners confused with Deniz's whistle from moments before. "Shut up with that!" a few shouted, interpreting the noise as a further provocation.

Another half dozen police left the precinct's offices and gathered by the cell door. They formed up in a line, gripping their black batons. From inside the cell someone reached through the bars, grabbed one of the officers by the belt and pinned him in place. He thrashed about for a moment but couldn't move, and in that moment someone snatched the steel handcuffs looped onto his belt and managed to secure the free cuff to one of the bars, locking the officer to the cell. In a panic he seized his canister of pepper spray, which he emptied indiscriminately. All of the prisoners had time to turn away except Peter. Crouching in the corner, he couldn't see the stream coming at him.

But he felt it as it seeped into his skin's already clogged pores and coated the membranes of his eyes. Whether it was the noise of Peter's screams, or the realization that the police would willingly stand behind the cell bars and douse every person inside into compliance, the result among the prisoners and even the officers was silence.

The cell door rolled open.

The officers stood in the threshold. They clutched their batons, their round knuckles bulging tightly beneath the skin. The only noise came from Peter.

He lay on his side, his legs pumping and his heels stamping the floor as the burn continued to spread. Deniz struggled to lift him as he kicked. "Calm down," he whispered to Peter, trying to remain calm himself as he hooked his arms beneath Peter's and hoisted him toward the cell's exit. "Give him some help!" Deniz shouted at the officer who had sprayed Peter and whose colleagues had managed to unlock him from the bars where he'd been cuffed.

Deniz impatiently heaved Peter up once more and motioned to leave the cell. The officer raised his baton. He would strike if Deniz attempted to cross the threshold. Undeterred, Deniz shifted his weight forward.

"Let him out!" In the open door at the far end of the corridor, from where the police had emerged, stood a man in plainclothes. He hadn't shaved and wore jeans and a cheap leather jacket. Although he didn't have a uniform, he had the same black shined police boots. "Are you trying to kill him?" he said.

Deniz stepped across the threshold in defiance of the other officer, who moved aside, casting a resentful look at the plainclothes detective, who seemed to be his superior. "Help him into the infirmary," ordered the detective, nodding down the corridor that ran next to their cell and into the parts of the precinct that were lit up and clean.

Hearing this new voice, Peter took a deep, calming breath. He tried to open his eyes. The pain was searing. His vision came down to a near pinpoint of light as he almost lost consciousness.

"We need to use a phone," said Deniz.

The detective glanced inside the cell, where the other officers brandished their canisters of pepper spray or clutched their batons by both ends, like rolling pins, as they efficiently restored order. The officer who had been rough with Peter carefully helped him along the corridor with another officer, who had also come to his side. This left Deniz alone with the detective. He asked again about the phone call.

"We'll handle all of that," said the detective. "But your friend doesn't listen."

"He didn't do anything," said Deniz. "They sprayed him for no reason."

"That's not what I meant," said the detective. "I told him to be careful when I first met him. He didn't listen."

Deniz silently followed the detective. The rubber soles of his black boots squeaked down the corridor as they walked toward the harsh lights and linoleum floors of the infirmary. Behind them the cell had returned to silence and it seemed, finally, that everyone had chosen to go to sleep.

"He's an American?" asked the detective, glancing in the direction Peter had been taken.

Deniz nodded.

"It's always good to have an American who owes you a favor," continued the detective. "But I imagine you know that."

Two-thirty on that afternoon

⌒‿

Their cab stops right as the rain starts. Catherine has made a plan with Peter and she needs to keep to it. So she wanders into the park. She stands with William beneath a row of elms. The air has measurably cooled and William clutches the white, nameless terrier's warm body to his own. The occasional raindrop navigates through the weave of overhead branches with their broad flat leaves and finds its way onto William's exposed neck, or into the dog's gray eyes. Across the grass is a vast playground, and as the rain picks up, heavier drops hit the hollow plastic slides and the sound is like a drumroll, as if some incredible stunt were about to be performed.

The more rain that falls on Catherine, the more her expression sets with determination. Peter's plan to meet here, outdoors, hadn't been a good one and she needs somewhere else to go.

Behind the playground is a parking lot with a small tollbooth that houses an attendant. The lot is empty, so the booth is likely empty as well. Catherine removes her black jacket and hangs it from one of the low, bare branches that jut like pegs from the side of the tree. "We're going to run over there," she says to William, pointing across a muddy field with puddles to the booth. "Hop up on my shoulders to keep your feet dry." She grasps William under his arms, as if to hoist him in a single thrust above her head. Murat often carried William in this way, lifting him in a clean jerk, his technique as perfect as that of any weight lifter. When Catherine bends to try, she realizes that she isn't quite strong enough. William then sets his dog on the wet earth and shimmies up the side of the tree, high enough to dangle by his arms from one of the limbs. Catherine tucks her head between his legs. The nameless dog nervously runs figure eights around her feet while she regains her balance.

"Hold my blazer over your head," she says, her voice choked with the effort.

William asks about the dog.

Catherine glances down, bends her knees slightly as if to pick him up, but stumbles. "Don't worry," says William. "He'll follow us."

"Ready?" she asks.

Before William can answer, she strides out into the rain.

Catherine runs quickly, but unsteadily. William holds her blazer above their heads; when it catches the breeze, it tugs upward like an insufficient wing. With his hands occupied, William's balance is off and he totters on Catherine's shoulders. She lurches from one side to the other with each of her uneven footfalls, nearly toppling into the mud as they chart their way out from under the trees, past the playground and then finally onto the parking lot. By this time the cadence of her steps has slowed. She falters through the deep puddles in the chipped and uneven macadam. She grips William by the ankles. Each of her fingers presses firmly into his skin, holding him more tightly the closer she comes to falling herself. "Too tight," he protests. She apologizes under labored breath. Then, losing her balance, she clamps down once again.

They arrive at the tollbooth. Catherine collapses at the waist, nearly dropping William, who still holds the blazer above their heads. The two of them become tangled in it as they try to stand. She tugs on the shut door. When it unlatches, she releases a single expiring breath, which she quickly muffles with a confident "In you go" as she rests her hand on William's shoulder and sweeps him inside.

William stops her when she reaches to pull the door closed.

The terrier saunters in their direction from across the parking lot, holding a steady pace, in no rush it seems, as if accepting that he cannot get any wetter than he already is. Catherine calls after him, yet he refuses to hurry. He processes with a great dignity, even stopping at one point to have a drink from one of the puddles, his spry tongue lapping up the fresh water. It is only when Catherine motions to shut the tollbooth's door a second time that the small dog chooses to cover the last few meters between them.

Catherine places William on a three-legged stool, the only spot to sit in the booth. A single lightbulb radiates above them. Catherine glances at it, concerned—though for the moment she chooses to ignore the question of who left it on and whether they might return. Water trickles down the backs of William's legs, pooling beneath his shoes. Catherine clamps her hair at the neck in a ponytail and wrings it out. Droplets speckle the dust on the plywood floor and form into puddles. Catherine unhinges a small panel window above a shelf and this allows the air to circulate. Spread across the shelf are a phone book, some tabloid glossies and a portable television the shape of a cinder block with a transistor receiver jutting from its top.

Catherine lifts William from the stool, sits herself down and then places him on her lap. She fiddles with the dial on the television, tuning through static and a few daytime talk shows, until she eventually finds some cartoons in black and white. She kisses the top of William's head and smooths out his hair, which is mussed from the rain. "This isn't so bad," she offers, but she speaks as if convincing herself. William leans against her. The dog curls up in a dry corner beneath the shelf.

"How long are we going to stay here?" asks William.

"Until the storm passes."

"Then we'll go home?"

Catherine begins to thumb through one of the glossy magazines.

William asks again.

"Watch a little television," she says, keeping her eyes fixed on the pages. "The rain will let up soon." She has found one of William's favorite shows, but he fidgets restlessly on her lap as he watches. Without color, the story no longer holds his attention.

❈

Twenty minutes have passed when the front door swings open. A man dressed in a yellow waterproof suit kicks the toe of one of his molded rubber boots against the threshold, knocking the mud loose. His head is bent forward, beneath a hood. He doesn't notice Catherine or William as he wheezes into his closed fist as if coming down with an ailment lodged in his chest. He raises his head to step inside and then freezes. By reflex, Catherine clutches William tightly toward her. Before the man can say anything, or Catherine can offer an explanation, the terrier begins to bark violently from under the shelf. The noise of his yips pierces the quiet and a snarl reveals the small, sharp rows of his teeth. The man removes his hood.

Outside the rain has picked up, lashing against his bare head as he comes to a crouch in the doorway. He holds out his hand, palm down, offering his scent to the dog. His skin is as black as the dog's muzzle. The barking stops. He cradles the dog's head in his palm and scratches him beneath the chin. The man steps into the tollbooth. "Welcome," he says, glancing down his long hawkish nose at Catherine and her son.

Removing his slicker, he apologizes as rainwater trickles off the hem. He hangs it by the hood on a peg nailed to the back of the door. His rain pants are clownishly baggy, cuffed several times at the ankles, and held up by a set of wide suspenders, which cling to his narrow shoulders. He wears a white polo shirt with the logo of the parking lot company embroidered over his heart. "Excuse me," he says, reaching toward the back of the tollbooth.

Catherine makes way, pressing herself against the wall. The man lifts a canvas bag from beneath the narrow shelf. He rummages through its contents, an empty sandwich wrapper, an apple core and whatever else he's had for lunch. He then removes a thermos. He loosens its cap and pours out its steaming contents, which he offers to Catherine. "Would you like some tea?"

She refuses.

"But you are freezing," answers the attendant. He points to Catherine's clasped hands, which she holds in front of her. For the first time she notices how she is shaking. Her reaction is to check on William, who sits next to her on the stool. His shoulders have also begun to tremble with cold. A wave of expansive, nearly unmanageable guilt possesses Catherine. Soaked, freezing, huddled in a parking attendant's booth—this is where she has led her son, gone are the four corners of his vast room, with its toys, its sprawling wood floor covered by three carpets. Each involuntary shudder of her body against the cold threatens to knock loose the tether of control she holds over her emotions. She tries to swallow but can't. She feels dangerously close to a precipice, as if she might collapse into tears. And she won't do this in front of William.

To avoid those tears she takes the tea and drinks. After a first and then a second sip she feels more in control of herself and the paralyzing tightness in her throat dissipates. The cup has warmed her palms and she places one on the back of William's neck. He turns toward her, a generous smile on his face, and she offers him some of the tea, which he takes without hesitation. William empties the cup and returns it to the attendant, who pours him another.

"Such a miserable day," the attendant says to himself, craning his neck toward the window. The rain comes in violent whorls, slashing against the tollbooth, receding to little more than a drizzle, and then slashing again.

"I don't think anyone will be visiting the park," answers Catherine, who listens intently to the man's voice as she tries to place his accent.

"No, I suppose not."

"We'll leave as soon as this weather lets up."

"You are my guests," he says. The corners of his mouth creep upward and he offers a slight, subservient bow of his head. "Please stay as long as you like." The attendant reaches beneath the narrow shelf, where, bent over, he searches for something and awkwardly brushes up against Catherine, who, avoiding him, presses herself against the shut door and nearly topples back out into the rain. From a nylon backpack the attendant removes a collapsible stool.

As he unfolds the stool's metal legs and pulls its canvas seat taut, Catherine glances into his open backpack. She notices a sleeping bag, a hiker's water bottle and a toiletries kit. The contents puzzle her. Glancing out of the window once more, she sees an orange cone blocking the parking lot's entry. If the lot is closed, then why is the attendant working? In fact, she realizes, he isn't working. Like her, he has nowhere else to wait out the rain. This also explains his hospitality. This tollbooth is his home, or the closest thing he has to one.

She sits on the stool that he offers.

"I'm Catherine. This is my son, William."

"A pleasure to meet you both."

Catherine waits for the attendant to volunteer his name, but it isn't forthcoming. Instead he stands and bent at the waist works over his backpack as he quickly returns its contents. He then stows it under the shelf and leans against the tollbooth's corner with his arms crossed. Catherine notices his wedding ring, a slim gold band. "Do you have family here?" she asks.

The attendant shakes his head. "No, my wife and daughter are in Germany. It was the only place that would help us." If he is reluctant to offer his name, the attendant is not reluctant to offer other particulars of his life. He goes on to explain that he and his family had fled their home three years before. When Catherine asks where that home was, the attendant refuses this detail, answering only "North Africa," and then, to clarify his separation from his family, he adds, "The money I earn goes to them. Work is easier to find here, but without a permit it's dangerous. So I have to be careful. I was a lawyer before. Now I park cars."

Catherine glances around the tight quarters. The air is dank, thick with recycled breath and heated only by their bodies. William seems to be ignoring their conversation. Instead he watches the small television. Catherine imagines the countless hours this man has spent, huddled in his tollbooth—freezing in winter, sweltering in summer—watching that same television and parking and reparking cars.

"And you," asks the attendant, "you are American?"

Catherine nods, but she feels that the attendant asks not so much to discover the answer to this question, which he must have already surmised from her accent, but rather to acknowledge a specific disparity between them: one's nationality when an expatriate confers a certain status, although not without the complexities that so often accompany—and in their way diminish—privilege.

The attendant glances down at William, who continues to watch the television in black and white. He then reaches over the boy's shoulder and toggles a hidden switch in the back of the set. The screen lights up with color. William beams upward at the attendant, who tussles his hair. "My daughter is around his age," he says and then offers Catherine a weak, closed-lipped smile.

"How much longer until you see her?"

"Until I can afford a passage on the ferryboat."

The rain shows no sign of letting up. It continues to strike the side of the tollbooth, making a rasping sound as if on the television white noise had replaced William's program. Catherine stamps her feet against the cold. The attendant offers to brew more tea. Catherine refuses. She no longer wants to take anything from him. The attendant folds his arms across his chest, leans against the wall and gazes outside into the bleak, monochromatic day.

Catherine again glances at the attendant's wedding ring. The gold band is likely valuable, perhaps worth enough to secure his passage on the ferryboat he'd mentioned, so that he could join his family. Had she known him better or been certain it wouldn't offend, Catherine would have asked him why he didn't sell the ring. Considering this suggestion shames her. This man isn't like she is. He had sacrificed his entire life's happiness to secure the happiness of his family. He had sent them across a sea so that they might have a future while only able to make half the journey himself. She can predict his reply to her suggestion: that he'd rather never see his wife again than present himself to her impoverished and having pawned their last shared possession. The joy his wife would feel on their reunion would soon temper when she imagined the indignity of him hawking his wedding ring. There is a moral hollowness, which all through her life Catherine has suspected herself of and learned to conceal. Her well-cultivated instincts tell her not to suggest to the attendant that he try to sell the ring.

"What if it doesn't let up?" she asks, her eyes fixed on the rain and what seems to be some immovable point in the distance.

"It will eventually."

They stand next to one another and William remains perched on the stool in front of them. Minutes pass. There is the sound of approaching thunder. The terrier begins to yip skyward, turning circles, as if chasing some invisible pursuer. Static clouds the television screen, and then overcomes the image altogether as the brunt of the storm passes above them and scrambles the signal. Without anything to watch, William glances at his mother. "Are we still meeting Peter?"

That the weather would keep Peter away had not occurred to Catherine. She reaches into her pocket, removing her phone. She has no messages and debates whether to call him. She surmises that Peter is with Murat but wonders what has delayed him. Perhaps Murat has convinced Peter to abandon her. Perhaps the weight of meeting her husband has proven too much for Peter. Then of course there is the truth about William. Would Peter care? Catherine had always thought the fact of William's adoption would simplify his relationship with Peter. After all, her son isn't Murat's by blood. Peter wouldn't have to contend with having betrayed William's father. Everything but blood is erasable. Without blood William could be one man's son as much as another's.

The attendant glances at the phone in Catherine's hand. "Let me step outside so you can have some privacy for your call." He takes his waterproof jacket from its peg on the door. Catherine refuses, insisting that the weather outside is too bad, that she doesn't need anything.

"No, no, you have your private business," says the attendant. "It's no trouble. I should really check the drains around the lot. They often clog and then flood over." Before Catherine can say more, he is out the door. She can feel William staring up at her. His look falls like an accusation, as if he were asking his mother why she couldn't convince any good man to stay, no matter how insistent she was. Spurred on by this look, she dials Peter.

It rings, but no answer.

She tries a second time and then a third. While she listens to the ringtones she wonders how she could have allowed herself to become dependent on Peter, so much so that she can't even get out of this tollbooth without his help. He had offered her money, which she had refused. Now she can't afford even a cab, and if she had money for a cab, where would she go? Home is no longer an option, neither is Peter's apartment. She stands, motionless, with the phone to her ear. Each ring that passes unanswered sounds like a jubilant ridicule, a chiming laughter that proclaims all of her weaknesses, all of the many ways she has made a mess of her life. She wants so desperately for Peter to answer, for his voice to interrupt and claim the line. When she tries a fourth time, there are no rings, not the slightest hope that he will pick up. Her call goes directly to voicemail.

Catherine tucks her phone into her pocket. Her first instinct is to step to the window, which is right above where William sits, and to look out into the storm in search of the attendant. Then she hears the toes of his rain boots striking the threshold as he knocks the mud from their soles. The door swings open. Rivulets of water pour through the creases of his rain jacket and pool on the floor. He rushes to close the door behind him in an effort to shield Catherine and William from the weather outside. When he appears, Catherine feels as if a weight she had not yet noticed is suddenly lifted from her chest. An involuntary smile forces itself upon her.

"Let me help you with that," she says, grasping the attendant's jacket at the shoulders while he makes an awkward turn in the cramped tollbooth and frees his arms from the sleeves.

"Thank you," he says, nodding sheepishly.

She imagines it has been some time since anyone has taken care of him and she can feel her power to grant him this. She takes the wet jacket by the hood and rehangs it on the peg behind the door. She offers to make him tea. Again, he thanks her. When he stands in the corner, she insists that he sit on the canvas stool he had taken out for her. She then asks him where to fill the electric kettle. He tells her that he has another water bottle in his bag. When he motions to get it for her, she won't hear of it. She rummages through his personals, quickly removing the bottle. She sets out a cup for him, places a tea bag in it and waits for the water to boil. William continues to watch his television. Aside from the program's low rhythms the tollbooth is quiet.

Catherine stands across from the attendant. Chilled from the storm, he begins to rub his hands together, blowing into his clasped palms to warm them. She flirts with the idea that he might help her, that if Peter never answers her calls the attendant might care for her, at least for a bit.

His tea is ready. Catherine pours his cup and steam uncurls across its surface. The attendant nods gratefully. When he reaches for the tea, she carefully passes it to him. Then she notices something on his hand. The rainwater has left a stain around his ring finger. Before Catherine can get a better look, the attendant sits back on the stool and begins to sip his tea. A green color faintly bleeds onto the attendant's dark skin. What is it, she wonders. Each time he raises his cup to his lips, Catherine stares. The attendant smiles self-consciously in return. He asks if she is sure that she doesn't want a cup of the tea for herself. She only shakes her head, refusing his offer with silence while she continues to puzzle over where this stain has come from. Then she realizes—the color is seeping out from his wedding ring, which isn't gold after all, but rather forged from some other, less valuable substance, which would have sold for nothing and taken him nowhere.

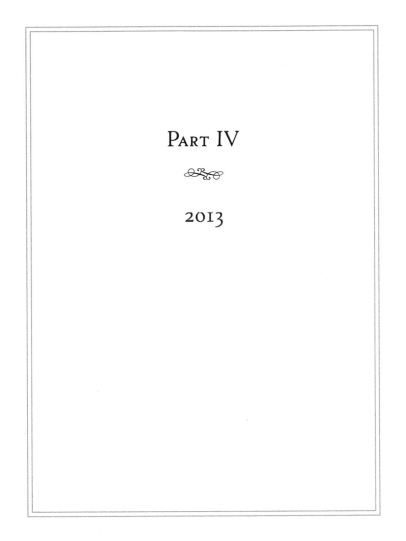

PART IV

2013

Three o'clock on that afternoon

⌒

Peter sits on his sofa and through the silence he listens for Murat. The toilet whines as it refills. Water hisses out of the sink. The metal ring with the folded hand towel swivels on its joint, clanging against the rectangular subway tiles. By these sounds Peter tracks Murat as he moves through his apartment. He visualizes Murat's every step. Straining to keep track of him in this way requires complete focus and for this reason Peter is startled when his phone rings.

He thrusts his hand in his pocket to mute it.

"Get that if you want," says Murat. He ambles into the living room but doesn't sit next to Peter. Instead he steps to the rain-streaked window that overlooks the Bosphorus. The apartment is warm, fogging the pane. Murat wipes a circle with his hand and looks outside. Before the storm arrived, most households had taken their laundry down from the wash lines strung between the buildings. Peter imagines the heavy, damp heaps scattered across kitchen counters and over the backs of sofas in the many cramped apartments whose occupants can't afford a dryer. The wash on a few of the lines hasn't been taken down. A child's brightly colored shorts. A patterned housedress. White shirts flapping like so many flags of surrender. Perhaps these households hoped the storm would clean their laundry twice over. These abandoned possessions dance mournfully above the street, like the torn sails of a ghost ship.

Murat turns away from the window. He sits next to Peter on the sofa, crosses one leg over the other and folds his palms across his knee. "Take the call if you need to," he once again insists. He then leans forward and thumbs through the books scattered across Peter's coffee table, editions of photos mostly. Murat offers Peter no privacy, for he must know that it is Catherine who's calling and he must relish forcing Peter to sit with him while her calls go unanswered.

If Peter had anticipated a heated confrontation with Murat, it doesn't manifest. An hour before, when Peter had exited the taxi and approached Murat's double-parked Mercedes, he had half-expected their introduction to turn violent. Peter had his fists clutched to his sides in expectation, hoping that if provoked he might be the one to land the first blow, assuming things would come to blows. Instead, Murat had approached him with his hand outstretched. "You must be Peter," he had said. Peter didn't answer, but rather unclenched his fists so that the two of them could shake hands. Murat had then parked his car in an empty space on the street and invited himself up to the apartment. As they climbed the stairs Murat had asked about the building—the terms of Peter's lease, if utilities were included, whether the landlord was responsive to maintenance requests, what Peter thought about the planned renovation to the building's modest façade and the inevitable disturbance this would create with workmen climbing on scaffolds, obscuring his view, at least for a few months. Murat had inquired about this last subject as Peter was unlocking the front door and Peter had said that he didn't know of any planned renovation. "Ah, well, perhaps they haven't told the tenants yet. I came across the approved paperwork a couple of weeks ago." Then when the door opened, Murat had added, "That's a shame, too, because you have such a nice view."

Murat had settled himself in the middle of the sofa so that Peter would have to sit awkwardly close to him, or stand. When Peter had offered Murat a drink—tea, coffee, water—Murat had asked if he had anything stronger. Peter had disappeared into the kitchen and returned with a tumbler of whiskey. The previous tenant had left behind the bottle. Peter had never touched it, but it was all that he had and he thought nothing of serving something of questionable palatability to Murat. For himself, he poured a glass of tap water.

Neither of them had wanted to raise the issue of Catherine and William. That first hour was spent in a collegial standoff. "I understand you take photographs," Murat had said. Peter had looked up at the walls, at his portraits that he had framed and hung. "I do," he had replied. Murat had mentioned his involvement with the Istanbul Modern, how he had overseen plans for its renovation and expansion. "You've visited, of course?" Murat had asked. "Of course," Peter had answered. Murat had guided their initial back-and-forth, dictating its pace. Like sportsmen warming up before a match, they had volleyed genial snippets of conversation to one another. Neither of them had said much, asking simple questions, giving simple answers. Murat had then excused himself to the back of the apartment, ostensibly to use the toilet. When Murat returned, he didn't sit on the sofa, he stood by the window. And Peter now watches him as he looks out across the city, toward the water and in the direction of the park with its shaded elms and empty playgrounds where, unknown to Murat, Catherine waits with their son.

"So where is she?" Murat asks.

Their entire interaction up to this point has been framed around this single question. Peter can feel how Murat has lured him in, establishing a rapport between them, no matter how tenuous, so that he can strike out after this one fact. He hadn't said Catherine's name, only *she*. By acknowledging that he understood Murat's question, Peter would be affirming what exists between him and Catherine, the depths of their relationship, its illicit nature, that when speaking *she*, Catherine is the only person to which either of them could be referring. Peter understands the weight of his own response. His answer could free him from Catherine, and from William. A sickening temptation invites Peter to reveal their location, which would return his interrupted life to him. He glances at Murat, who continues to look away from him and out of the window. The rain has been falling steadily for the past hour. He remembers the birds from that morning, how he had taught William to photograph them in the instant when they would land or take flight. He wonders where they have flown off to in the storm. When the weather clears, they will return, fluttering between his window ledge and the others. After he leaves this city, whenever he decides to journey home across the ocean, someone else will watch them from this same window. It is inevitable. And jealously, he recognizes this inevitability, and that he will have to answer Murat's question.

"She doesn't want you to know where she is."

Murat turns away from the window. He steps around the back of the sofa so that he stands menacingly beside Peter. Murat inhales once, heavily, bows his head and then clasps his hands in front of him. "Okay, but now I am asking you to tell me."

"Have you tried calling her?"

Murat unclasps his hands and crosses his arms over his chest. "Why don't you call her for me?" He glances down at Peter, toward his pants pocket and the phone that had been ringing earlier.

"I'm not going to do that."

"Why?"

"Because I'm not going to trick her into speaking with you," says Peter.

"That would be a betrayal?"

Peter returns his glance, sensing the trap he's been baited into.

"Do you think she hasn't already betrayed you?" adds Murat. He sits next to Peter, who edges away from him on the sofa. "Did she ever tell you the truth about William? Perhaps you should call her and ask."

Peter stands. "What are you talking about?"

"I'm not his father, surely she at least told you that."

If before Peter had felt concerned that Murat might lose control and turn their altercation physical, now he feels that he might be the one to lose control. His hands once again ball into fists at his sides. "Who is the father?" Peter asks, forcing the question out of his clenched jaw.

"I have my suspicions," answers Murat.

"Suspicions? You don't know?"

"I never wanted to."

As he makes this admission, Murat's eyes dip toward his hands, which are clutched together in his lap. Peter's first and most obvious inclination is to assume Murat is emotionally shut off and that this is the reason he doesn't want to learn who William's father is. Or perhaps Murat fears that an inquiry into William's paternity might reveal further—yet to be imagined—infidelities on Catherine's part. Peter can imagine whole rosters of lovers before him who had sustained her through the course of her marriage. Parsing the details of those liaisons would only further humiliate her husband and interfere with what Murat could offer the boy. Murat had remained willfully ignorant not only as a protective measure for himself, but as a protective measure for his son, who isn't really his son, just a child, as anonymous as any he could hope to encounter in the street. And in Peter's mind a question forms: Would it make sense for him to remain similarly ignorant if he were to factor into William's life?

"Why don't you try to reach her?" says Murat. "Ask her who William's father is." He again gestures toward Peter's phone, further asserting that he knows it was Catherine who had been calling. "I have every reason to believe she'd tell you." He pauses for a moment, his eyes shuttling to the ceiling as if imagining how the scene might play out. Then he returns his gaze to Peter. "In fact, you would be doing Catherine a favor. It would be a relief for her."

"I'm not calling."

"Then I will." Murat dials her number. He waits on the line as it rings and then clicks over to voicemail. He calls once more, again with no answer. Shrugging his shoulders, Murat slides his phone back into the breast pocket of his gray suit jacket. "This is all very embarrassing for me. And bad for business, too."

At the mention of Murat's business interests, Peter stands and approaches the window. "I think you should leave." Sitting alone on the sofa, Murat ignores Peter's request and continues to complain about his real estate holdings, the depressed market since the Gezi Park riots and the depreciating Turkish lira. He speaks at length about the incomplete Beşiktaş football stadium and the incurred losses on Yaşar Zeytinburnu 4. "This scandal in my personal life won't help me get any relief from my creditors." He jabbers on, behaving as though he were playing a part Catherine had assigned to him, that of the inattentive and business-obsessed husband. Eventually his monologue comes to an end. An uncomfortable silence ensues. Peter glances over his shoulder. Murat's left leg is still crossed over his right and his arms are now spread along the back of the sofa, as if he owns it, while in one hand he palms his phone and lazily sorts through emails and surfs the Web, navigating the interface with only his thumb.

Peter again asks him to leave.

"That's fine, but I am asking you to tell me where she is." Murat returns to his phone, apparently engrossed in whatever he's reading, welded to his spot on Peter's sofa.

Rain continues to streak the glass. The wind comes in uneven gusts, jerking the clothing that has been forgotten on the wash line. Among the trousers, shirts and socks, Peter notices a dress. It is a deep red, stained almost maroon by the rain, but Peter imagines that when it is dry it would be a bright red, like the woman's dress he had photographed months before. The photos he had taken of her had gone nowhere. They existed for his personal collection alone. The other image of the woman in the red dress had achieved a singular status, capturing the consciousness of an entire movement, a consciousness which has since dissipated. However, for Peter, that photo serves only as a reminder of his own inadequacies. In someone else's hands the woman in the red dress had become an iconic subject. In his hands the subject had been relegated to nothing, to obscurity.

"How long are we going to wait here?" Murat calls over his shoulder.

Peter continues to stare out the window.

"I'm not leaving until you tell me where they are," Murat adds.

Peter doesn't respond, instead he continues to look at the red dress flapping on the wash line. The wind has pulled it free from one of the clothespins and it twists around itself. Peter worries about Catherine

and William. They have no money and he can't phone them with
Murat in the apartment. He doesn't know if they've found refuge from
the storm. He hopes that they've managed to get out of the rain. Peter
had been telling Murat the truth when he said he didn't know where
they were—for Catherine and William most certainly aren't waiting
outside in Bebek Park.

Murat gets up from the sofa and stands uncomfortably close to Peter
at the window. "Let's go and find them," he says. "If she doesn't want
to come back with me, I won't make her. But it's no good for her and
William to be out in this weather."

Peter turns to Murat, so the two of them are staring squarely at one
another. "You won't force her to go back with you?" he asks.

"I could have forced her to stay."

Peter can't help but see the logic in Murat's answer, and the insan-
ity of Catherine wandering penniless through the city in a storm with
her son.

"You should think about whether or not you want to know who
William's father is," Murat continues. "But you should also consider
something else."

"What's that?"

"Whether you want to know who William's mother is."

Peter had never considered that William wasn't Catherine's son.
Turning away from Murat, he looks back out the window. The red
dress is gone. The wind has taken it away. Peter searches the streets
below, the adjacent rooftops, the terraced balconies that pour rainwater
from their gutters—nothing. Peter's gaze wanders, flitting uneasily over
the distance as he searches for some fixed object to rest his eyes on, so
that he won't have to stare at Murat.

He can't find anything.

May 29, 2013

⌒

Kristin had taken a white sedan from the consulate's motor pool, a Chevrolet, American-made per U.S. government regulations administering vehicular acquisitions. The small fleet of cars she used to meet with the locals who peddled her information were less conspicuous. They didn't have diplomatic plates, or seat belts for that matter, and were manufactured by companies based everywhere from France to South Korea, but none of those were right for this job, in which she wanted the full weight of the U.S. government behind her. For this job, she needed the white Chevy.

When she had received the phone call from the detective at the Twenty-second Precinct, inquiring about an American photographer who claimed an affiliation with the consulate, she knew that her visit would be in her titular capacity as the cultural attaché, as opposed to her nontitular capacity, the one which centered on her collateral duties, those duties for which she used the other, non-American cars.

The sun was rising. She jostled the transmission into drive, tugging down a curious doglegged gearshift affixed to the base of the steering wheel. The streets were empty. The garbage trucks had already made their rounds and the water trucks had passed by, tamping down the dust. The morning commute had yet to begin. The traffic lights shifted

onto the wet, empty roads, their glare like a palette of spilled water-
colors which cast reflections of red, yellow, green. Taksim's Gezi Park
was a few miles off. As she drew closer to the city center, checkpoints
appeared. The white Chevy's official plates would ensure that the police
let her pass. The citywide demonstrations had lasted for nearly a week,
and the officers manning the checkpoints had a famished, hollow look,
as if they'd been on duty for the entirety. Few had shaved. Their uniforms were wrinkled, as if they'd slept in their patrol cars. Their breath
stank from tea and cigarettes as they queried Kristin, wanting to know
where she was off to so early in the morning. To a man they were irri-
table. Their eyes made a cursory search of her vehicle, but they couldn't
do anything more, even though they seemed to want to out of sheer
spite. Rumors had already begun that a western conspiracy had fueled
the demonstrations. The same old three-lettered foreign agencies came
under suspicion, their almost unspeakable acronyms articulated in cautious whispers with each of the letters evoked like an individual head of
a hydra that would need to be slain. Kristin knew better than to credit
any of these agencies, even though she wished the theories were true,
even though she wished her organization, or the others like it, possessed
such powers, or even such competencies.

At each checkpoint she recited the badge number of the detective
she had spoken to at the Twenty-second Precinct. He hadn't offered
his name, which had seemed odd to her, although not too surprising
given the mistrust of foreigners Kristin had become accustomed to. The
detective had called from Peter's phone to explain to her the situation,
which was that Peter had been detained when despite prior warning he
had wandered into a restricted area.

"What restricted area?" Kristin had asked.

"The protest zone."

"So what's the charge?"

The line went silent for a moment. "Trespassing," the detective had
said.

"Trespassing?" Kristin had asked incredulously.

She had heard what sounded like a metal door slamming in the background, followed by curses in the guttural Anatolian accent common to the country's remote interior. She had then heard the detective's stifled voice added to the chorus, as though he had muffled the receiver with his palm. Then he had returned to the line. "If you come and pick him up, all charges will likely be dropped. But for now, the charge is trespassing."

Since the demonstrations had begun a week earlier, the phone call on Peter's behalf was far from the first cry for help that Kristin had received from her network of assets strung throughout the city. In a moment of crisis, when the network she had developed was obligated to stay in place and report, she had found herself receiving hardly any information from them at all, rather only their requests for rescue, evacuation, asylum—these were some of the terms they used when pleading with her. She had chosen to help no one. If at the first sign of trouble an asset wanted to flee the country, then in her estimation that person wasn't worth helping. This did, of course, establish a contradictory paradox. When Kristin's help was needed the most, it wasn't on offer.

Peter was her exception.

From the instant she had received the call on his behalf, Kristin had known as an embassy official that she was obligated to come to his aid because he was, to her great annoyance, a U.S. citizen. While she navigated the checkpoints toward the precinct, inching along with traffic and passing through a warren of one-lane streets flanked by rickety gecekondus, she knew that she had no choice in the matter.

Of all her assets, the one she felt most concerned about was Murat. She had heard nothing from him. Although she felt certain that he was physically safe, she had begun to speculate about how the demonstrations might affect his financial interests, which, as he often complained, existed in a state of perpetual volatility. She imagined his government partnership on the football stadium would likely dissolve. After his failed project at Zeytinburnu 4, Kristin's superiors would balk at bailing him out of another deal gone crosswise. She stood to lose him if his business collapsed. And if her conscious mind was focused on getting Peter released from prison, her subconscious was calculating the various options that would ensure Murat weathered the current upheaval, if not for his benefit then for hers.

Kristin pulled up in front of the Twenty-second Precinct. It took her two tries to align the wide Chevy into one of the diagonal parking spaces arrayed along the curb. She levered the gearshift into park. On the seat beside her, she gathered up her diplomatic credentials as well as the project proposal Peter had submitted the year before, which was still, as of yet, untitled. She had by her own admission neglected Peter and his work for too long. This seemed like the appropriate time to direct his efforts more clearly, even if she wasn't certain how.

She tugged the Chevy's door handle. It had a tendency to stick, so she put her shoulder into it. The latch sprang open and the edge of the door smacked into the car next to hers. A few of the officers who lingered by the precinct's front steps took notice. She wondered if they'd get involved, but they didn't. With complete indifference, they resumed smoking their cigarettes and reading headlines from their cellphones.

Kristin crouched next to the glossy black door opposite hers, checking for a dent. She thought she felt some unevenness beneath her fingers but wasn't certain. A little of the white paint from the Chevy had flecked onto the black, but she was able to scrape it away with a dab of spit and her thumbnail. When she stood, she caught a glimpse into the backseat. Hanging in a dry cleaner's bag by the window was a familiar charcoal gray suit. Her eyes ran toward the hood ornament, a Mercedes's silver tripartite circle. It was Murat's car.

※

Kristin approached the precinct's booking officer. He sat opposite the entrance, behind a chest-high desk on a stool. In front of him was a single partition of bulletproof glass. Behind the glass, officers pored over written forms or sat with their glazed eyes fixed to computer screens as they triaged the massive arrest rosters from the night prior. From a steel door at the far end of the precinct, the detained were paraded out to complete paperwork from what Kristin assumed was a holding cell. She glimpsed Peter sitting at a desk among the officers. He was cuffed to his chair, fastened to its arm by a single plastic zip tie. Deniz sat next to him and was similarly cuffed to the desk, which was empty except for a roll of dry paper towels, a mound of wet ones, and a carton of half-and-half creamer. Halogen bulbs ran in a centerline down the ceiling of the Twenty-second Precinct, their glare reflecting off the well-buffed linoleum floors. Outside, the morning light was gentle. The light here was not. Everything was very clean and adding to the harsh light was the antiseptic smell of bleach. Mixing with it all, Kristin could smell the creamer.

Deniz clumsily poured the creamer from the carton and across the paper towels with his one free hand, making a wet compress that he laid against Peter's eyes; it stuck to Peter's skin as thick and sticky as papier-mâché. This was an old trick, one Kristin had seen in the aftermath of other protests in other countries. The alkalinity of the cream would gradually counteract the acidity of the pepper spray, diminishing its effects. Kristin hadn't seen, let alone spoken to Deniz in longer than she could remember, but the manner in which he took care of Peter indicated a closeness between them, a connection that Kristin could ill afford to remain ignorant of if Peter was—as she assumed—nominally within her sphere of control.

The booking officer was reading a magazine. While barely lifting his eyes from the page, he asked Kristin what she wanted. She presented her diplomatic credentials, sliding the documents through a slot beneath the glass partition. The booking officer rested his flattened palm on top of them while in earnest she explained herself, as if her credentials might be returned only if her reason for being here proved satisfactory. Kristin pointed over the booking officer's shoulder, at Peter, saying that she had come for his release.

The booking officer closed his magazine. His mouth bent into a considered frown as he made a closer examination of Kristin's documents. He then slid down from his stool and lumbered toward the back of the precinct, offering Peter and Deniz a scrutinizing glance as he passed them by.

Behind the rows of steel desks, which made up most of the precinct's
work space, there was a bank of a half dozen glass offices. All of the
offices were empty, except for one, whose door was shut. But through
the floor-to-ceiling glass Kristin could see a plainclothes detective leaning casually against a desk. A gold badge hung around his neck, glinting in the harsh light. His holstered pistol peeked out where the zipper
of his faux leather jacket fell on his hip. A woman sat across from him
in a chair, her back toward Kristin. The booking officer stepped inside.
The woman in the chair turned around as the door behind her opened.
Her eyes met Kristin's. It was Catherine.

On reflex, Catherine jerked back around in her seat. Kristin watched
as a quick, confused exchange took place between the booking officer
and the detective. Kristin's credentials were handed over, reviewed and
then handed back to the booking officer, who then recrossed the precinct and reassumed his perch on the stool. "Follow me, please." He
reached beneath his desk and pressed a buzzer that unlatched a waist-
high gate. He waved Kristin through, holding the gate open for her
with one hand.

In his other hand he clutched Kristin's credentials. "May I have
those back?" she asked. The booking officer glanced down, as though
he had forgotten that he carried them. "You'll have to ask him about
that," he said, pointing to the glass office and the detective, who had
resumed his conversation with Catherine. "And no speaking to them,"
whispered the booking officer as he nodded toward Deniz and Peter,
whose head was tilted upward as he leaned back in his chair, the compress over his eyes.

As Kristin walked toward the glass office she passed by them. Peter
stank of the cream. It had soaked into his shirt and onto the floor
around him. It was a sickly sweet odor, a vagrant smell and an inadequate remedy to the violence the police had done to his eyes. Kristin
didn't want to stare at Peter for too long and she knew that Deniz
wouldn't acknowledge her, that despite his characteristic bravado he
could exercise a well-practiced discretion bordering on invisibility when

circumstances required. However, through a single glance she could see
Peter's vulnerability and intuit his fear. His vision was his livelihood
and so he sat, cuffed to his chair, hoping that it might return.

The detective held open the office door and the booking officer
once again handed him Kristin's diplomatic credentials. "Are you who I
spoke with earlier?" Kristin asked. She rifled through her bag, searching
for the slip of paper where she had scribbled the badge number. While
she looked she dabbed a drop of Purell on her palm from the bottle
she kept and wrung her hands together. Before she could find the slip,
the detective told her that he was the one she had spoken to. He also
apologized for the confusion. Kristin recognized his voice and then
glanced toward Catherine, who sat with her back to the door. Catherine
seemed uncertain whether or not to acknowledge her relationship with
Kristin to the detective, while Kristin's mind immediately turned to the
Mercedes parked outside. Catherine never drove herself anywhere in
this city. That she would drive here, for Peter, caused Kristin to suspect
that what had passed between them had more depth than a casual
affair. A beat of silence interrupted their conversation as Kristin and
Catherine choked on their suspicions of one another.

"Pleasure to meet you," said the detective. He offered his hand.

Kristin shook, but with a moment's hesitation, one only she
perceived—her reflex was to keep her hands clean. The booking officer returned to his desk and the detective offered Kristin a seat next to
Catherine, who continued carefully to ignore her.

"I apologize, but when she arrived"—and the detective nodded in
Catherine's direction—"I assumed that she was you, that she was from
the consulate. An honest mistake. You can see the chaos around here."
The detective looked past both of them, through his window and into
the precinct. "It's been like this all week." He then returned his focus
to Catherine and Kristin. "So you are both his friends?"

Kristin glanced at Catherine, curious as to whether she would answer
this question and define the nature of her relationship with Peter—one
that had clearly evolved considerably since their introduction. It wasn't
only that Catherine had driven herself here, to a police station in the

earliest hours of the morning, on Peter's behalf—a friend might do that for a friend, particularly among expatriates—but the way Catherine averted her eyes to the floor and the hesitation that accompanied her every movement, as if she'd determined that each gesture needed its justification, that a single motion if not properly measured could reveal her. Recognizing this, Kristin knew that Catherine wouldn't speak first, so she did. "Yes, we are his friends."

The detective nodded, slightly pursing his lips as though he were considering the nature of their friendship with his mouth, as if the idea had a taste. "He faces a charge of trespassing—which of you did I tell this to?" Kristin lifted her hand. "The man he came in with, Deniz, he faces the same charge. Did you know Deniz is also his friend?" The detective's mouth ticked upward, forming a nearly imperceptible smirk, which accompanied the sly insinuation that Peter's arrest alongside Deniz had revealed some illicit sexual preference that neither of these women knew.

Kristin was well aware of the vagaries surrounding Deniz's sexual proclivities, but she doubted the inference the detective made about Peter and, even if it were true, she didn't care. Kristin glanced at Catherine, whose focus was on the confusion of papers strewn across the detective's desk. Her passport lay next to his computer, alongside Peter's. From a side table, a fan rotated on its axis. It generated a gentle breeze. Each time it passed over the detective's desk it was as if an invisible hand flipped through the passport's mostly unstamped pages. Kristin possessed a reasonable understanding of what the authorities could and could not glean from the records connected to a passport, but she wondered if Catherine understood the same.

"I introduced Peter to Deniz," Catherine offered.

The detective nodded. "And . . . ?"

"And what?" said Catherine.

"Where did they meet? How do you know them? How long have they known one another?" The detective had been leaning casually against his desk, but he now circled behind it, sitting at his computer with his back straight and arms extended. His fingers began to work furiously at his keyboard while he floated a staccato of interrogatories in a flat, disassociated voice that became only more pointed as he gathered information from Catherine. If she hesitated in her responses, the detective would peer from behind his computer screen and ask her, "Anything else?" or "Are you sure you don't remember?" and then resume typing for a few menacing seconds as he made some further entry.

Catherine unspooled her story. Much of it confirmed what Kristin had already learned from Murat. Kristin couldn't say for certain that the detective knew who Catherine's husband was, but he likely did, or at least knew the Yaşar family, and the insider's look into that family which the detective now elicited took on a voyeuristic air. Many of the detective's questions seemed designed to inform his own curiosities as opposed to Peter's relation to Deniz and the current charge of trespassing.

As an official from the diplomatic corps, Kristin could have intervened on Catherine's behalf, curtailing this extraneous line of inquiry. Yet she didn't. The detective had embarked on an interrogation of Catherine that filled holes in Kristin's understanding as well. Most fundamentally, she witnessed the lengths Catherine would go to in order to protect Peter.

"Do you know where he lives?"

"Yes."

"How do you know?"

Catherine went silent.

The detective again peered around the side of his computer screen. Soft furrows took shape across his forehead. He asked her once more, but with a gentler voice, coaxing her.

"He told me."

"So you've been to his apartment?"

"Yes."

"Alone?"

Catherine glanced at Kristin with pleading eyes, as if not understanding why she wouldn't help her. Kristin stared away. If Catherine had any inclination to lie, claiming someone else had been with her and

Peter, Kristin's apathy must have convinced her that the truth would do no harm. "Yes, alone," Catherine said.

The detective resumed typing at his computer.

"How do you know Peter's friend Deniz?" the detective asked.

"Deniz is my friend," answered Catherine. "I introduced him to Peter."

The booking officer wandered back into the office. He carried a tray of tea and a plate of sugar cookies. The detective offered them each a glass, which they took. They had been speaking for some time and it was well past breakfast.

"I apologize," said the detective, his mouth now filled with a cookie. He took a sip of tea and swallowed. "How do you know Deniz?"

"We work together."

"Where?"

"At an art museum."

"Which art museum?"

Catherine reached for the plate of cookies, placing one into her mouth. She chewed slowly, buying herself a few seconds. "Is that relevant?" she asked.

The detective didn't answer. Instead he dipped behind his computer screen. He registered a few strokes on the keyboard and clicked at his mouse. Reading from his screen, he announced, "The Istanbul Modern."

Catherine glanced over her shoulder at Kristin, who leaned closer and speaking in a whisper advised, "Don't assume they're asking you because they don't know." Kristin then settled back into her chair.

Catherine sat up a little straighter. "Yes, the Istanbul Modern," she said to the detective, who nodded with a false appreciation.

"You mentioned that you work there as well?" asked the detective.

"I do."

"I have no record of that."

"I am a trustee of the museum."

"There's no record of you working for the museum," he repeated.

"To what record are you referring?" asked Catherine. Impatiently, she stood from her seat and leaned over his desk, trying to glimpse his computer screen. On reflex, the detective angled the screen away and asked her to sit down, which she did but only after Kristin instructed her to as well.

"I am looking at the payroll for the Istanbul Modern," explained the detective. "You aren't on it. So how is it that you work there?"

"Trustee isn't a paid position," answered Catherine.

She then guided the detective to the Istanbul Modern's website, where a few tabs deep into its interface a page lurked with the photographs and biographies of the dozen or so trustees. "So you don't work there," answered the detective, after inspecting the website.

"The work isn't paid," said Catherine, "but I work there."

An irreconcilable gulf existed between Catherine and the detective. Kristin thought to insert herself into the exchange, to attempt to explain to the detective Catherine's role at the Istanbul Modern as a patron of the arts, but she decided against it, feeling certain that trying to convince the detective to decouple pay from work was a fool's errand, one she would surely fail at because she wasn't certain that she could make the leap herself.

"When did you first meet Deniz?" asked the detective. He stared at his screen, the answer clearly before him.

"If you already know," said Catherine, "then why are you asking me?"

The detective asked again.

Kristin interjected, "I'm going to instruct her not to answer unless you can explain to me why this is relevant." The detective leaned back in his chair, his arms crossed over his chest. "This man, Deniz, is a person of interest to us, a troublemaker who has incited riots against his government." Then the detective pointed an accusatory finger at Catherine. "She is deeply connected to him."

"They work together, that's it," said Kristin. "This questioning is uncalled for."

The detective motioned for Kristin to step behind his desk. Two documents split the computer screen. The first was the payroll from the

Istanbul Modern, which listed Deniz's steadily increasing salary dating from late 2006, when he had presumably begun work there. The second document was a scanned form from the Central Authority dated only a few weeks prior to the first salary entry. It was William's birth certificate. Aside from William's name there were only two others on it.

Kristin read over the document, glancing at Catherine, who had now clasped her hands together and pulled them between her knees, hunching into herself. Outside the glass office Deniz tended to Peter, who stubbornly tried to open his eyes, but without success. "Is it illegal for an American to adopt a child in this country?" asked Kristin, but her voice was heavy, tinged with defeat.

The detective ignored her, resuming his line of questioning with Catherine. "Your husband is Murat Yaşar?"

Catherine nodded almost imperceptibly.

"This boy William is his adopted son?"

"What difference does that make?" asked Kristin, but the detective continued.

"Who else knows who the boy's father is?"

"How is that relevant?" asked Kristin, cutting off the line of questioning.

The detective planted his elbows on his desk and wove his fingers together. "You're right," he said. "It isn't relevant to this arrest. We just thought you and your colleagues at the consulate would like to know what we know about Murat Yaşar."

"All right then," said Kristin. "Now we know."

"Good," said the detective. "And so do we." Kristin stepped out from behind the desk. She took Catherine by the arm, guiding her to her feet. "She is married to an important man," the detective continued. "I don't think he'd like this information about his wife and son out in public."

"Are you going to let Peter and Deniz go?" Catherine interjected.

The detective shuffled through his desk drawer, producing two notarized forms replete with stamps and official seals. "These are copies of their release orders. We'll have them out of here this afternoon."

He offered up the documents to Kristin, who folded them in half and tucked them into her coat pocket. Kristin then led Catherine toward the door, where they passed unnoticed by Peter, who still struggled to see, and by Deniz, who attended to him.

It was late morning and outside the precinct the day was clear and bright and a steady wind was coming from the east and it smelled like the sea. Catherine and Kristin said awkward goodbyes as they approached their cars. Catherine offered to let Kristin pull out first. Kristin then fumbled through her purse. A general anxiety—only heightened by the protests—had caused her increasingly to misplace her keys, though she soon found them. Reversing into the street, however, Kristin noticed Catherine as she approached the passenger side of her black Mercedes. Catherine crouched down, discerning something, and then she ran her fingers over the door, on the exact spot Kristin had dented a few hours prior. Catherine glanced out into the street, clearly recognizing the damage Kristin had done before she'd sped away.

Normally, Kristin would have stopped and taken responsibility, but she was in a rush. She was holding a single piece of information in her memory. Before she forgot the details, she needed to pull over and jot down a name and address she had glimpsed on the birth certificate the detective had shown her. It was the information on file for William's mother.

Three-thirty on that afternoon

The terrier begins to bark, its black and nimble mouth forming the piercing yips, which echo off the four cramped corners of the parking attendant's booth. Catherine lifts the dog into her lap, kneading at its white fur, trying to soothe it. When this doesn't work, the attendant opens a roll of crackers from his bag and offers a few to the terrier, who turns his nose away. "Maybe he's cold," says William, and the boy removes his sweatshirt and wraps it around the dog so that only the terrier's head sticks out. This does nothing to silence the barking. And now William sits in front of the television in only his T-shirt, so Catherine removes her blazer and drapes it around the boy's shoulders. The parking attendant then offers Catherine his coat, but she refuses, not wanting to wear his clothes. She tries to suppress a chill, but once again begins to shiver.

The dog continues to bark. William chooses to ignore it. He returns his attention to the television. The attendant wipes the fog from the window, searching outside. Perhaps the dog is trying to warn them of something, but through the curtains of rain the attendant can at best see only a few feet ahead. Catherine glances down at her phone. She has tried Peter more than a half dozen times. None of her calls have gone through. Her anxious mind projects a series of worst-case scenarios:

perhaps Murat has intimidated Peter into abandoning their rendezvous, or perhaps Peter has confessed her location to Murat and her husband is on his way to the park at this moment, or, and worst of all, perhaps nobody is coming for her and William, not Murat, and not Peter. She imagines that maybe both her husband and her lover have determined she is no longer worth the trouble.

She can't figure out what to do next. She can't hear herself think in competition with the television and the dog, which are both her son's, and so she can't hear herself think in competition with him. She continues to shiver, while in a similar nonvoluntary response, tremors of resentment spread from her center toward her limbs, directed at William, as if she might reach over and strike him in desperation. Instead, she snatches the dog from his lap.

"Give him back!" William leaps up from his stool.

"He's too loud," says Catherine. "He's going outside for a minute." She peels the sweatshirt off the terrier and makes for the door, so that her back faces William, who then lunges after her, reaching for his dog, who, strangely, has fallen silent in the struggle over his fate.

"He's not too loud for me," says the attendant.

Catherine turns to look over her shoulder and her stare darts back at the attendant. When their eyes meet, he immediately falls silent and casts his gaze toward his feet. With the terrier cradled under her arm, Catherine opens the front door and sets the dog down on all fours. The terrier sniffs the earth. He doesn't protest, or try to run back inside. He simply holds his nose to the ground for a moment. Then he raises his head and wanders out into the storm.

Catherine stands with her back to the door and her hands palms down against the frame, as if someone much larger than she threatens to enter. Her son broods by the television, his attention absorbed by the screen, avoiding hers. She focuses on his eyes, to see if he is crying, telling herself that he can't be too upset if he isn't crying. From beneath her arm, she offers William his bundled sweatshirt. He ignores her, so she sets the sweatshirt on the small shelf where the television is perched. She then takes back her blazer and removes her phone from its pocket, leaving William's birdlike frame covered by nothing more than his T-shirt.

Her screen lists the many incomplete calls to Peter. None of them have connected and she has no reason to believe that another will, but she doesn't know what else to do. He had said that he would meet her in the park. It is now well into the afternoon and it will be dark soon. She needs somewhere to go, so she dials Peter's number yet again. As she raises the phone to her ear, William stands, presenting himself in front of her.

In a single, nearly reflexive movement, William swats the phone from her grasp. "You ruin everything," he says; his voice is measured and calculated, speaking with hardly a hint of emotion, although he is shivering, just as she had been moments before.

The phone careens across the floor, landing at the feet of the attendant. William sulks in front of the television. The attendant slowly bends down and hands Catherine the phone, which now has a hairline crack across its dark, lifeless screen. She tries to power it back on, but with no luck.

The attendant reaches into his pocket, removing a single bill. "This is enough for a taxi," he says, offering the bit of money.

"Please, put that away," she says.

"I don't think your friend is coming, so take it."

She glances down at what he offers, which should be enough to get her across the city. Before she can refuse more stridently, the attendant politely, yet firmly, explains. "I have my own troubles and can't have you fighting here. I am asking you to leave, so again, please, take this."

"My problems are as serious as yours," says Catherine.

"I'm not questioning that they are, but if you sat across from anyone and both laid your troubles on the table, you would choose yours every time. So now it is that time; please, take your problems with you and leave me with mine." The attendant continues to hold the money out for Catherine. She knifes the bill into her coat pocket. Glancing at her broken phone, the attendant asks whether there is someone he could contact on her behalf. Catherine considers asking if he would try Peter just once more, but thinks better of it, knowing that he won't answer. She thanks the attendant but declines his offer.

Catherine wanders into the rain with her son. Staring across the park, she can see the crawling traffic on the road and the hesitant red brake lights of the cars flashing as the drivers struggle to navigate through the storm. She spots an approaching taxi. To flag it down, she and William will need to run. When she snatches his hand in hers, William pulls away. He is searching desperately for his dog. "We have to go," says Catherine.

"But where is he?" William asks.

Catherine tells him that she doesn't know, but that the terrier will be fine.

"How do you know he'll be fine?"

Catherine ignores her son's question, rushing the two of them toward the road instead as she flails her arm above her head, hoping that the taxi will see her before it passes. William follows, walking clumsily, stumbling across the undulating ground as he keeps his gaze fixed over his shoulder and into the park behind him, where he continues to search for his dog.

The taxi pulls over. Catherine opens the door and lifts her son into the backseat, then slides in beside him. Before she can offer the driver a destination, William asks where they are going. "To see Deniz," answers Catherine.

William returns a blank stare. "Who?"

"My friend that you met last night," says Catherine, feeling the guilt of an answer which is far from complete when describing Deniz's relationship to her son. William glances out the window, back toward the park. He asks his mother how she can know that the terrier will be fine.

"Because he left," answers Catherine. "If he needed us he would've waited, even in the rain. But he knew that he would be fine without us, so he left."

❋

"You must have known she wasn't William's real mother," says Murat.

He and Peter sit across from one another on the sofa, their backs to the living room window, which pours in a sodden, gray light, devoid of the late-afternoon brilliance that accompanies the end of clearer days. It would be dark soon. And the truth was Peter hadn't known. He is reluctant to admit this to Murat. He doesn't want to seem like a fool. The signs had been there, of course, the greatest of which wasn't that William looked nothing like his mother, or his father, but that Catherine was so reckless. Emotional connection, physical attention, even love, all of those elements were present between him and Catherine, but the overarching impulse that had brought them together was recklessness. And even now, when confronting all Catherine had withheld from him about William, the greatest challenge facing Peter is how to contend with the scope of her recklessness.

"I suppose it makes no difference that you didn't know," adds Murat.

"No difference to what?"

"To what happens now." Murat fishes around in the pocket of his charcoal gray suit jacket and removes a pack of cigarettes. He lights one without asking Peter's permission and then reclines deep into the corner of the sofa, his arms rising behind him, his legs extending without aim. A ribbon of idling smoke trickles toward the ceiling. Murat glances back at Peter. "I'm sorry," he says. "Would you like one?"

"No," says Peter. "I don't smoke in the apartment."

Murat nods, as if agreeing that this is a good policy. "Were you surprised when my wife showed up this morning?" He gazes at the ceiling, where the smoke from his cigarette hovers like a cloud of flash powder.

"I wasn't," answers Peter.

"You weren't?"

He shakes his head. "No, I was surprised when she showed up last night."

"At your exhibit?"

"Yes, and with your son."

Murat kneads his chin between his thumb and index finger, figuring why this was the most surprising development to Peter. "So you knew then."

"Knew what?"

"What she was going to do."

Peter suppresses an anxious laugh. "You mean leave you?"

"No," says Murat, returning a laugh of his own. "She's aiming to ruin me. There is a difference. When you own a family business and that family comes apart, it obviously affects your business."

A coil of ash threatens to topple from Murat's cigarette. Peter ducks into the kitchen and returns with a saucer, which he rests on the sofa's arm. "I'm sure your business would recover," he says.

"What could you possibly know about that?" says Murat. He jabs a finger toward Peter, one of the two with the cigarette pinned between them. Ash tumbles onto the sofa. Murat curses and then apologizes weakly, brushing at the upholstery but leaving tiny gray streaks behind. "Who is to say that my interests would recover if I faced such a scandal? You know the Beşiktaş football stadium? The debt on that property is mine. You were at Gezi Park. The plunge in the real estate market that followed ruined some of my competitors. It nearly ruined me." Murat stubs out his cigarette in the saucer, freeing his hands to gesticulate more aggressively at Peter.

"How do you know that I was at Gezi Park?" Peter asks cautiously.

Murat lifts an eyebrow, not answering right away. He keeps Peter suspended in a quiet that is charged with the prospect of all Murat knows and the lesser prospect of what he does not know. Then Murat nods across the living room, toward the table scattered with Peter's portraits, his abandoned project. "In case you forgot, you inscribed a book of your work to my wife. I've since kept track of your photos and have seen in the press the ones you took at Gezi."

Peter leans back into the sofa. He takes a deep breath. Until this afternoon he and Murat had never met, although they had both assumed outsize roles in one another's lives. Peter feels a degree of hesitation when dealing with Murat. Bound up as they are, it seems counterintuitive to Peter that Murat should know so little about him.

But at the same time, it seems utterly plausible that Murat's only connection to Peter would be through his photographs. After Peter had gifted Catherine his book, he had hidden his involvement with her, so what else could Murat really know? But as this calming idea asserts itself in Peter's mind, Murat lights another cigarette and lets slip, "... or was it Kristin who first told me you'd been at Gezi Park? This was the time you were arrested, no?"

Murat's elbow brushes against the precariously balanced saucer. It plunges to the floor, shattering. Murat comes out of his seat and apologizes as he sweeps the jagged fragments into his cupped hand. "Look at this mess I have made," he says absently, seeming to speak only to himself.

Peter remains on his side of the sofa, sitting very still. "And how do you know Kristin?"

"Where is your trash?" Murat stands in front of Peter with the largest shards gathered into his palm.

Peter doesn't move.

"In the kitchen?" asks Murat, and then he disappears to the back of the apartment, where Peter hears him opening and closing cabinets until he finds the waste bin. Murat returns to the living room. "How do I know Kristin?" he asks ponderously, picking up their conversation as he wipes his hands together and clears off the last sticky flecks of porcelain. "You could say that I know her in much the same manner that you do. She paid you to do work for her, did she not? She's paid me to do the same."

"She gave me an artistic grant," says Peter, as if the word *grant* ennobles his work. "Also, there was an exhibit last night."

"So I heard," replied Murat. "At Deniz's apartment."

"Yes," Peter says. "At his apartment." He hesitates, uncertain of Murat's connection to Deniz and uncomfortable with their perceived familiarity.

"And was your grant for this?" Murat asks while approaching the photographs scattered across the table. His open palm hovers over their surfaces as if he is casting a spell on them, and then he picks up and shuffles through a few of the black-and-white prints. "What was the concept?"

"I wanted to show how people keep one another in check," says Peter, "or how sometimes a person's conflicting character traits might do the same. The idea was to pair photos that would reveal this."

Murat lifts a portrait in each hand, sighting down his arm for the effect Peter was trying to evoke. He ranges over the black-and-white prints, lifting one and then another, searching for a pairing like a card-player in search of a winning hand. "It's an interesting concept," says Murat, eventually setting down the photos.

"The project hasn't worked," Peter confesses.

"Maybe you can't see how it all comes together yet." Murat ambles back to the sofa. "The idea makes sense."

"You mean pairing the photos?"

"I can't say about the photos," answers Murat, "but the concept that people hold one another in place. Let me ask you something: Did it ever occur to you that Kristin had an ulterior motive when providing you with your grant? Did you ever think that she wanted you to meet my wife?"

"She introduced me to Catherine, of course she wanted us to meet. Kristin thought Catherine could be helpful with my work."

"No," says Murat. "Did you ever think that your work had nothing to do with it? Did it ever occur to you that Kristin understood what you just described? That she knew how one person could hold another in place."

Peter points toward Murat's coat pocket, to where he keeps his cigarettes. "May I have one of those?" he asks. Murat sets the packet between them and Peter fishes one loose. He borrows Murat's lighter and inhales deeply. "You think Kristin engineered my relationship with your wife?"

"Catherine has been threatening to leave me for years."

"And . . . ?"

"I'm very important to Kristin." Murat's phone rings. He digs it out of his pocket and glances down at the screen, a wry smile expanding across his face. "Ask her yourself." He tosses the ringing phone to Peter, who answers it.

"I know where she is." It is Kristin.

Peter remains silent on the line.

"Hello? Hello? Murat?"

"No . . . it's me," says Peter, who glances up as Murat crosses the room and returns to the table of photographs, which he continues to sift through, seeing if he can find a matching pair.

June 21, 2013

⌒

"I wanted you to know that I knew," said Kristin.

She was having one of her regular lunches with Catherine, they'd met again at Kafe 6 in Cihangir. The day was turgid and the summer air lay stalled all around them. They sat in the empty garden, at one of a half dozen small round tables set out beneath a lattice that in spring had bloomed with violet explosions of wisteria, but for now was merely a tangle of strangling branches baking in the heat.

"And why do you think that's important?" asked Catherine. She then lowered her eyes, her gaze resting on her bowl of cooling soup, her spoon hovering above its surface. Several weeks had passed since she and Kristin had bumped into one another at the Twenty-second Precinct. Catherine had seen Peter almost daily since then. The two of them had resumed their relationship with vigor, as if by so doing they were asserting that nothing had happened, that they hadn't been found out and that, perhaps, they could carry on as before.

"Do you care about him?" Kristin asked.

The door from the restaurant's kitchen was flung open and the chatter of lunch-hour patrons who had chosen to sit cramped inside beneath the air-conditioning spilled out to the garden. A waiter presented Kristin with the salad she had ordered, an ultranutritious mix of greens and root vegetables. She removed a bottle of Purell from her purse, squeezed a dab into her cupped hand and then unwrapped her knife and fork from a paper napkin. Catherine remained silent until the waiter left. "Of course I care about Peter. He lacks confidence in his work, but he has talent. You see it, too. That's why you introduced us, isn't it?"

"I am talking about your husband. Do you care about your husband?"

Catherine took a sip of her soup, which burnt her tongue. "I don't know."

"Is Murat a good father?" Kristin asked.

Catherine dropped a pair of ice cubes from her water into the bowl, stirring them into the soup. She pondered the question as she watched them melt. "A good father?" she asked herself. "He works incessantly. He's hardly ever at home, not that I really want him in the house. When he takes William to school, that's nice ... I don't know. I haven't thought about whether or not he's a good father, at least not for a long time."

"Are you being fair to him?"

"Fair?"

"He provides well, doesn't he?"

"What has that got to do with him being a good father?"

"Everything," answered Kristin. "He takes care of you. And of William."

"It's surprising to hear such a conventional attitude from you," answered Catherine. She set her spoon down on the table and kept her eyes fixed on Kristin.

"Each of us has to live," said Kristin. "No matter how we do it. Do you think that I take my daughter to school each morning? If that were my measure as a mother, I would be failing. But I know how to provide for a child. I do that part of the job and do it well." Kristin glanced impatiently at her slim triathlete's watch, and Catherine could imagine her waking up each morning as her daughter slept, running however many miles she ran before sunup while she used that same watch to time herself.

"You're misunderstanding me," explained Catherine. She then paused, momentarily weighing whether or not to be explicit as to all she understood about her husband's relationship with Kristin. "Murat's business would be nothing without you. So you are our provider, not him. You are the one taking care of us while he does whatever it is he does for you."

Kristin stabbed her fork into her salad. She took one bite and then another, contemplating whether or not to acknowledge any of the myriad sensitive tasks Murat performed on her behalf and the many ways her interests, Murat's interests and Catherine's all aligned. "Let me ask you a different question," said Kristin. "If I am the one who has been taking care of you, if I am in fact the person who has ensured that your husband's business hasn't collapsed, don't you think that you owe me something?"

Catherine took another spoonful of her soup. She glanced up at the tangle of blossomless wisteria above, contemplating the invisible tally of debits and credits that existed between her and Kristin. "And if I do owe you something?"

"Then we both need to consider that," answered Kristin. She leaned over the table, closing the distance between her and Catherine. "My concern is that you might do something rash, especially as it relates to Peter."

"Like what?"

"Let me ask you this another way," said Kristin. "If you returned to the U.S. with William and Peter, do you think it would be good for either of them?"

"Is that what you're worried about? That I'll leave Murat and return to the U.S.?"

"Shouldn't it be?"

Catherine pushed her meal away and leaned forward, matching Kristin's posture. "Why did you introduce me to Peter?"

"I thought you could help him with his work."

Catherine leaned back in her chair, annoyed by this response.

"Thank you for lunch," she said, and then turned to flag down their waiter, whose eye she caught through the window.

"Stop it," said Kristin. "Why did I introduce you to Peter? Because I thought he might give you a reason to stay. And after seeing you at the precinct, I'm worried that Peter might have given you a reason to leave instead. But have you thought about him and what would happen if he quit his work? And your son, what would happen if he lost his father? You can't afford to only think of yourself in this."

For the briefest of moments, Catherine felt a twist of guilt as Kristin held up a mirror to her selfishness. But undermining this interpretation of events were Kristin's own interests in the matter. Kristin needed Murat. She needed his calibrated understanding of a corrupt system, one that Kristin couldn't navigate herself and that her invisible superiors demanded she report back on with an impossible degree of clairvoyance. Here, in this city, there was no one above Kristin in authority. She was spectacularly alone. However, a dependency existed between Kristin and Murat. Although the framework of that dependency was not entirely clear, Catherine recognized how Kristin would never permit her to disrupt that framework by leaving, even if Catherine tried. No threat had been made, it didn't have to be, the facts were evident and Catherine felt certain of Kristin's willingness to go far further than a pleading over lunch when it came to safeguarding her position in relation to Murat.

"What would it take to keep you from running off?" Kristin asked.

Before Catherine could answer, the waiter emerged with their check, which was inside a fist-size wooden box inlaid with semiprecious stones. He set the box between them. "What you've said about me isn't fair. I want what's best for my son. I want what's best for Peter. I even want what's best for my husband, and I'm not certain that you can say the same."

"So what does that mean?"

"It means if Peter stays then I will."

"How do we do that?"

"Help him get his work shown," said Catherine, "so he doesn't give up on it."

"I have helped."

"Not enough. Perhaps you could speak with Deniz? When I asked him to show Peter's photographs at the Modern, he refused. Perhaps there's something the consulate could do that would convince him otherwise."

"I'm not certain that would work."

"Why not?" asked Catherine. "You haven't even tried."

"I guess you didn't hear."

Catherine shook her head.

"Deniz was fired two days ago, after word got out about his arrest." Kristin opened the small wooden box with the bill. She dipped her eyes and gave it a quick once-over as she pulled a credit card from her purse. "Listen, as long as you and I have an understanding, we'll figure something out regarding Peter."

Catherine removed a few banknotes from her pocketbook.

"My treat," said Kristin. "I'm the one who invited you to lunch."

But as much as Kristin insisted, Catherine refused. Standing from her seat, Catherine examined the bill. She made absolutely certain to leave no less than her half of the cash on the table.

Four o'clock on that afternoon

⌒ ⌐

They leave Bebek Park and ascend the terraced folds of the city. The Bosphorus disappears from view and the urban sprawl of the interior swallows them. The rain gentles into a mist, which lingers like disappearing crowns among the uppermost stories of the darkened skyscrapers that line their route with shadows. Their taxi has come to a standstill in the traffic. While William waits for them to inch forward, he traces the cityscape on his window's fogged glass. The outline appears like an uneven staircase, climbing and then falling for no discernible reason. The traffic eases as they pull onto Barbaros Boulevard, which leads them out of the city's interior, back to the Bosphorus, toward the Kabataş ferry terminal, where on the overcrowded decks rush-hour commuters finish their day huddling beneath a black mosaic of umbrellas.

The Kabataş ferry terminal reminds William of his father and the afternoon of their failed excursion to the Princes' Islands. Staring out of his window, through the cityscape he has traced, William asks if his father will be where they're going. But Catherine doesn't answer him. She sits with her hands in her lap, clutching her broken phone with its dark, cracked screen, as if she believes that a call from Peter still might come.

Past the Beşiktaş football club's incomplete stadium, their taxi enters a warren of incomprehensible side streets, which eventually dumps them onto İstiklal Caddesi. "This is where we were last night," William observes.

Catherine turns toward her son. "Yes, it is," she says, and then leans forward from her seat, passing the driver some last instructions on where exactly to drop them. Glancing back at William, she explains that they are going to see if Deniz is at home.

"Are we going to stay there?" William asks.

"Maybe."

"Why can't we stay at our home? Or with Peter?"

Catherine reaches into the pocket of her blazer. She clutches the single bill that the parking attendant had given her. It won't be quite enough to take them to Deniz's apartment, so she asks the driver to stop. They will walk the remainder of the way. As they step out of the cab onto the İstiklal's cobblestones, William asks once again about his father. "Am I going to see him?" he wants to know.

"Yes," says Catherine. And she sounds certain of it.

❈

"Cat, I wish you hadn't come." As Deniz opens the front door, his voice is flat, constricted, as though these words are the first he has spoken after a long sleep. The figure in the doorway bears little resemblance to the glamorous man William had met the night before. A day's coating of stubble has collected along Deniz's cheeks like some leveled ruin. A freshly lit cigarette dangles nervously from his lips. He kneads his palms against his reddened eyes, which betray that he has just woken from a nap. Deniz allows his gaze to dip toward William. He offers the boy a smile, exposing his perfectly arrayed and brilliantly white teeth, which with wiring, bands and bleach he has hewn into something more presentable than the misaligned smile he was born with.

"I'm sorry to impose," says Catherine. She drapes an arm over William's shoulder, pressing the boy beside her. "We had nowhere else to go."

"You should come inside," says Deniz, but the tired edge in his voice no longer seems to indicate a nap interrupted, but rather a defeat. With this slight change of inflection, Deniz pushes the front door all the way open. Sitting on the sofa is Murat. He still wears his coat and it doesn't seem as if he has been waiting for very long. Then, from the white painted room where he had displayed his photographs the night before, Peter emerges.

Catherine turns around, as if she might run out the back of the apartment with William. But before she can take a first step, she hears the rhythmic tick-tock of heel strikes coming from down the corridor. Someone else is ascending the stairs toward Deniz's front door.

July 7, 2013

⌒

Kristin did her best thinking at the gym. Her most original ideas occurred to her while she was exercising. Perhaps it was the clarity associated with early mornings, or maybe it was the meditative qualities of listening to her heart pound out its beats as she struggled to maintain a certain speed on the treadmill, or hold a specific rpm on the stationary bike. She had read articles about how endorphin releases and highly oxygenated blood led to revelatory thinking, although she absorbed such conclusions with a healthy dose of skepticism.

She logged the progress of her workouts carefully. By her calculations she was a first-rate triathlete, posting many of the same times as professional competitors. About once every two months she would wake impossibly early on a Sunday morning and put herself through an Olympic-distance race. She would begin in the lap pool, then move to the stationary bike, and finish on the treadmill. Her overall times—all of which she tracked on the digital watch clasped to her wrist—she kept only for herself, allowing her the quiet satisfaction of knowing the many unclaimed medals, sponsorships and accolades to which she would have been entitled had she ever chosen to compete.

On one such Sunday morning, a couple of weeks after her most recent lunch with Catherine at Kafe 6 in Cihangir, Kristin was hunched over the handlebars of the stationary bike. Twenty-three kilometers into the forty-kilometer bike leg, her cadence held strong but lagged enough to take her off pace for any personal record. Throughout the preceding swim, her mind had looped over the end of that meal, specifically Catherine's disconcerting insistence on paying her half of the bill. The gesture was no small refusal. Kristin understood that Catherine was beyond her control. How to solve this liability was the problem she focused on as she pedaled.

Her legs pumped, holding at slightly above one hundred rotations per minute, and the entire bike had begun to purr. Steady, single droplets of sweat migrated from her forehead and then gathered on the tip of her nose. She counted them as they fell to the floor and concentrated on her breath, which punctuated her thoughts. *Inhale.* She suspected that she had, perhaps, played herself to a standstill. *Exhale.* That if Catherine was dead set on leaving her husband, there was nothing Kristin could do. *Inhale.* Except for manage the fallout. *Exhale.* She glanced down at the odometer, 120 rotations per minute. She needed to slow down, or risk burning out her legs.

Her breathing evened out. The task set before her became clear. If Murat remained in his job and continued his work for her, then everything would be fine. This much was obvious. This was all that mattered. To achieve this result, Kristin needed Peter to stay in Istanbul so that Catherine wouldn't have anyone to run off with. That meant giving Peter something. The grant Kristin had arranged from the consulate had been insufficient. It had allowed him to stay in the city, but it had afforded him none of the recognition he craved. Kristin knew she would have to make a more active intervention in Peter's career if she was to convince him not to decamp to the U.S. She would have to facilitate the success that had eluded him. Catherine had spoken to Deniz about arranging a show for Peter at the Istanbul Modern, but she had been refused. And now Deniz had been fired from his post at the museum after his arrest at Gezi Park. This offered Kristin an opportunity, because all of this could be fixed, at least she could fix matters for Deniz. Kristin could simply instruct Murat to rehire him.

And then, owing his job to Murat, Deniz would be more than willing to show Peter's work at the Modern.

A sense of contentment took hold of Kristin. By giving Peter what he wanted, both she and Murat would receive what they wanted. Kristin glanced down at the odometer. The glimmering red digital display hovered above one hundred rotations. Kristin felt satisfied that she was on pace, maybe not for a personal record but for a respectable time. She allowed her mind to go blank. For the next half an hour or so she continued to pedal, head down, oblivious to anything except the three digits an arm's length from her face, which, without too much struggle, she managed to keep above one hundred.

After forty kilometers, she leapt off the bike. Her running shoes were staged next to a treadmill in the opposite corner of the gym, which was still empty. She slid them on. More than the swim or the bike, the run was the portion of the race where she lost herself. On the treadmill there was no odometer she was trying to rev to a certain level, no number of laps she was counting and struggling to complete in a certain time. On the treadmill, she set the pace into the computer and then she ran. The motor on the machine would take over. She would try not to fall off the back. The swim and the bike set her up for this final struggle, one where all of her efforts concentrated on just holding on.

She inputted her pace and then pressed start. The belt on the treadmill engaged, lurching forward. The motor accelerated, releasing a high-pitched whine. Her steps landed in quick succession, sounding wild as native drums, the rhythm of which ferried her away into a pain-induced trance. Her thoughts returned to Catherine and the solution she believed she had found. Deniz was the linchpin that would hold both Peter and Murat in place, but what satisfaction existed for Catherine in this arrangement? Would she be content to carry on as Peter's mistress?

Kristin could feel herself slipping toward the back of the treadmill. A stitch clawed into her side, slightly beneath the ribs. She rolled her shoulders. She breathed deeply, attempting to relax.

For Peter and Murat—and even for Deniz—she had come up with a solution that would maintain the status quo, in effect suspending them in a construct created by her. Kristin could see how each of their interests might balance the others'. Murat would return Deniz's job. Deniz would exhibit Peter's photographs. Peter would secure Murat's personal life by not running off with Catherine.

What about Catherine?

The stitch in Kristin's side threatened to spread. Her muscles cramped in a form of contagious hysteria. Instead of focusing on her breathing, or rolling her shoulders again, Kristin turned her energies to the unsolved problem before her. How would she convince Catherine to stay? Her love for Peter—if that's what it was—wouldn't be enough. It would quickly erode in a construct where Peter remained in Istanbul for his best interests as opposed to hers.

Kristin made the mistake of glancing down at the treadmill's screen. The remaining time seemed like an impossibility. She could no longer hang on. Her hand reflexively wanted to lift from her side and dial down the speed. But whatever short-term relief this might have provided would be far less than the frustration she would feel at quitting. She refocused and, once again, turned her attention to the problem of Catherine, not only so she might solve it but also so she might lose track of time through its contemplation.

If Catherine's love for Peter was conditional, Kristin knew that Catherine's love of William was not. And if this was so, it was William who could keep Catherine in place. He was the key. Kristin recalled a piece of paper on her desk: the name and address listed for William's birth mother. The Central Authority had registered this information. A single claim made by William's birth mother to the local authorities not only would be enough to forestall the boy's departure from the country but could go as far as threatening the legitimacy of his adoption. Catherine was, after all, a foreigner. Would the threat of William's birth mother be enough to hold Catherine in place? Kristin suspected so, and as she came to this conclusion, she felt the stitch in her side dissipate. She had been running as though guarding a wound. Without that liability, she straightened up. Her gait lengthened. Her movements became fluid. For moments at a time she had the sensation of hovering as she ran.

When she again glanced at the display, she noticed more time had passed than she had expected. If she dialed up the speed slightly, she would be on track for a personal best. She hazarded to do so. The new pace didn't challenge her as she thought it might. The sensation of hovering endured. She heard the door open behind her. Glancing over her shoulder, she saw a young man, still in his twenties, a gym towel, which he clutched at both ends, slung behind his neck. He was a new consular officer who had arrived only a few weeks before. He wished Kristen a good morning. She replied with little more than a nod and a grunt, not wanting to waste her breath as she closed in on the finish.

Kristin glanced down at the treadmill's timer. About nine minutes left. She increased her speed by one tenth of a mile per hour. This would place her ahead of her previous best time by under ten seconds. The distracting clank of free weights shuttling in and out of their cradles echoed from across the gym. The noise was accompanied by the pleading grunts of the young consular officer as he began his workout. Kristin wondered if he would make a habit of exercising early on Sunday mornings and if the solitude she had found in the gym would be forever compromised by his arrival. How much of her life, she thought—or at least the portions of her life she prized most—existed in a delicate, interruptible balance. These Sunday mornings existed only for her. She hurt no one by taking this time. Her daughter and husband had been asleep in their beds when she left. They would be asleep in their beds when she returned. If later in the day she felt tired—in the afternoon at her desk, for instance, or in the evening if she was meeting with one of her many contacts, like Murat—she would embrace that feeling, satisfied by the knowledge that on this one day, as opposed to all of the others, her exhaustion served as a reminder that she had done something for herself.

She could feel the young consular officer lurking behind her, unwittingly robbing her of that solitude. He approached the stereo bolted on the side of the gym's wall. He asked to turn it on. She ignored him and he substituted her silence on the matter for her consent, tuning the radio to a techno-pop station. The music blared and the sound of Kristin's steps—the heel-to-toe percussion of each foot meeting the treadmill's belt, which she had followed hypnotically all through her run—suddenly disappeared. And her thoughts dissolved amid the woofing thump of bass line that emanated from the stereo.

Kristin's concentration lagged until she felt herself lulling toward the back of the treadmill. She then shot a glance at the display, which flashed up her remaining time: less than six minutes. With the last of her energy she corrected her stride, which had become pigeon-toed and sloppy. She did her best to tune out the young consular officer's music, the rhythm of his grunts and the sense of loss and imbalance she felt when considering that every Sunday morning he would now, unavoidably, be in the gym with her.

Then everything shut down. The lights. The music. And the treadmill.

Kristin stumbled forward, taking a full step in the darkness so her ribs crashed into the treadmill's crossbar. Across the gym she heard a breathy curse as the young officer dropped his dumbbells on the rubberized flooring, where they landed with a dull thud. Kristin shot her hand up to the treadmill's control console. She tapped at the buttons, trying to restart the machine—nothing. The power was out. She glanced at her digital watch. The seconds bled away from her. The record she was chasing would soon be lost.

The young officer asked if she knew where the light switch was.

Kristin crossed the gym, feeling her way toward the switch on the wall. She maneuvered blindly through the pieces of equipment, whose positions she had memorized after countless workouts. The young officer sat on his weight bench in the darkness, not moving, although Kristin could hear his labored breaths mixing with her own. Her fingertips found the switch, which she toggled on and off to no effect.

"Does the power often go out?" asked the young officer.

The power had never gone out before, at least not at this time on a Sunday.

"It usually cuts out about now," Kristin lied.

The young officer stumbled forward, navigating toward Kristin's voice and what he thought was the door. When he spoke again, he was much closer to her. "Do you know what time the power comes back on?"

"In the afternoon." Again she lied to him; she didn't know about the power.

"I guess I'll have to work out later," he said. His hands groped around the door, clutching after the knob, which he couldn't find, so Kristin reached out and opened it for him. The threshold passed into a darker corridor, which led to a locker room lined with a few windows, whose light would help the young officer find his way out.

Kristin felt no guilt about the lie that she had told. This was her time. These Sunday mornings kept her level through the week. It would've been far worse for her to pretend otherwise. Although she had not beaten her record, standing in the darkness, she considered the morning to have been a success. She had figured out how to preserve her relationship with Murat. Like the protected space around her morning workout, it required the creation and maintenance of a well-calibrated equilibrium. She would have to lie, or to at least fashion a few mis-truths, which in her mind were less malicious than lies and more akin to the factual error she had offered the young consular officer, who would now likely change his gym hours, leaving her alone.

Kristin stood calmly in the dark. She heard the gym's front door slam shut. Two or three minutes had passed, perhaps slightly longer. She had caught her breath. Her muscles had begun to cool. Then the power came back on. The stereo picked up. The treadmill revved into gear. Kristin glanced at the display, which held the remaining time and distance. The machine hadn't reset itself, and according to its clock she had lost only seconds. She crossed the gym and turned off the stereo. She then leapt back onto the treadmill, rejoining her race at nearly the exact spot where she had left it. She doubted the young consular officer would return. She also doubted that Catherine would ever be able to leave. As she drew these two conclusions, she noticed that despite the prior interruption she was still on track to achieve a personal best. And minutes later, in the silence of the morning, she did.

Five o'clock on that afternoon

William glances down the hallway toward the creaking stairs. Standing at their top is the woman from the consulate, the one who had made the speech at the exhibit the night before. The boy knows that, like her, he is an American. His mother had occasionally emphasized this part of his identity, although his father never did. His mother had even once shown him his first passport, a blue book with empty, unstamped pages that had a photo of him when he was little more than an infant. When this woman emerges at the landing, William can feel his mother's grip on him tighten. With both of her hands placed over his shoulders, she pins him to her front in the way she sometimes did when they stood waiting to cross the street, the merciless traffic zipping past so close that the air would stir at their faces.

"What are you doing here, Kristin?" his mother asks. The hallway channels her words, changing the timbre of her voice so that it sounds as hollow as an echo.

"I had a hunch this is where you'd show up." A grin pinches upward from one corner of Kristin's mouth. "We need to have a talk," she adds, and her eyes wander toward the door. As Kristin closes the distance between them, William can feel his mother pressing him ever more forcefully toward her. Kristin stands next to Catherine but won't enter the apartment before she does.

A standoff ensues until Peter approaches from the living room. "Catherine . . ." he says. His mouth remains agape, ready to give some long explanation. His shoulders are hunched forward as if he is dislodging from inside himself certain assurances and optimisms, but when none of those words manifest, Peter's open mouth repeats her name once more, without context, "Catherine . . . ," and then, with his eyes casting down at the boy, he mutters only, "It's time to come inside."

Before Catherine can cross the threshold of her own volition, William pulls away from her. He has caught a glimpse of his father, who sits on the sofa, hands pinned between his knees. Seeing William rushing toward him, Murat stands. His son embraces him, his cheek pressed to Murat's belt buckle. Catherine remains alone in the doorway, then, reluctantly, follows her son into the apartment.

Inside it is more cluttered than during the exhibit. The open living room—furnished the night before with only a couple of chairs—is filled out with a pair of sofas divided by a coffee table. Kristin gestures for Catherine to sit next to her. Peter takes a place across from them on the sofa, so does Deniz. William has climbed back up into the bay window, where he had sat last night looking out at the haloed streetlamps, which now, in the late afternoon, are about to flicker on. He is favoring Murat in much the same way he had favored Peter the evening prior, lavishing attention on the man whom he feels might lavish the most attention on him.

"Are we going to go home now?" William asks his father.

Murat gazes out at the city, at the buildings which had made him his fortune and which have just as quickly threatened to ruin him. "Soon, I think," he says to his son.

"If we're going to talk," says Catherine, "someone please take William outside." At the sound of her voice and his own name, William glances back to his mother, whose eyes have never left him. Through her look, the boy feels how his question about going home and Murat's response threaten her. Catherine's definition of home has changed from his. The place William considers home is now foreign to her, a place to be escaped from, not returned to.

Kristin is perched next to Catherine on the sofa, their knees angled toward one another, nearly touching. Catherine repeats her request for someone to take William outside. Kristin stalls for a moment, as if reluctant to allow anyone to leave the apartment after her efforts to unite this group. She then glances up at Deniz. Perhaps he would take William.

Deniz comes to the window, where William sits contentedly with Murat. He suggests that they wander up to the İstiklal. "Your father will be here when we get back," Deniz says, releasing the word *father* into the air like a noble concession, like the announcement of an entire fortune being gifted as charity. William turns a desperate stare toward Murat, who glances away.

William then turns to his mother, who, like Murat, looks away, refusing to weigh in with a gesture or a remark as to whether or not William should follow Deniz outside. This decision, unlike any other William has known, is entirely his to make. He offers his hand to Deniz, who grips it firmly as they head for the front door.

"Back in an hour?" Deniz asks Kristin, who nods in return.

William and Deniz descend the apartment's stairwell. Standing in the street, Deniz asks William what he usually does when he's out with his parents. "My father," says William, "takes me to look at buildings."

"At buildings?"

"I tell him how much I think each is worth and he tells me if I'm right."

"And this is a fun game?"

William considers the question for a moment as they wander down the block, toward a tangle of alleyways and tributary roads emptying onto İstiklal Caddesi. "Knowing what things are worth is how my father makes money. He says that someday I'll make my money doing the same thing, by being the best at this. He says I'm already good at it, that I'm observant."

"Maybe you can teach me," says Deniz, who still holds William's hand.

The echo of their steps carries cheerfully down the road. As they turn off the block of Deniz's apartment, they pass by a large white Chevy parked at the corner. They both notice the car, which stands out among the few others scattered along the roadside. But neither of them notices the woman who waits in the passenger seat.

※

Kristin begins to explain herself. The men are on one sofa, the women on the other, the coffee table between them. They sit, the four of them—Murat, Peter, Catherine and Kristin—in the awkwardness of a moment, which each must have known their collective choices over the years had driven them toward. And as Kristin talks of their interests and of hers, the many points of intersection, the logic of what each of them should do next—whether it is Catherine giving up her plans to leave, or Murat agreeing to support Peter's ambitions—Kristin realizes that she isn't so much explaining herself to them, but rather explaining each of them to themselves. She attempts to speak in a level, even-mannered tone. She had hoped—and continues to hope as she feels their skeptical gazes boring into her—that they will subscribe to her logic of their best interests.

They wait, their bodies settled in three different angles of repose. Murat thumbs through a magazine with his legs crossed one lazily over the other, while Peter sits plank straight like a child who with great effort is demonstrating good posture for an adult's behalf, and Catherine is leaning forward with elbows perched on her knees as if she might lunge after Kristin, who prattles on:

"Murat, if you're willing to help reinstate Deniz to his position at the Istanbul Modern, I know Deniz would be willing to reconsider some of Peter's photographs for an exhibit and perhaps even the permanent collection." Murat doesn't reply, but Kristin knows how to interpret his silence, which isn't a manifestation of disagreement, but rather a quiet acquiescence to the inherent logic of the bargain. "And Peter," Kristin continues, "an exhibit at the Istanbul Modern would be a significant opportunity. An opportunity I imagine you couldn't afford to miss."

Like Murat, Peter doesn't reply. And if Kristin doesn't know Peter as well as she knows Murat, if she doesn't understand the topography of his silences, Catherine surely does. Catherine turns her head toward Peter, so that her profile faces Kristin, who can see Catherine's clenched jaw and the muscles in her cheek flickering like a candle near the end of its wick. Kristin imagines the flood of accusations screaming through Catherine's mind as she stares Peter down, knowing that he is weighing the merits of betraying her happiness against the merits of assuring his own success.

"What about Catherine?" Murat interrupts the silence. He has uncrossed his legs and come forward on the sofa. Leaning toward Kristin, he asks her again, "If Peter remains here for work—and if Catherine chooses to stay as well—then what happens to her?" Catherine turns away from Peter and toward her husband. The tension in her jaw eases, her shoulders relax.

"I'm not sure I understand," answers Kristin. "Where would she go?"

Peter, Murat and Catherine shuttle confused glances between themselves as if uncertain how Kristin could have suddenly become unaware of Catherine's intention to leave with William, the very same intention which has triggered this current crisis.

"She would return to the U.S.," says Peter.

Kristin allows Peter's words to hang in the air for a moment. The idea of Catherine leaving can't sustain itself and it dissipates the longer it goes unacknowledged, like a ribbon of clouds at dawn, or dew on the ground, or any number of whimsical and vanishing distractions.

"How would she do that?" Kristin asks.

Catherine straightens up. "It's my right to return home."

"That it is," answers Kristin.

A beat of curious silence passes, in which Catherine glances at Murat and Peter, as if taking a final measure of what she might choose to leave behind and then, as if finding the pair of them insufficient reason to stay, she stands and asks Murat if she can have the passports.

"Those won't do you any good," answers Kristin.

Addressing Murat and not Kristin, Catherine stands with her hand extended. "If you don't give them to me, I can always have another passport made—"

"For you," interrupts Kristin.

"I'm sorry?" says Catherine.

"You can always have another passport made *for you*," repeats Kristin. "William is a different matter." Before Catherine can respond, Kristin continues, "Leave if you want, but you won't bring your son along. Even that idea, that he is your son, is a matter that could easily be refuted. You're an American woman taking away the adopted child of a Turkish citizen." At the mention of William's paternity, Catherine glances out the window, toward the İstiklal, where Deniz has taken him. "Don't worry, they'll be coming back," adds Kristin. A tinge of malice sharpens her voice, an effect she believes Catherine deserves. Although a part of Kristin pities the manner in which events have conspired to trap Catherine, she also resents Catherine's inability to appreciate—or at least to acknowledge—the web of other people's interests, of which she is a part.

Kristin rises from the sofa and gestures for Catherine to join her by the window. They stand shoulder to shoulder and beneath them is the street, with the echoing conversations of passersby, with the trash huddled in piles under fluorescent bulbs, with the parades of stray cats either rummaging in those very same piles or sitting erect with a calm, cynical clairvoyance. "Do you see my car?" asks Kristin, pointing toward the corner, where she has parked the same white Chevy that had dented the door of the black Mercedes weeks before.

"I see it," Catherine says.

"What if William's mother knew that you were going to take him away?" asks Kristin, and she is no longer looking out the window, but rather at Catherine, whose stare is fixed on the white Chevy, where a meek, fidgeting silhouette sits in the front seat. "Do you think if she knew her son was going to be taken from the country that she might reconsider her decision of many years ago?"

"I have a right to go home." Catherine repeats this several times, but each time she speaks her words, they are already long gone.

"And her?" asks Kristin, who nods toward the white Chevy.

"She gave up her right to my son."

"Did your son give up his right to her?"

Catherine's eyes narrow, and she looks out at the city with unshielded contempt, as if it isn't Kristin, Peter or even Murat who has conspired to undermine her escape, but rather the monster of a city itself, the undulating skyline, the large buildings that look down on small ones and the small ones that had once been large, only to find themselves outpaced by newer, more innovative forms of construction. Arcing steadily across the evening sky the blinking signal lights of airliners trace irregular flight patterns, making it difficult to know which are returning and which are departing. Catherine stares upward, trying to solve the many riddles of their direction.

"Deniz and William will be back soon," says Kristin, interrupting the mournful silence Catherine has escaped into. In a form of threat, Kristin tosses her eyes up the road, to where William and Deniz will return. Then she shifts her gaze to the parked white Chevy and its passenger. "I suppose we might be witness to a reunion of sorts," mutters Kristin in almost an afterthought.

Catherine's expression is alive with the implications of such a reunion, as if a synaptic jolt has, at last, forced a decision, and, upon recognizing that she needs to intervene to keep William from meeting this woman—at least at this moment—she also recognizes that she still needs her husband's help to do this. Catherine bolts for the door, but not before offering a single pleading glance to Murat. What she is pleading for is forgiveness, or enough of it so that Murat won't abandon her, so that he might come with her after their son. And upon his eyes meeting hers, Murat finally gets up from his seat. He has made his choice and it is to follow her. The patter of their footfalls descends the hallway, and then the stairs, and lastly their voices can be heard in the street as they walk head down with shoulders forward past the white

Chevy and toward a fissure of narrow, ascending pedestrian thorough-
fares which will take them to the İstiklal, where they might find William, only to take him home and to then, if they are lucky, find a way
to resign the day's events to a single episode in an otherwise fruitful, if
at times uneven, marriage.

Kristin sits heavily on the sofa next to Peter. With her elbow
propped on its arm, she leans her head into her hand and has an impulse
to put her feet up on the coffee table but thinks better of it. Whatever
future Peter and Catherine had with one another—no matter how
improbable—has walked out of the apartment door. The vacuum of
that loss leaves a silence in the room. Peter lights a cigarette.

"I never realized you smoked," said Kristin.

He leans forward on the sofa, searching the coffee table for somewhere to put his ash. The cigarette dangles from his lips as he casts
Kristin an incredulous sidelong glance. "So that's the one thing about
me you didn't figure out," he says, standing. He walks into the kitchen,
where he smokes by the sink, finishing one cigarette and then lighting
another as he tips his ash into the drain. He then crosses Deniz's apartment and enters the room he had converted into a gallery the night
before. His photographs still crowd the walls, a perimeter of faces, battered and unbattered impressions, lending to an effect Kristin wasn't
certain Peter ever quite achieved. Peter lingers in the exhibit's center,
as if to feel the weight of each glance on him for a final time before he
takes his work down.

Kristin steps into the empty doorway to speak with Peter. What
she wants to offer him are assurances: that Deniz will be in touch to
begin plans for his exhibit at the Istanbul Modern, that she will ensure
another grant is forthcoming to cover his expenses, and that, ultimately,
he has done the right thing by supporting Catherine when she seemed
poised to make a ruinous decision—even though that decision involved
coupling up with him. However, before Kristin can say any of this, Peter
gently lifts the first of his portraits off its hook. One by one the photographs are removed from the wall. As Peter stacks them in the center

of the room, the somnolent dismantling of his work silences Kristin. Gathering her coat, she heads for the door. She has a great deal to tell Peter, but she will do it later.

❊

When Kristin steps from the apartment, the street is empty. She fumbles through her purse searching for her keys. After a couple of seconds, she finds them in the interior pocket of her suit jacket. The day had been a busy one, stressful, leaving her preoccupied. Misplacing keys has become too common a tic, like a geriatric placing dishes in the laundry hamper or books in the dishwasher. To Kristin it's a sign she's slipping. It frightens her, this slippage, for Kristin has lived continually not only on her guard against others, but also on guard against herself.

As soon as she resolves the detail of her misplaced keys, she unlocks the white Chevy. When she hears steps approaching, Kristin glances up—it is Deniz, returning from the İstiklal. Kristin now realizes that she has made another and far more severe oversight. With the door to the Chevy open, Deniz can clearly see the woman inside, the petite silhouette which Kristin had used to menace whatever equilibrium still existed in Murat's and Catherine's lives.

"You're leaving?" Deniz calls out.

"Yes, but we'll be in touch about everything," says Kristin, sliding into the car. Their voices carry and Kristin thinks that perhaps their conversation won't travel as far if she sits inside the Chevy.

"And who's this?" asks Deniz, stepping beside Kristin's door.

The slight woman in the hijab glances at Kristin like an actress who has forgotten her lines, or worse, like an actress dealing with another actor who has gone off script. Kristin shifts her eyes to Deniz, answering as she turns on the ignition. "She works with me at the consulate."

Kristin puts the Chevy into gear. Deniz straightens himself and then, as if sensing shifting weather overhead, he glances up, to where he catches a glimpse of Peter, who is standing in the open window of the apartment. Deniz waves at him good-naturedly. Peter has been watching the entire time and he shuts the window behind him.

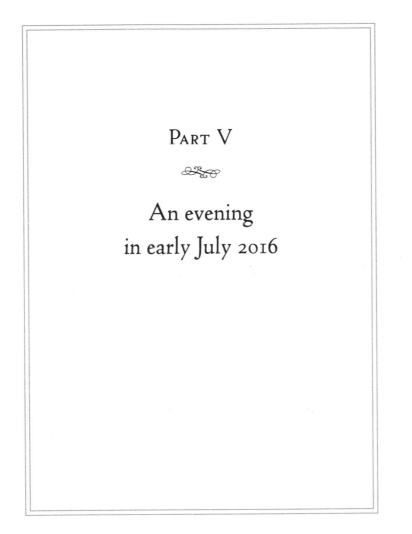

PART V

An evening
in early July 2016

How it glimmers. Encased in glass, the renovated wing of the Istanbul Modern invites the light. During the day it shines and shines along the bank of the Bosphorus, radiating like a second sun. At night the boat lights, the bridge lights, even the passing gridlock along Cevdet Paşa Caddesi reflect kaleidoscopically from its windows, behind which a priceless mélange of contemporary and classic collections hang the interior walls, adding their value to the exterior glass walls, which Murat Yaşar has built to house them. A year before, Peter had his first show in the Istanbul Modern's old wing, which by all accounts was a wild success. Scheduled to run for two weeks, it was extended to three months. The coverage Deniz arranged in the Turkish press had been both rampant and generous. Venerable European auction houses took notice and began to inquire about Peter's work, and the museum had gone on to purchase a half dozen of his photographs for its permanent collection while the consulate had purchased a half dozen more, even providing him with another grant, which he no longer needed but happily pocketed and then used to purchase his rented apartment.

On opening night of the Istanbul Modern's new wing, Peter dresses next to his bed in that apartment. His sheets are predictably mussed, the evidence of another afternoon spent with Catherine, who still insists

on their series of knocks and counterknocks, even though on the occasions when she cannot easily find a cab she's had Murat's driver deliver
her straight to Peter's front door in the black Mercedes. Standing in
front of a full-length mirror, Peter struggles to articulate the series of
cinches, twists and pulls that will construct his bow tie, the last detail
on the tuxedo he has rented a half dozen times over the past year, a fact
which has led Catherine—and the tailor who rents him the tuxedo—to
ask why he simply doesn't purchase one. A question he has yet to find
a satisfactory answer to, except his nagging hunch that each celebration
of his talents might well be the last in what has become an unsettling
string of successes.

In the back of the taxi Peter steals glances at himself in the rearview
mirror, specifically at his bow tie, of which he has made a shoddy job.
Something is off about the knot, which isn't quite straight, so the bow
tie keeps unscrewing a few degrees to the left. Peter twists it back to
center, but it then stubbornly propellers to its natural, off-kilter position. Changing lanes, the taxi driver glances in his rearview mirror. A
laugh escapes him as he notices Peter's determined effort. Peter slinks
into his seat. From his interior coat pocket, he removes the engraved
invitation which Catherine had hand-delivered to him several weeks
before. It is printed on heavy stock, the edges brushed with gold paint
and lettering to match. Listed in a curlicuing font on the back of the
invitation are the dinner's cochairs in alphabetical order, aside from
Catherine and Murat, who despite the first initial of their last name
have been placed on the top, as in *Murat and Catherine Yaşar, along
with . . . invite you to . . .* and so forth.

Peter touches his bow tie. It has again unwound into its off-kilter
position. He knows that he cannot fix it in the back of the cab and that
he will have to remember to tend to its stubborn unwinding until he
finds an opportunity to retie it himself. It occurs to him that if Catherine had been in the cab, if the two of them were traveling together to
this opening like any normal couple, she would have simply turned to
him and fixed his tie in the backseat. But things have never been and

will never be this way between them. He returns the engraved invitation to his coat pocket.

In front of Dolmabahçe Palace traffic congeals to a near standstill. A match between Fenerbahçe and Beşiktaş has released a roiling mass of drunken fans into the late-afternoon darkness. Their bodies filter between car fenders, which lie against one another like so many bricks in an impenetrable wall of traffic. Clad in black and white, the Beşiktaş fans chant in one singsong cadence, while the navy-and-gold-clad Fenerbahçe fans rise up in another voice entirely. Peter asks the driver if he knows who has won the match. "Nobody win," says the driver. Around the time of Peter's first show at the Istanbul Modern, Murat had managed to refinance the construction of the new stadium through "unidentified sources" as the newspapers had reported it. Since its completion the year before, the games—popular as they are—have crippled the city's transit system. "Nobody win," repeats the driver, with a hint more vitriol.

They pass directly in front of the stadium and the pulsing artificial lights from its exterior jumbotron cast shadows inside the taxi. Squinting upward, Peter catches dramatic replays from the match and then the final score: nil to nil. All of this commotion over nothing, he thinks. And then he eases back into his seat and shuts his eyes to the relentless light.

A phalanx of security men in dark suits lingers at the entrance of the museum. In the spots where the temporary offices had once been, Mercedes, Bentleys and Audis are parked. Their sleek curving black chassis are menacing, like a pack of predatory cats. All except for one. Parked in a far corner, as if it must have been the first to arrive, is the white Chevy. Atop a marble flight of stairs with a crimson runner, a woman in a ball gown cradles an iPad. She checks Peter's name against a list and then opens a glass door for him.

The soft and pleasant sound of intelligent conversation, which in any language forms a universal melody, fills his ears. A waiter in a white waist jacket offers Peter a flute of champagne. As he takes it from the silver tray, he hears his name called from across the grand atrium, as if it were being called not only for his behalf, but also as an announcement to the entire party. With a wide heedless grin, Deniz approaches him, his arms outstretched as if he were pacing a high wire and might, at any moment, lose his balance and topple back to earth from the altitudes where he walks. He grabs Peter by the biceps and kisses each of his cheeks, causing a measure of champagne to splash across the bib of Peter's tuxedo shirt, but Deniz takes no notice as he places his arm triumphantly around Peter's shoulders and surveys the party with him. "You're late," says Deniz. "I was worried you might not come."

"I hit some traffic."

"Because of tonight's match?"

Peter nods.

"Who won?"

"Nil to nil."

"He's printing money with that football stadium," says Deniz. His eyes cast out over the teeming atrium, to its center, where beside an abstract stone and plaster sculpture Murat entertains an ever-widening circle of guests, the men in black tie with lithe, ornamental women affixed to their arms, the weighty hems of their gowns brushing the polished marble floors, and the patrons of the museum, women so bedecked with jewels that it seems as though their husbands serve no other purpose than to catch a necklace or bracelet if its clasp might fail. Catherine stands among them, next to her husband, and her forced smile seems to rise and fall as unconsciously and with as little joy as the tide against an abandoned beach. "I suppose we can't complain about the traffic," Deniz continues. "The stadium has, after all, paid for this." He glances up at the museum's vaulted ceiling and the glass walls which miraculously carry its burden, and then Deniz kicks the toe of one of his patent leather slippers at the floor. "Have you seen Kristin?" he asks.

"Not yet," says Peter. His eyes avoid the crowd where she likely lingers.

"I imagine she'll find you."

"Did my finished frames arrive?"

"They did," answers Deniz, nodding toward the main gallery, a cavernous white room off the atrium. "You want me to take you to see them?"

"I'd rather see them on my own."

"Why this mystery about your next exhibit? You haven't shown me a thing."

"If you didn't like the work, would you still display it?" asks Peter.

Deniz reminds Peter about the Karsh exhibit, how he disliked Karsh and thought he was little more than a paparazzo, but nevertheless his photographs remain hung in the permanent collection. "So yes, I would still display your work if I didn't like it."

"Then why should I show you—or anyone—the photos in advance?"

Murat's voice breaks above the crowd, cutting off Peter and Deniz's conversation. He calls across the party for his son, gesturing with a wave of his hand toward the boy, who stands in a nearby corner. In the past few years, William has taken on an uncomfortable resemblance to Deniz, which is to say it has become increasingly evident that he bears no resemblance to either Murat or Catherine. In response to this, Murat has taken greater pains to keep William close by his side, as if proximity might quash any speculations about his son's paternity. If Murat can't replicate a genetic resemblance to his son, he's engineered that resemblance in other ways. William's impeccably tailored tuxedo matches his father's down to the studs, and although Peter can't hear from such a distance what they're talking about, he can see the way William holds the crowd in suspense and the manner in which Murat shows him off, as if the boy's innate grace evidences Murat's own brilliance in much the same way the light of the moon is, at night, the clearest and only evidence of the invisible sun.

Murat drinks deeply from his champagne, ensconced in his happiness and expensive clothes, as his son carries his fair share of the conversation with their guests. William addresses those gathered around him with whole paragraphs, his words garnering appreciative nods, both for the elegance with which he speaks about the museum and for the well-bred young man he has so unmistakably become. Murat glances about for a server and, unable to find one, he carelessly places his empty flute on the pedestal of the nearby sculpture. Deniz curses under his breath and barrels across the party, elbowing his way through the knots of patrons who, thanks to either a hefty check written to the museum or a favor granted by one of the sizable donors, received invitations to the evening's celebration. The group encircling Murat continues to listen with rapt attention as William holds forth on the design specifics of this new wing, the particulars of which he has learned through the afternoons he apprentices in his father's office.

Deniz fails to break into the circle where his son now stands at the center. When he reaches after the empty flute of champagne, he catches a disapproving glance from Murat, who doesn't appreciate Deniz's proximity to William in a crowd, which could, conceivably, discern the resemblance between them. Before Deniz can step away, a few of those who have been listening to Murat and William notice him clearing the empty champagne flute and they offer him their empties as well. Deniz doesn't protest. He bows his head, not so much in subservience but rather in a reflexive fear that he might compromise his son in some unforeseen way, and with the stems of four or five empty crystal flutes hanging from the spaces between his fingers, Deniz shuffles into the kitchen in search of someone to pass them off to.

※

"Not even a thank-you from Murat," says Kristin.

Peter hadn't noticed her come up alongside him. Her arms are crossed, she drinks a large glass of rosé instead of champagne, and instead of a ball gown she is wearing a black, knee-length cocktail dress, which is wrinkled in a few places, as if she had taken it from a drawer where it had lain unused for many months. Kristin sips from her glass and continues, "How's Catherine?"

"Fine," answers Peter as he glances in her direction.

Standing next to her husband, Catherine wears a white low-cut evening gown, which is brutal in its elegance, its front dipping into a slim

V that exposes a plunging strip of skin, which, familiar as her body is to Peter, appears illicit in such proximity to her husband and son. He wonders how Kristin's relationship with Catherine has developed in the many months since that afternoon at Deniz's apartment. Catherine and Peter never again spoke of the twenty-four hours when she had tried to leave Murat. All they could do was carry on. And this is what they have done, with Kristin's help. If Kristin had engineered the events that brought about that crisis, she similarly engineered the events that had allowed Catherine, Peter, Murat, Deniz and even William to reconcile.

Kristin glances curiously at Peter's neck. "Your bow tie," she says, reaching toward him. "It's crooked."

Peter feels beneath his chin. He torques on the knot, trying to fix it.

"That won't do," says Kristin. Without asking permission she yanks on the running end. She hands Peter her drink, so that both of his hands are occupied. She then begins to reassemble the knot as she continues, "I overheard that the photos for your next exhibit have arrived," she says. "What's the theme?"

"You'll have to wait for the opening. I'm not telling anyone."

"Why's that?" Kristin asks.

"Maybe I just want to see who will come knowing nothing about the photographs except that they were shot by me. You'll be there, won't you?"

"Straighten up," Kristin orders while finishing the last twist on his bow tie. Peter squares back his shoulders. "There," she says, making a final adjustment. "You're a mess without me." She takes her rosé from Peter and has a sip, admiring the work she's done.

"You'll be at my exhibit, won't you?" he asks again.

"No, unfortunately I won't be, Peter."

He says nothing, demanding an explanation through his silence.

"I've been meaning to speak with you about it," says Kristin. "A cable arrived earlier in the week. It's time for me to go."

"To go? Go where?"

"Back to the States until I get my next posting sorted out."

"The States?" Peter's voice mixes with his suddenly elevated breath.

A shot of panic stabs him in the stomach and then flows gradually outward, like blood from a wound, pooling into his legs, feet, arms, hands. His mouth is dry and he closes and opens it once like an idiot. He looks above him and feels as if the roof might tumble down, as if this building made of glass is no building at all, but rather an illusion for him to be crushed beneath.

"I had requested another extension on my tour, but it got denied."

Peter shuts his mouth. He wills the roof above him to lift, and gradually it does as time and space reassume their familiar proportions, those infinitely small units of measure that are finite all the same. Peter begins to nod and slowly his face contorts into a slight expression of disgust at the irony. The only person among them who can escape the web of interests and counterinterests that have kept them in place is Kristin herself, the architect of it all. "It doesn't seem fair," says Peter.

"What doesn't seem fair?" asks Kristin.

"You leaving after you convinced all of us to stay." Peter draws silent for a moment. "You leaving after you convinced Catherine to stay."

"Catherine made her own decision, so did each of you."

"The woman in your car that day, William's birth mother, where is she?" Peter asks.

Kristin stares across the room, to an unknown point.

"Answer my question," says Peter. "That afternoon, when Deniz was walking back from the İstiklal, I was watching from the window. Deniz didn't recognize that woman in your car. So who was she?"

"I don't see how it's relevant," mutters Kristin.

"That wasn't William's mother."

"No, it wasn't."

"After that day I traveled to the Central Authority," says Peter. "I waited in the lines. I even paid a bribe. Do you know what they showed me in their records? That William's mother has been dead for eleven years. If you leave, I'll tell Catherine."

"And why would you do that?"

"Because you convinced her to stay on false premises."

"You won't do that," adds Kristin.

Approaching them through the crowd is a man, conspicuous in that he doesn't wear a tuxedo, but a pair of khakis, a white oxford shirt and rep tie with navy blazer. The rubber soles of his docksiders squeak meekly on the marble floor. He is muscular but gangly, like a rower, with a well-brushed drape of sandy brown hair. He carries his drink, a bottle of IPA, with his elbow bent at a perfect right angle. "There you are," he says, the relief evident in his voice as he finds Kristin. "Sorry, the caterers had me go all the way to the kitchen to find a beer." Then he stops, holding up an index finger. "Wait, don't tell me," he says. "You must be Peter." Kristin introduces them properly and her husband has the personality of a Labrador retriever, saying how Kristin has always kept "her work at work and her home at home," and how after hearing so much about "the elusive Peter" he wondered if he'd ever have the chance "to at least meet before we leave." Their conversation then turns to that departure, to the scramble of packing up their house, to the question of where their daughter will go to school in the States, and to what they plan to do with their last week or so in the city. "We are treating ourselves to one thing," he says, glancing sheepishly downward at his docksiders. "It's a total splurge. We're going to get a suite at the Çıragan Palace Hotel. Neither of us has ever been. I hear it's got the best view in the city."

He smiles at Kristin. But she is staring fixedly at Peter.

Then the squelch of a microphone interrupts them. Deniz mounts a black stage in the corner of the atrium. He pulls down the microphone stand, which has been adjusted for a much taller man's height. He makes brief introductory remarks, which welcome everyone to the opening of the museum's new extension, and then he offers a summary of some of the Istanbul Modern's upcoming programs, to include Peter's "highly anticipated sophomore exhibit."

Peter listens, but he hardly hears the words. What he is thinking is that Kristin has, of course, been to the Çıragan Palace Hotel. According to Deniz that's where the two of them first met. Why would she lie?

Murat then assumes the stage with Catherine and William dutifully standing alongside him. He begins to speak about his family, their support of his various enterprises, and how he has asked them to the stage because he could not claim any success without acknowledging their contributions. When Murat offers a toast to his wife and son, the crowd lifts their champagne. So do Peter and Kristin, but neither of them drinks. They have already emptied their glasses. When Kristin's husband swallows the last of his beer, he notices their empties. "I'll get us another round," he says but fumbles nervously with the glasses as he takes them and disappears across the reception.

With Murat's remarks out of the way, the gentle hum of conversation has resumed among the crowd. Once her husband is safely out of earshot, Kristin turns to Peter. "Did they tell you at the Central Authority how that girl died?" Peter gazes up at the stage, to where Deniz has taken the microphone from Murat and is now attending to the evening's festivities. "You could have asked Deniz about William's mother," Kristin continues. "It would have saved you the trip . . . and the bribe."

"What does it matter how she died, all that matters is—"

Kristin cuts him off. "A suicide, Peter. The girl whose name you saw was a suicide. But she wasn't William's mother, just a name, one that everyone else was ready to forget." At the foot of the stage, a small, impenetrable circle of celebrants has once again formed around Catherine, Murat and William and a ripple of laughter rises up from the group. Deniz climbs down the stage behind them, again avoiding his son.

But regardless of whatever claims Kristin makes about this anonymous girl's suicide, Peter continues to fixate on the Çırağan Palace, on catching Kristin in this lie. Why would she tell her husband that she'd never been? And the language he'd used to describe the place, that it "had the best view in the city." Peter had heard that before. It was how Deniz talked about sunrise from a suite . . .

"So who is William's mother?" Peter asks clumsily, wishing to retract his words as soon as they depart, because he has already answered the question for himself. Kristin meets his awkwardness with a conversely elegant silence. "But why?" Peter eventually says, but he hardly speaks, it is as though he only mouths the sentence. "Why?" he repeats a bit louder.

"Why," answers Kristin, as if *how* is the question she's prepared for, and had it been asked she would've explained her single night's indiscretion with Deniz at the Çırağan during a low point in her marriage after her husband had refused to follow her here, how she had thought to get rid of the child but couldn't bring herself to, how her husband had eventually agreed to stay with her but only if she'd register the child at the Central Authority under a phony name and never speak of it again, how she had used her position in the consulate to find Catherine and Murat, and, lastly, how from there she had arranged everything— Murat's relationship with her, Peter's relationship with Catherine, all of the events that had led up to this night. She had arranged it all to create a stable framework for her son, one that would keep him proximate to her, one that would allow her to glimpse him from time to time at her meetings with Murat, or to hear about him at her lunches with Catherine, a structure that allowed her to hold at least a tangential influence over his life, and now that he was grown, or at least grown enough, she had to move on. But Peter's question, *why?* She struggles with the word.

"I made a mistake," she says.

"A mistake?" says Peter.

Kristin explains to him the *how,* but he is unsatisfied.

"Why?" he asks again.

"Is it so improbable," she says, "that a well-planned life can be built around one single mistake?"

"We're all bound up in one another."

"And . . . ?" asks Kristin.

"And I thought you were, too," says Peter. "But you're not. You can leave."

"So can you," she says.

Peter's racing mind catalogs all that he would lose if he chose to abandon this place and, as he unhinges his jaw to speak, Deniz rejoins them. "It's come off beautifully, hasn't it?" says Deniz. And for a moment, Peter feels uncertain as to what Deniz is referring to. Peter casts his gaze out over the crowd, at Murat, at William and at Catherine in her elegant gown. Then he looks beyond them, to the Bosphorus, which reflects the ceaseless, churning lights of the city. There is nowhere else he can go—or Catherine can go, or William, or Murat, or even Deniz—where in some way they won't be diminished from what they are now. No place can match this one, he decides, and because of this they would remain.

"Yes, it came off beautifully. A lovely evening," says Kristin. "Congratulations." She glances across the reception, to where her husband is approaching with their three drinks cradled in his large grip.

"Did she tell you her news?" Deniz asks Peter.

"Yes, she told me. I guess we'll have to get along without her."

"It's not that bad," says Deniz, and then he turns to Kristin. "Didn't you say your replacement was coming soon?"

"Three weeks."

"Nothing will change too much," says Deniz. "Will it?"

Kristin turns to Peter. "No," she says. "Nothing will change at all."

※

The frames are stacked in the middle of the gallery. Peter unwraps them from their plastic packaging and leans them one by one against the wall. He can hear the dissipating conversation and laughter from the museum's atrium as the party ebbs to its conclusion. He works slowly, evaluating each of his photographs in context with the others before selecting its position. The photos aren't portraits and this is something different for him, a change. Their composition is more complex and in each of the frames he has shot there is movement. In some of the pictures there is so much movement that the image appears as a blur. He isn't certain who might appreciate images that convey so little clarity.

His glasses are perched down his nose. He had long ago pulled loose his bow tie and he had dropped his rented tuxedo jacket in a corner of the gallery. With his attention deep in his work, he is interrupted by a set of footsteps approaching the door. It is William.

The boy stands on the threshold. It has been months since Peter has seen him, perhaps even a year. He has grown. Perhaps it is just the tuxedo William wears, but Peter doubts it. William seems to have crossed some frontier of awareness, and when their eyes meet across the gallery, Peter feels with complete certainty that William understands everything and that, perhaps, the boy had come to understand long before he had.

"Come in," says Peter. "You'll be the first one to see it."

William crosses the gallery so that he stands in its center. Unlike Peter, the boy had not removed his tuxedo jacket as the night wore on and the knot of his bow tie remains set tightly in place where an Adam's apple will soon form. Standing next to Peter, he folds his arms and examines the first few photographs in the exhibit. "Were these taken from your apartment?" William asks.

"You remember," says Peter.

Hanging in front of them, or stacked neatly on the floor or against the walls, are dozens of images of birds in various degrees of flight. The shots had all been observed from Peter's window, but with different exposure lengths and in different seasons and light conditions. "What I like about the birds in these prints," says Peter, "is that it's difficult to tell whether they're taking off or landing. There is lots of movement in the frame, but you're not sure exactly what direction it's going in."

William continues to browse through the photographs. Then he stops at one. He looks intently into the frame. "I took this," he says, glancing over his shoulder toward Peter. It is of a perfectly black bird and a flawlessly white one, the pair of them lifting into flight.

Peter steps alongside him. "It's my favorite of these."

The two of them begin to work. "Do you think your father will let me show one of your photographs alongside mine?" asks Peter. William is quiet for a moment, and then says that he isn't sure. "Will you ask him?" adds Peter. William glances up with an uncertain gaze. Then he nods. They hardly speak as they arrange the remaining pictures. Although they don't have time to hang all of the photographs, they finish laying out the order of the exhibit, so that each frame leans against its place on the wall. The two of them stand in the center of the gallery, making a last examination of their work, when Murat appears in the doorway.

"William, it's time to go home," says his father, who then steps cautiously into the gallery and glances at the walls. "Is this your latest exhibit, Peter?" Murat clasps his hands behind his back as he strolls the perimeter with his head craned forward, making a careful examination of each photograph. "You usually do portraits. What gave you such an idea?"

"Do you like it?" Peter asks.

Murat takes a few more paces around the gallery. The echo of his steps is the only sound as Peter awaits a verdict. "In fact, I do. Much more than your other work." Murat unclasps his hands from behind his back and leans deeply toward the photograph of both the white and the black bird. "This one in particular, the symmetry," he says. "The two birds perfectly balance one another." Murat offers his hand to Peter. "I suppose congratulations are in order."

Peter nods gratefully and the two of them shake.

"We'll see you at the opening in a couple of weeks," says Murat. He then places his arm around his son's shoulders and pulls him close. "It's late and he has school tomorrow and then work with me afterward." Peter glances down at William, encouraging him to tell Murat and to take credit for his work so that it might hang on the wall of his father's museum. As Murat leads him away, William turns his head toward his father, as if he might ask him something.

Murat cuts him off. "Hurry, your mother is waiting. She's tired and wants to go home." And so father and son walk out the door, to search for Catherine, who lingers in the thinning crowd.

Acknowledgments

⌒

With gratitude to Diana Miller, Vanessa Haughton, PJ Mark, Robin Desser and Sonny Mehta for their friendship and support at home; and with gratitude to Kemal Egemen İpek and Özgür Mumcu for their friendship and support in Istanbul; and with gratitude to Lea Carpenter for her love in both places.

A Note About the Author

Elliot Ackerman is a National Book Award finalist, author of the novels *Waiting for Eden, Dark at the Crossing* and *Green on Blue,* and of the non-fiction book *Places and Names.* His work has appeared in *Esquire, The New Yorker, The Atlantic, The New York Times Magazine* and *The Best American Short Stories,* among other publications. He is both a former White House Fellow and a Marine, and served five tours of duty in Iraq and Afghanistan, where he received the Silver Star, the Bronze Star for Valor and the Purple Heart. He divides his time between New York City and Washington, D.C.

A Note on the Type

This book was set in Cloister Old Style, a revival of the Venetian types of Nicolas Jenson, designed by Morris Fuller Benton for American Type Founders in 1897.

Typeset by Scribe, Philadelphia, Pennsylvania

Printed and bound by Berryville Graphics, Berryville, Virginia

Designed by Betty Lew